NORTH SHORE PUBLIC LIBRARY

3 0651 00298 2589

S0-BJO-274

THE
OUTSIDER

First published in 2013 by Portnoy Publishing

1

Copyright © Arlene Hunt, 2013

The right of Arlene Hunt to be identified as the Author of the work has been asserted by her in accordance with the Copyright, Designs and Patents Act 1988.

All rights reserved. No part of this publication may be reproduced, stored in a retrieval system, or transmitted in any form or by means, electronic, mechanical, photocopying, recording or otherwise, without prior and express permission of the publishers.

This book is sold subject to the condition that it shall not, by way of trade or otherwise, be circulated in any form or binding other than that in which it is published.

ISBN: 978-1-909255-06-7

All characters in this novel are fictional. Any resemblance to real persons, alive or dead, is coincidental.

Printed and bound by CPI Group (UK) Ltd, Croydon, CRO 4YY

Cover design: David Rudnick
Typeset in: Adobe Garamond by Sheer Design and Typesetting

Portnoy Publishing
PO Box 12093, Dublin 6, Ireland
www.portnoypublishing.com   Twitter: @portnoypub

ARLENE HUNT

THE OUTSIDER

Portnoy

P U B L I S H I N G

NORTH SHORE PUBLIC LIBRARY
250 ROUTE 25 A
SHOREHAM, NEW YORK 11786

For Bryan

NORTH SHORE PUBLIC LIBRARY
250 ROUTE 25 A
SHOREHAM, NEW YORK 11786

FOREWORD

It's a rainy Thursday in Dublin, 3rd of October. According to my daughter I am dressed like a scuba diving spy: but she likes to dissect my outfits and label them. There is a one-eyed cat asleep in his basket on my desk, and Archer, the German Shepherd, is dozing under my chair, filling the office with eau d'wet dog.

I envy their peace of mind. For I am sitting here attempting – for the third time – to write some kind of small dohickey for this novel, and am once again stumped.

What is it I can tell you about The Outsider that you cannot read for yourself? It's a novel about misunderstanding, loneliness, bravery, isolation, love. It's about a girl who may or may not be on the autism spectrum; and her brother, who is her protector, her tormentor, her blood. It's about failing and triumph. It's about horses. It's about kindness; it's about the evil that resides in the human heart.

I don't really know any other way to describe The Outsider.

It's a book I wanted to write so I wrote it, and I hope you enjoy it.

Arlene Hunt.

CHAPTER 1

January 1990

The body lay at the bottom of a water-filled ditch. Larry Green wiped the rain from his face with his hand and took a step closer to get a better look. His breath formed a white plume in the bitterly cold air. It was December 27th, the day after St Stephen's Day.

'Eddie!'

Eddie Yates, a mountain of a man clad in a green waxed jacket and green wellingtons, shuffled up beside him. Rain spilled from the brim of his cap.

'What?'

'Down there.'

Eddie looked.

'Ara Jaysus, sure it's no wonder we couldn't find him.'

'Aye, he must have been lying under the snow.'

'If it hadn't a rained we'd a missed him.'

The two men stood shoulder to shoulder. The bulk of the body was submerged under the brackish water, but tufts of hair breached the surface, as did part of a shoulder and a section of a white curled finger.

Eddie's cocker spaniel Lulu – named after the singer – saw what they were looking at, raised her hackles and growled.

'Stick her on the lead there,' Larry said. 'We don't want her disturbing things.'

Eddie pulled out a length of twine from one of his many pockets, made a noose, and looped it over the dog's neck. He yanked it a few times until, eventually, she sat down. 'Is it definitely him?'

Larry glanced at Eddie to see if he was being serious or not. How many bodies did he expect to find in the hills above Killbragh? But Eddie's broad face displayed no hint of sarcasm or guile.

'Sure who else would it be?'

Eddie shrugged, turned his head and spat. 'Should we pull him out do you think?'

'I'm not touching him.'

'I'll go see where the rest are so.'

'Aye,' Larry reached into his pockets for his cigarettes, 'you go on. I'll stay here.'

Eddie grunted and left, dragging a reluctant Lulu behind him. Larry lit a cigarette and stood huddled against the rocks on the opposite side of the track while he waited. He was already on his third cigarette by the time he finally heard voices.

Eddie came into view first, followed by a garda, and behind him, Arthur Donovan, looking grim-faced beneath his flat cap. Larry stamped on his cigarette butt and swore under his breath. Although he had little time for Donovan, he wouldn't have wished this moment on his worst enemy.

'Is it him?' Donovan called, his voice taut stretched thin over the beating rain. He overtook the garda, who was slipping and sliding in the mud in his regulations shoes.

'Aye, I reckon so.'

'Mr Donovan, wait.'

Donovan paid the garda no heed. When he reached the track where Larry stood, he looked down into the ditch. His hard, maimed face gave nothing away, but Larry wasn't fooled. He'd lost a child once too, a son, stillborn. That had hurt – it still did from time to time – he couldn't even begin to guess what Donovan was feeling.

'I'm so sorry, Arthur.'

'Help me bring him up.'

'Mr Donovan!' The garda was upon them. He glanced down and then quickly turned his face away again. The garda's uniform was destroyed by mud and he was breathing hard. A bloody townie, Larry thought uncharitably. He's not used to tramping around the wilds. 'Mr Donovan, you can't…you have to leave him as he is.'

Donovan removed his coat.

'We can't move him until the pathologist takes a look at him. Please, I've radioed for the Inspector. He'll be here in a minute.'

He was, Larry realised, looking at him, appealing for some sort of back up. Larry looked away.

'I'll not leave him down there,' Donovan said through clenched teeth, 'not like that.'

'Please Mr Donovan …'

Donovan tossed his coat onto the briars. The garda looked at him, helpless, in his oversized coat and sodden peaked cap. He was a kid, Larry realised, like all of them seemed to be these days. Jug-eared, freckled, not much older than the boy lying in the water below them.

A savage gust of wind drove the rain horizontally. Donovan rolled up the sleeves of his shirt and began to descend the bank. The garda made one last effort and tried to grab a hold of his arm, but Donovan shook him off easily.

'We can't disturb the scene!'

'Give me a hand here lads… help me.'

Eddie handed Lulu's makeshift lead to the exasperated garda.

'Here, make yourself useful and take a hold of her.'

Lulu was none too happy with this arrangement. She barked and whined after Eddie as he scrambled down the bank behind Donovan and landed in the water with an enormous splash. Donovan plunged his arms beneath the surface and felt around.

He leaned back, grunting, claiming what was his from the muck and the filth.

Larry heard the garda mutter under his breath. Eddie grappled the legs, lost his footing, slipped and went down, soaking himself in the process. Taking this as his cue, Larry removed his own coat and went to help.

Between them they managed to haul Gully Donovan's body out of the water. They carried him up the bank and onto the track.

Larry stood up and stared at the boy's claggy eyes. He located his hip flask, opened it and took a slug, felts his guts roil as he passed it to Eddie, who took more than a mouthful.

Gully's face was bloated and mottled, marbled almost. Donovan's shoulders shook as he slid his hands under the boy's shoulders and lifted him onto his lap. The head rolled back, revealing a wound that made Larry gasp. The garda, still holding Lulu, staggered back and managed to make it to the rocks before he vomited.

Days in the water, Larry thought, taking another slug, feeling the liquid burn hot and settle his bile. Sure how could it look any different?

Donovan cradled his son's head in his lap, smoothing back strands of black hair from Gully's forehead. Without being asked, Eddie fetched his coat from the briars and draped it over Donovan's shoulders.

'Here, put this on you. You're frozen.'

'Look what they did to him, lads,' Donovan said, his voice wretched. 'Look what they did, oh look what the bastards did to my boy.'

Larry lowered his head, embarrassed to be witness to this grief. His hands dangled uselessly by his side and no words of comfort came to him, no soothing gesture. Donovan continued to cradle his son's remains. After a while, Lulu began to whine and then to bark; she kept it up until Eddie yanked the lead from the garda's hand and gave her a quick kick in the ribs. With that, she fell silent.

CHAPTER 2

1971

Evelyn Finchley was twenty-three years old when she did two things that shocked and scandalised everybody who knew her: she confessed her love for a dark-haired Catholic farmer; informed her family he had asked her to marry him, and that she had said yes.

Evelyn's father, Albert Finchley, was a District Court judge. A man who was committed to his Protestant faith, he received the news of his daughter's romantic entanglement while seated in his favourite chair by the fire. It was the last weekend of October, and the autumnal sun had long since dipped behind the sycamores surrounding the family's imposing Georgian home. The judge, an intemperate man at best, was in the process of digesting a splendid Sunday roast with all the trimmings. He had loosened his waistband and was in no mood for surprises of any kind, certainly not one as unwelcome and as startling as this

Having listened to what Evelyn had to say, he removed his pipe and gaped at her, his newspaper momentarily forgotten.

'What did you say?'

Evelyn, tall, slender, with alabaster skin and a shock of auburn hair, straightened her shoulders and repeated her lines.

'I said Jack Byrne has asked me to marry him, and I said yes.'

'Jack Byrne?'

'Jack Byrne.'

The judge looked to his wife for some sort of clarification. Evelyn's mother, Violet, a soft-spoken, gentle woman who hated any kind of fuss, gave an almost imperceptible shrug. This, it seemed, was news to her too. The judge stared at Violet for a moment, clamped his jaw and returned his gaze to his only daughter.

'I don't know what sort of a joke you're trying to play, Evelyn, but it's not very funny.'

'I am not making a joke. He's just bought a farm and we are to be wed,' Evelyn said, hearing in her voice a little less conviction than she had hoped it might carry.

'Byrne?'

'Yes.'

The judge's eyebrows scurried down his forehead to become one. 'Are you talking about the Widow Byrne's lad?'

'Yes. Jack. His name is Jack.'

Violet put down her book and rising out of her chair said. 'Evelyn, I really don't think this is the time–'

'Have you taken leave of your senses?'

'Father I–'

'Because you must have, if you think any daughter of mine is going to marry one of them. You mustn't have a brain in your head if you think that.'

Evelyn's fine head rose an inch.

'One of… them?'

'*A Catholic!* You're going to stand there and tell me you're taking up with a bloody *Fenian*? You're going to stand there and say that to me, in *this* house? This house where your own great-grandfather was murdered by Fenian scum on his own bloody front doorstep?'

The judge flung the newspaper aside, scattering pages everywhere. Sweetie, Violet's asthmatic corgi who had been sleeping on the mat in front of the fire, woke and began to bark in fright.

'No daughter of mine is going to marry that sort. I can tell you that right now.'

'Jack has nothing to do with any of that. He's a good man and I love him.'

'Love…what the hell do you know about love? Would you go away out of that!'

'I know enough about love to know who I want to marry.'

'You can't marry him! He's a bloody Catholic.'

'His religion is not important.'

'Oh *is* it not?' the judge replied, savagely. 'Well then, what about yours?'

'I–'

'What about any children you might want to have? Will it be important to you then do you think?' The judge threw up his hands in disgust. 'Go on, go on now, I won't hear any more of this nonsense. What did I tell you, Mother?' He shot Violet a disgusted look. 'Always with her nose in those blasted romance books, filling her head with rubbish. Go on, go on. Let me read my paper in peace.'

Evelyn glared at him and clenched her fists.

'I am twenty-three years old. I don't *need* your permission to marry Jack.'

Violet took a step towards her. 'Evelyn please–'

But it was too late.

'My permission, oh will you listen to her now?' the judge said, using a voice that could strip paint. '*You don't need my permission.* Is that what you think?'

'Father, I'm trying to tell you–'

'You don't tell me a thing. Not in this house, not in this life-time. I'll send you away, you hussy, the cheek of you. You won't shame this house, by God, *you won't*. I'll tell you…after all we've done for you…I won't have this…this…sort of carry-on under this roof.'

'There is nothing to be had. For God's sake, I am not a child, and this is not terrible news. I am to be married. I would like you to be happy for me.'

'*Happy?* How in the name of God could any man be happy about th<u>is</u>?'

Colour rose in Evelyn's cheeks. 'Well happy or not, I'm marrying Jack Byrne.'

The judge vaulted out of the chair and grabbed Evelyn by the shoulders. He shook her so hard her head snapped backwards and forwards uncontrollably.

'Albert!' Violet darted between them and tried to wrench her husband's nearest arm free.

Sweetie barked hysterically, dancing around them

'*You won't, you won't sully this family name with that dirt.*'

'*Albert!*'

And then, the unthinkable: Judge Finchley drew back his hand and struck his daughter across the face. Violet gasped. Evelyn staggered backwards, but remained on her feet. She stared at her father in shock. He had never struck her before: despite his fierce reputation, he had never raised a hand to any of his children.

Puce-faced and breathing hard, Judge Finchley raised his hand and jabbed a thick warning finger in her direction.

'If you have decided think to go ahead with this abomination… you can get out! You can get the hell out of here before I put you out!'

Evelyn walked stiffly from the room and closed the door behind her. In the hall, she found her brother, Clive, sitting on the stairs with a medical book open on his lap. He was eighteen years old, slender like her, bookish and shy, off to college soon.

'I heard shouting.'

Evelyn glanced towards the living room door, behind which the judge was bellowing at Violet.

'Is it true?'

'Yes.'

'Your lip is bleeding.'

Evelyn touched her mouth with her fingers and examined them for signs of blood.

'So it is.'

'You should put some ice on it, to stop it from swelling.'

Evelyn laid a hand on her brother's shoulder and gave it a quick squeeze, stepped past him and went upstairs to her bedroom. She locked the door, sat at her dressing table and stared at her reflection in the mirror. She was frightened, close to hysterical, yet giddy, and filled with emotions she had never felt before. None of it mattered – not the fight, not the split lip, nothing; her only thoughts were of Jack.

CHAPTER 3

They had met at a dance in Ashford six months before.

Evelyn had been standing at the bar, a whiskey and club soda by her elbow. She disliked dances and had only gone along to keep a heartbroken friend company, a gesture that now seemed wasted as she watched her friend happily allowing herself to be swung around the floor by a succession of men, her heartbreak all but forgotten.

As the evening wore on, Evelyn considered whether or not to go home, and was just about to leave when a dark-haired man walked up to the bar, ordered a pint, turned to her and said: 'Awful, isn't it?'

He flashed a shy smile, showing even, white teeth.

'Yes, yes it is.'

'I'm not one for dancing.'

'Is that what they're calling it?'

He laughed. 'Well, whatever it is, it's not for me.'

'Me neither.'

The barman delivered the pint, smirking as Jack dug a fistful of change from his pocket.

'How's she cuttin' Jack, how's the form?'

'Grand, Ben.'

'Can I get you anything else there?'

Jack pointed to Evelyn's glass, but she shook her head.

'I'm Jack,' he said, when the barman moved away to serve another customer.

'So I gathered. I'm Evelyn.'

'You're not Judge Finchley's daughter are you?'

'There's no need to look so horrified. I don't bite.'

'It wasn't your *teeth* I was worried about,' he said, with a glint in his eyes. 'Who are you here with?'

'A friend.'

'Oh? Would I know him?'

'What makes you think it's a he?'

He shrugged and took a sip of his pint, his eyes scanning the room.

She studied him without making it obvious. Though she was sure she had seen him around before, she could honestly say she had never noticed how handsome he was. His hair was wavy and near black, his eyes deep brown, and his skin clear and weathered tan. He was six feet tall, neatly put together, with broad shoulders that filled his jacket nicely.

She looked out across the heaving floor and, after a moment, said, 'I suppose we could give it a try though.'

'What?'

'Dancing of course. What did you think I meant?'

He smiled again, and at that moment Evelyn Finchley knew, with concrete certainty, that this was a man she would like to get to know better.

'Shall we?'

'Like I say, I'm not much of a dancer.'

'Will we wing it?'

He offered her his arm.

And she had taken it. Now, here she was: staring into a mirror with a swollen lip while her parents were having a massive row downstairs.

She would think of that day, many years later, and wonder at such an inauspicious start to the rest of her life. But, at that moment, Evelyn Finchley was in love, and that was all that mattered.

Evelyn left her father's house the same night and walked three miles to the nearest phone box where she called Jack and asked him to come and pick her up. When Jack eventually cooled down about her swollen lip, he drove her and her single suitcase – hastily packed while her mother stood wringing her hands in Evelyn's bedroom – to a guesthouse in Rathdrum.

Later, they sat together on the hard sofa in the front room, their knees touching chastely, both acutely aware that the landlady was hovering in the hall outside, ready to pounce at a moment's extended silence. It was late and she had already made a point of telling Jack that she locked her front door 'promptly at ten o'clock, no exceptions'.

Jack took Evelyn's hand in his. His skin was warm and rough, his fingernails unexpectedly square.

'I will understand if you want to go home.'

'I don't want to do any such thing.'

'This is a big step.'

'I know that Jack, but I've made up my mind.'

'What about the rest of your family?'

'What about them?' Evelyn said, rubbing her thumb against his. 'Are *you* having second thoughts, Jack?'

'Indeed and I'm not.'

'Well then, neither am I.'

'Good.'

'Good.'

They managed a kiss and an embrace before the landlady entered the room, clearing her throat theatrically.

The following Thursday, Jack and Evelyn married at a registry office in Dublin with only the landlady (who was being paid for her efforts) and Jack's friend, Pat Kinsella, as witnesses. It was a sombre affair, but neither Jack nor Evelyn noticed or cared.

Money was tight, so the best they could do for a honeymoon was an overnight in the Harbour Hotel in Courtown. The next day, Jack drove them back to Wicklow, parked his Ford Escort in front of a near-derelict farmhouse and opened the passenger door for his new bride.

Evelyn climbed out of the car and gazed around her in silence. Jack cleared his throat.

'Well, what do you think?'

'I think it's a little more than a – what did you call it – a fixer upper?'

'Aye, well…it's not much to look at now, I know. But it's a solid enough house: there're two bedrooms upstairs, and three rooms below, with plenty of space to add on…' he blushed a little, 'if we need it. A bit of plaster, some paint and she'll look good as new.'

'And the roof?'

'What about it?'

'Don't we need one of those?'

'Oh *that*? That's nothing to worry about. I'll have it fixed up in no time.'

Evelyn gazed up at the tattered roof. The eaves were visible in places where the tiles had long since fallen off. As she counted the holes, a wood pigeon flew out through one of them and disappeared from view.

'Got a parcel of five acres to go with it. Grand bit of land it is too.'

Evelyn said nothing to that. She had glimpsed the surrounding fields on the drive up the overgrown lane towards the house; scrubby, filled with weeds, thistles and rocks, and precious little else.

'So, what do you think?'

She looked at the sagging front door, the crumbling bricks, rotten sash widows and cracked paving stones. She thought of her family home, the Georgian lodge she had left behind, with its large comfortable rooms and neatly tended lawn that led down to the lake. She felt tears threatening somewhere behind her eyes. But, when she turned her head to speak, she found herself staring into Jack's hopeful face and realised what this crumbling wreck and the scrubby land meant to him: to this man, her *husband*. For better, for worse, that was what she had promised on her wedding day.

'It has…a certain charm to it. Definite potential.'

Jack beamed and slipped an arm around her waist. 'Come on and I'll show you where I'm going to put the milking parlour. Pat had a dowser out last week, and he says there's water aplenty under that back field'

'That doesn't really work, does it? Finding water underground using sticks?'

'Oh it works all right.'

'How do you know?'

Jack looked at her, taken aback. 'Because he…well the sticks point down wherever there's water.'

'It sounds a bit dubious to me.'

'It's not a con. It's an ancient tradition.'

Evelyn wanted to say 'so was cockfighting', and that her father routinely jailed people for partaking in that, but something about the set of her new husband's jaw made her hold her tongue. If he wanted to believe in a bit of magic, who was she to stop him?

Over the following months, Evelyn and Jack saved every penny and worked every hour they could, slowly turning the homestead into a home. During the week, Jack also worked as a labourer on Pat Kinsella's large dairy farm; but on the weekends and evenings he grappled with his own land. He sank a well behind the house and bought a tractor at auction – a machine so old it seemed to be held together more by rust than by metal. He and a number of his friends tackled the meadow to the front of the house clearing many of the rocks and the boulders by hand, carting away the debris in trailers and barrows, ploughing and harrowing long into the evening, until the meadow was eventually clear.

Slowly, the farm began to take shape. By late summer of the following year, they had reaped their first crop of barley from the reclaimed meadow – the same meadow some old gouger up the road had offered Jack a pittance for, claiming the soil was 'rancid'. Locals began to remark that Jack Byrne was the sort of man who could turn his hand to anything, little realising that in order to do so, he had worked every waking hour, with a now-pregnant Evelyn matching him stride for stride.

It wasn't all sweetness and light. The more Evelyn's belly grew, the deeper she felt the loss of her family. She missed her mother terribly, and was vexed that Violet would not stand up to the judge. She missed her brother, who was now away at university. One evening, driven by hope and loneliness, Evelyn called the house from the phone box in the village. Her father answered, heard her voice and hung up. That night, Evelyn cried so hard she gave herself hiccups. She prayed her father would reconsider, but two months after the phone call, he walked straight past her in the local post office as though she were invisible.

The work on the farm began to take its toll: some nights Jack was so exhausted he fell asleep halfway through his dinner. Whenever this happened, Evelyn would rouse him and help him upstairs to bed, before returning to the kitchen to finish working on curtains and the bedspread she was making, her chair pushed back from the sewing machine to allow for her rapidly expanding stomach.

Work on the milking parlour finished in late September. Jack took out a loan and bought five cows at auction and a part share, along with Pat, in a young Holstein bull, named Jericho. It was a gamble, but one he had to take; Jack hoped the bull would inject some quality into his poor breeding stock.

By the time the twins, Anthony and Emma, were born in early December, Evelyn realised that though she loved her parents, she had her own family to look after now; and that, she vowed, was exactly what she would do.

CHAPTER 4

Evelyn stared at Dr Williams's self-satisfied face, feeling bewildered and close to tears. Was the man blind? Was he deaf? She wanted to scream at him until her throat burst into flames. She wanted to grab him by his stupid, ridiculously long sideburns, pull him out of his damn chair and shake him until he told her exactly when Emma would stop crying.

'What do you mean she'll grow out of it? She's nine months old. *When* will she grow out of it?'

Dr Williams placed his pipe in the ashtray, leaned forward on his desk and linked his long bony fingers together.

'Children develop at their own pace, Evelyn. I cannot give you absolutes.'

'But…I'm not looking for absolutes… You don't understand. She hardly ever sleeps and this crying…' Evelyn looked down at her daughter, who was red-faced and howling up a storm on her lap. 'It's constant. I'm worried that–'

'*Evelyn*, children cry. It's what they do.'

'But there must be something wrong for her to be crying like this all the time.'

Dr Williams glanced at his watch. A tall, hawk-faced man with sandy hair, he made no effort to disguise his irritation at her questions. Evelyn felt her cheeks redden. She swallowed and pressed on.

'Please, I really think something is not right. Anthony is trying to talk. He has some words already. He knows what things are. He knows who *we* are. Emma doesn't make any effort to call me or Jack Mamma or Dadda. She won't even look at us when we call her by her own name.'

'There's nothing unusual about that. I've tested her hearing and it's perfect. As I told you, children develop in their own time. You can't force these things. Just keep doing what you're doing and make sure the children are getting plenty of fresh air.'

'*Fresh air!*' Evelyn sorted derisively, unable to help herself. 'You think her symptoms are down to a lack of fresh air?'

'I assure you, *Mrs Byrne*,' he said, emphasising her name in the most patronising of tones, 'your daughter is perfectly healthy, a little slow perhaps, but–'

'Slow?'

'Perhaps if you could relax a little around her she might not be so easily upset.'

'I'm sorry, what do you mean?'

'You're so tense and highly-strung. Children learn from their parents, you know.' He glanced at her slyly. 'Particularly from their mother.'

'So, you're saying this is my fault?'

'Fault is not the word I would have chosen,' Dr Williams said, glancing at his watch again. 'Tell me Evelyn, have you ever considered that you might be depressed? Are you always this…close to hysteria?'

'I'm not hysterical.' Evelyn glared at him. 'If it's my fault, then why isn't Anthony like this? He hardly ever cries. I'm upset, Doctor, because I haven't slept a full night since Emma was born. I'm upset because I think my own daughter hates me. I'm upset because she cries if I pick her up, I'm upset because…I know *something* is not right here.'

Even before she had finished speaking, Dr Williams was scribbling on a notepad. He ripped out the page and pushed it across the desk towards her. Evelyn lifted it and read what was written on it.

'Valium?'

'It will help calm you down.'

'I don't—'

'Loosen up some of the tension in the home.'

Evelyn gave up. She gathered up her bag and her coat and carried Emma, screaming, through the waiting room. Of course it seemed like half the village was in there. She imagined everyone was looking at her, judging her and her screeching child. What a mother, they must think, what a failure. That's what happens when people marry outside of their own.

In the front hall of the GP's surgery, she struggled to get her daughter into her pram. Emma resisted her every effort, holding her tiny body rigid, screaming blue murder until Evelyn finally snapped and gave up on the straps. On the long walk back to the house she realised there were tears streaming down her face.

Valium. Maybe Dr Williams was right. Maybe all of this was her fault; maybe she was losing her mind. If only there was someone she could talk to, but none of her friends were married or had children – or, being totally honest, approved of her marriage for that matter – and she was loath to discuss her distress with the only other woman in her life, Jack's mother, Margaret.

It wasn't that she disliked her mother in law – in a way she admired her a little. Margaret Byrne was a no-nonsense woman who had single-handedly raised three children on pittance after the death of Jack's father, Malachy. The cost of this herculean effort had erased all the humour from her life and, over time, she had replaced it with an overbearing piety that confounded people and repelled only the most intrepid conversationalist. She was, nevertheless, well regarded in the village, although no one held Margaret in esteem quite as high as the esteem in which she held herself. Jack was Margaret's only son, her youngest child. She loved him fiercely, even though he had taken up with a Protestant.

Margaret liked to think she bore her troubles stoically.

'You're back then,' Margaret said, opening the front door as Evelyn struggled with the pram across the broken cobbles.

'Yes.'

'What did the doctor say?'

'Can I get in first, Margaret?'

Margaret pulled her lips into a thin line and Evelyn felt her heart sink. Why was it that everything she said to her mother-in-law caused such offence?

She folded back the blanket and lifted Emma out of the pram. Despite Evelyn's attempts to be as gentle as she could possibly manage, Emma started to grizzle immediately. This turned to tears the moment she spied her grandmother. For this, Evelyn did not blame the child at all.

'I put on a bit of lunch, not much mind.'

'Oh…thank you.'

'I washed them floors too,' Margaret looked down and frowned at Evelyn's grubby shoes. Evelyn kicked them off.

'How was Anthony? I hope he didn't give you any trouble.'

'Good as gold, never any trouble that little maneen.'

Evelyn hugged Emma a little closer to her chest, and walked down the narrow hall to the kitchen. She was relieved to see Jack sitting at the table, with Anthony in his high chair across from him. Sweet, adorable Anthony, with his sunny smile and dimples: the apple of everyone's eye. Even Margaret fussed over him when she was certain no one was observing. Not like Emma, who, though she was no longer crying, was still blotchy from earlier, and her strawberry blonde hair was stuck to her head with sweat.

'You're back early,' Evelyn said, noticing, as always, that Jack never kissed her in front of his mother.

'I wanted to see how you got on. What did Dr Williams say?'

'He advises patience and fresh air.'

Evelyn put Emma into another high chair and pulled it so she sat next to her brother. The siblings exchanged gurgles. Evelyn kissed the top of Anthony's head, breathing in his clean, lovely smell as he patted her cheek.

'You should take her to see Hal Roach,' Margaret said over lunch. 'I'm surprised, Jack, you've left it this long. Didn't I tell you about him a while back?'

Jack glanced at his mother, looking a little uncomfortable.

'I must have forgotten.'

'Who's Hal Roach?' Evelyn asked, cutting up pieces of boiled ham for Emma, who turned her face away from it as though it was poison.

'He's a faith healer.'

'A *faith* healer?'

'He's very good.' Margaret pursed her lips, sucking hard on her dentures, a habit that set Evelyn's own teeth on edge. 'A lot of people have been cured by him.'

'Oh? What does he cure?'

'All sorts.'

'I don't know if he could help,' Jack said.

'Why couldn't he? Didn't he cure Paddy Clancy, and he driven half mad with a burst eardrum? And what about Phillip Green's sciatica when the doctors told him there was nothing they could do for him? He cured Olivia Doyle of the migraines, and wasn't she crippled with them so bad she had to take to her bed for a week at a time.'

'How does he do…this healing?' Evelyn asked, genuinely curious.

'He lays on the hands. Then he asks Our Blessed Lady to work through him.'

'Sounds rather odd to me, this laying–'

'I wouldn't expect a woman of your…faith to understand the power of the Blessed Mother,' Margaret cut across her sharply.

'But I am surprised that a mother wouldn't try anything she could to help her poor baba,' she said, indicating towards Emma with a jut of her chin.

Evelyn stared at Margaret for a moment. 'Of course I want to help Emma. I'm just not sure letting some strange man…man-handle her is the right thing to do.'

'You'd rather leave her to *fresh air*, would you?'

Evelyn gaped. Sometimes Margaret could really cut to the bone.

'It couldn't really hurt though, I suppose,' Jack said, glancing at his daughter, who was now carefully pushing away the pieces of chopped ham with the heel of her hand.

'Indeed and it couldn't,' Margaret replied. 'Somebody has to help that child, the dear Lord knows she's more to be pitied than laughed at.'

CHAPTER 5

The following Saturday, Evelyn and Jack loaded the children into a large basket, strapped it into the back seat of the Ford and left the farm.

The atmosphere in the little car was tense and unpleasant. Evelyn hadn't slept much the night before and rebuffed every attempt that Jack made to start a conversation. In the end, he gave up and concentrated his efforts on getting them where they were going in one piece, tensing his jaw as the roads became narrower and rougher.

Hal Roach lived in a mobile home perched on a scrubby patch of gorse-filled land. It was a desolate location, miles from the nearest house, and on that September morning, though the sun was high and bright, a savage wind carried with it the threat of winter. Scrawny sheep dotted the hillside, eking out a meagre existence among the bracken; a mangy-looking cat watched their approach from the top of a crumbling gate plinth, long missing a gate.

'Jack, I don't know about this,' Evelyn said, staring at the cat, which stared back through slanted blue eyes. 'This doesn't feel right to me at all.'

'Don't be worrying. He's well known.'

'This kind of thing, this laying of hands…how do we know it's the Lord's work?'

'What?'

'How do we know it's good and not…not some kind of other thing?'

'What kind of other thing?'

'I don't know. I've never done anything like this before.'

'My mother wouldn't mess with anything unholy,' Jack said, offended.

'I didn't say she would.'

'Then what are you saying?'

'I don't know. I just don't…like this place.'

Jack glanced over his shoulder to where the twins slept under blankets. Anthony was flat on his back, his thumb in his mouth; only the top of Emma's head was visible.

'We can go home if you want, but what if this helps her?'

Evelyn glanced at the cat again and bit her lip.

'All right.'

Jack reached across the handbrake and gave her knee a squeeze.

They took a child each and made their way across the ground carefully. Jack knocked, and after a few moments the door of the mobile home opened to reveal a middle-aged, bespectacled man who beamed at them. His hair was long, unkempt and grey; he wore a knee-length cardigan over an off-white vest, and check trousers of a kind normally worn by professional chefs. His feet were bare and gnarled.

'Good morning. A brisk day, thank our Father in Heaven! Come in, come in.'

'Mr Roach?' Jack said.

'Yes yes. Come on in, you look perished.'

They followed him inside and stood shoulder to shoulder in the cramped space as Hal wrestled the door shut again. There was hardly room to swing a cat. Towers of books teetered on every surface, and the air reeked of paraffin from two lamps hanging on the walls – walls, Evelyn realised, which were festooned with religious pictures: terrible images of the crucifixion, a headless John the Baptist, a gloating, naked Salome and, over the tiny sink beamed a surprisingly jaunty Christ with a glowing Sacred Heart.

Hal Roach squeezed past them and settled himself onto an L-shaped bench at a foldout table. There was an old-fashioned Remington typewriter on the table, with paper in the reels.

'Are we disturbing you?' Evelyn asked, making a mental note of the fact that he had not offered them a seat.

'Not at all. I'm answering a few letters. Can I get you some tea or some water? It's from the spring behind my home. Pure crystal mountain water, provided free by the Lord himself.'

'We're fine, thank you,' Jack said, shifting Emma from one arm to another.

Hal nodded as though this was expected. 'Tell me now, tell me what it is that troubles you?'

'Did my mother not mention what I, what we, were coming to see you about?'

'She said the little one is strangely affected. I believe Margaret fears for her well-being.'

'Yes…well, I don't know if I'd say affected exactly.'

'Oh?'

'Unsettled maybe. She…cries a lot and she doesn't talk yet.'

'And you've spoken with her doctor?'

'Yes. He said she was fine, medically.'

'Ah, doctors.' Hal pulled a face and shook his head and blessed himself. 'There is so much doctors could learn if they would only but open their hearts. I take it you're not convinced by his diagnosis.'

Jack glanced towards Evelyn, who remained stubbornly silent. 'No,' he said, finally. 'We're not convinced.'

'Nor should you be,' Hal said. 'For only our Lord God is infallible, despite what they would have you believe in Rome,' he tittered.

Evelyn frowned. She searched his face for any sign of insincerity but could find none. Even so, there was something off-putting about him: the relentless fixed smile and over-bright eyes unnerved her.

As though sensing her mother's discomfort, Emma stirred in Jack's arms.

'Speak to me now, Jack, speak openly and plainly and tell me what troubles your little angel. Be precise if you can.'

Jack explained their predicament, managing, somehow, not to cite Evelyn's disbelief or her discomfort about what they expected Hal to do. When Jack finished speaking, Hal was sitting forwards, with his hands on his knees and his eyes closed. He inhaled deeply twice, as though he needed to brace himself before he faced them with his verdict.

'Let me see the poor unfortunate who has been so ill-judged by our merciful Lord.'

Evelyn bristled. 'She has not been "ill-judged" by anyone.'

Hal ignored her and lifted the typewriter down onto the floor by his feet. 'Remove the child's coat and lie her down on the table.'

'Jack—'

'It's okay, Evie.' Jack removed Emma's coat and after a moment's hesitation placed Emma on her back on the table. Emma gazed around the small living area. The moment her eyes fell on Hal her face crumpled and she began to howl.

'Stand aside please.'

Jack took a step backwards.

Hal held his hands over Emma, muttering words and incantations that neither Jack nor Evelyn could make out clearly. When he'd finished, he looked to the ceiling, a faint sheen covering his forehead, as though some monstrous effort had overtaken him.

'Blessed Mother!' he cried. 'Hail Queen of Heaven, hear now thy humble servant.'

He removed a small vial from the pocket of his cardigan, opened it with his teeth and sprinkled liquid onto Emma's chest and face. Startled, Emma screamed. Evelyn took a step towards her.

'Please, let me—'

Hal raised his hand. The smile was gone.

'Our Lady tolerates your presence here, but under great sufferance. She knows the pain you are going through, she lost her only begotten son. But please, do not speak again or I'll have to insist that you wait outside.'

Jack took Evelyn's elbow and coaxed her back to where he was standing. Anthony was awake now too. He clung to the lapels on Evelyn's coat, with eyes wide in amazement.

Hal put both hands over Emma's sternum; his thumbs locked together, palms down.

'Oh Blessed Mother, we ask thee to pray for this child, pray for her, star of the sea, release her from her affliction, lead her from the darkness we ask of you, Blessed Virgin, Our Lady of Light. Hail Mary full of grace, blessed art thou among women, Holy Mary mother of God, pray for this lost child of light, pray for her spirit to be cleansed of her sin…'

He placed his hands on either side of Emma's cheek and lowered his face to hers and kissed her on the forehead.

Emma howled in terror. Her legs kicked against the Formica surface. Outside, the wind buffeted the mobile home on its concrete block base.

Evelyn shrugged off Jack's hand. 'Stop it, you're scaring her–'

'Pray for this sinner, pray for this victim of the fall. Release this poor child from her torment, through *your* love and *your* goodness, we ask that you ask our Holy Father to absolve this child from the sins of the mortal flesh. Through Christ we beseech thee, we ask you *holy radiant Mother* to speak to Our Lord, your only son, who gave up his life for us sinners, I ask of you Blessed Lady, to release this child. *Release her from her torments.*'

He splashed more water. Emma's screams filled the air, matched now by her brother's, in sympathy.

Evelyn had had enough; she thrust Anthony into Jack's arms. 'Take him.'

'Evie–'

'Take your son.' She whirled. 'Get away from her, get away from my daughter.'

'For now is the hour, now is the wisdom of—'

Evelyn shouldered Hal Roach out of the way. She snatched up Emma and headed straight for the door.

'Evelyn, wait.'

'No, this is outrageous. Have you lost your mind Jack? She doesn't need this, this is…it's like an exorcism!'

'Please Mrs Byrne,' Hal called after her. 'You don't understand, it's not—'

'And you. Stay away from me. Don't say another word, not if you know what's good for you. I'm going home now Jack. You can either drive me or I'll drive myself.'

'That little girl needs all the help we can give her. Her poor mind is in torment.'

'Ah torment my arse!' Evelyn yelled, slamming the door open so hard she broke one of the hinges. Then she was gone.

Hal Roach shook his head mournfully.

'There's none so blind as those who do not want to see, none so deaf as those who do not want to hear.'

'Sorry about the door,' Jack said.

The children clung to each other on the way home, only finally falling into a fitful sleep just before they reached the house. Evelyn carried them inside without waking them and put the basket in the sitting room, with the radio turned on low for company should they wake up. In the kitchen, Jack was waiting for her, leaning against the Welsh Dresser, his arms folded across his chest.

'Evelyn, listen to me—'

Evelyn closed the door before she spoke. Her face was white with fury.

'No, Jack Byrne, *you* listen to me. You take that woman's side over mine all the time and I'm *sick* of it. I don't care if she's your mother or not. I don't ever want to hear another word about faith healers or any other nonsense in my home ever again. I *mean* it Jack. If I do, I'll take the children and I'll go live on the street. Better for them to be raised destitute than with a father who thinks they're possessed or evil.'

'I don't think Emma's evil,' Jack said, shocked. 'Evelyn, I don't.'

'Then no more of…whatever that was.'

Jack pushed off the dresser and cupped her face with his hands.

'I promise you, no one is going to harm a hair on that child's head ever again.'

'They'd better not.'

Jack leaned down and kissed her, and after a few seconds Evelyn kissed him back.

CHAPTER 6

It had been almost been eight months since Jack had last laid eyes on Jericho, the Holstein bull he part-owned, but, even from across the yard, he couldn't help but give a whistle of appreciation.

'By God, will you look at the size of him now!'

'Oh he's been eating well,' Pat said. 'Good grass over in that valley. I'll tell you, he has the class of a show bull.'

At their approach, Jericho stamped his feet and raked his head along the wooden railings, testing them for any sign of weakness. He had a ring in his nose and it looked as though he had no neck to speak of, just a massive head sitting on a solid block of muscle. Yet, despite his bulk, Jericho walked with a light step and his small eyes were watchful and sharp.

Emma sidled up beside Jack and stared at the massive creature. 'What do you think, kiddo?' Pat asked her. 'Impressive isn't he?'

Emma shied in behind her father's leg. Though she had known Pat all her life, she rarely spoke to anyone outside the family. She was seven years old, light-boned and rangy for her age. She wore her strawberry blonde hair in ponytail, and her dark brown, almond-shaped eyes were rimmed with light-coloured eyelashes. Nobody, not even Jack, who Emma accompanied as often as school and her mother would allow, ever truly knew what went on behind those eyes of hers.

'Look at the head on him,' Jack said, with more than a hint of awe in his voice.

'Aye,' Pat pushed up his cap and scratched his forehead. 'I'm warning you though, Jack, he's a mean bloody brute. I'll tell you, so he is. I wouldn't trust him as far as I'd throw him.'

A cow lowed nearby. The small, fine hairs on Jack's arms bristled when Jericho lowered his head and bellowed in response.

'Doesn't look too happy, does he?'

'Took him out from them earlier today, fierce fight he put up too, he attacked one of the dogs.'

'Oh aye?'

'He clipped Duke, the poor old bugger. He was too slow, got himself tossed into the gate.'

'Was he hurt?'

'Broken back. Nothing for it, but I had to put him out of his misery.'

Emma glanced over her shoulder to where her father's collie, Shep, waited for them in the front seat of the car.

'Poor old devil,' Jack said.

'Ah sure, that's the way of it.'

'Short fuse on most bulls, Emma,' Jack said, absentmindedly patting her head. 'You need to remember that, never turn your back on them. Even if you've raised 'em from a calf, they'd turn on you first chance they get. Stallions the same.'

'He'll be grand enough when he sees the ladies you have lined up for him.' Pat clapped Jack on the shoulder. 'I'll get the lads to load him up. Come on into the house, Stella's got a brew on. Will the little one come in too?'

'No, she's grand,' Jack said. 'I'll stick my head in and say hello, then I'd better get on home.'

Jack walked Emma back to the car and put her inside, sitting her beside Shep.

'I'll be back in two shakes of a lamb's tail. I'm just going to say hello to Pat's wife. You stay here and be good now, won't you?'

Emma nodded and curled an arm around Shep's neck.

'Eoin!' Pat called across the yard to a skinny teenager wearing a red baseball cap. The kid was washing muck from his wellingtons using a hose. 'Get one of the lads to load the bull into the trailer and tell them to come in for a cup of scald when they're done.'

'I c-can do it Mr K-Kinsella.'

'No, leave it to Danny or Aidan.'

Pat and Jack watched him slope off up the yard.

'He's one of the Clancy lads, isn't he?'

'Aye, I took him on there a few weeks back.'

'How's he working out?'

'He'll be grand when he toughens up a bit.'

'Is he taking a bit of a ribbing?'

'They'd have your heart broke, so they would,' Pat said.

Jack knew he was talking about Aidan and Danny Flood, the two brothers who had worked for Pat for over a decade. There was no malice in Aidan, but Danny was a different story. Jack had happily worked alongside them for years, but they were hard men, hewn from the same rock, with little time for skinny lads who stuttered when under pressure.

Pat's wife, Stella, wouldn't take no for an answer on the subject of tea, so Jack and she were exchanging pleasantries when the dogs began barking savagely.

Pat walked over to the window to see what was causing the commotion.

'Shite!'

'What is it?'

'Bull's out.'

Pat sprinted outside, with Jack hard on his heels. Jericho was standing in the centre of the yard, scrapping the cobbles with his right front hoof. Pat's German shepherd, Bess, darted back and forth across the yard, barking in high-pitched distress, but it was Shep, snapping and snarling about Jericho's face that had the bull's attention.

Jack's heart nearly stopped dead in his chest when he saw Emma standing by the open door of the car. She was staring at the bull, her eyes huge. Jack took a step towards her, but, as soon as he moved, Jericho swung his massive head in his direction.

'Don't move Jack. He'll charge you,' Pat said, trying to keep his voice as calm as possible. 'Tell her to stand still and be quiet.'

'Emma, listen now, stay where you are! Don't move, don't move a muscle.'

'Ah Jesus,' Pat moaned. 'He got the young fella.'

Jack followed Pat's gaze: Eoin Clancy lay behind the trailer. He looked like a broken doll, crumpled, his hat lying a few feet away from his body.

Aidan Flood walked around the corner of the barns carrying his lunch box and stopped dead in his tracks.

'What the fuck?'

'Aidan, you see if you can distract him,' Pat said. 'I'll get the bull staff.'

Keeping close to the wall, in case he needed to jump up onto it, Aidan waved his hands frantically while Pat ducked into the shed to get the pole that clipped onto the bull's nose ring.

'Hisk Hisk!'

Jericho scraped the ground and tossed his head, but he ignored Aidan and took a step closer to the trailer. Shep sprang forward, jaws snapping, keeping his body between the prone boy and the bull.

'Hisk! Come on you fucker. I'm over here.'

Shep launched himself at the bull again. Pat came back with the staff in his hand. Jericho backed up a step and snorted. He bluff charged, nimble and dangerous, but as soon as he did, Shep circled him and bit him again on the back of the hock.

'Try herd him back towards the pen,' Jack called. 'Shep, away, away boy!'

'Hisk!'

Jericho turned his side to Pat, keeping his eyes on him. He tossed his head.

'Pat!' Jack called, 'Pat, get out of there, he's going to charge.'

'Shit.'

Shep shot forward and nipped the bull again, this time hard enough to draw blood. Jericho had taken all he was going to take. Without any warning at all, he charged Shep, covering the distance with terrifying speed. The collie held his ground until the last moment, sprang right and nipped the bull again as he hurtled past.

Jericho released an earth-shattering roar and kept going flat out towards the pasture where the cows had gathered at the fence to see what was going on. Taking his chance, Jack sprinted across the yard and snatched up Emma into his arms just as Jericho, without slowing a fraction, bulldozed his way through the fence, sending wood and splinters everywhere. A shaken Pat would stand in Lakelands Pub later that same evening and tell the assembled crowd that it looked like a wrecking ball had hit it.

Within moments, Jericho and the cows where hightailing it down to the bottom of the field, clods of muck flying, their cries ringing in the air.

Once he was sure Emma was okay, Jack put her down and hurried back across the yard to where Pat was kneeling beside Eoin.

'Jesus Christ, Pat, how is he?'

Then he saw over Pat's shoulder and swore under his breath. There was blood on Eoin's face and his lower jaw was crushed. His eyes stared sightlessly towards the sky above them.

'What happened?'

Aidan ran towards them, his hobnailed boots ringing on the cobbles.

'The fucking bull must have crushed him.'

'Where the hell were you? I told him to get you or your brother to move him.'

Aidan looked at the boy and looked away. 'I was up the yard, Pat. He never came or asked me nothing. And I haven't seen Danny since this morning.'

Emma crept out of the car and went to stand behind her father. She looked down at the dead boy but said not a word. Jack tried to take her hand, but she wouldn't let him.

'I'll have to call his mother, oh Jesus.' Pat said. 'I'll have to tell her myself.'

On the way home, Jack glanced at Emma, trying to gauge what she was thinking.

'You all right, chicken?'

'Yes.' She stared out the window, expressionless.

'Did you see…see what happened?'

'Yes.'

Jack swallowed, feeling sadness and great guilt. That was no scene for a child to witness; he should have left her at home.

'Emma, listen to me, it's okay; it's okay to be sad.'

She shifted a little in her seat and aimed her eyes at Jack's elbow.

'I am not sad.'

'Because it's okay if you are. You can talk to me or your mammy if you're sad or if you got a fright.'

'The boy was afraid.'

'The…oh, was he?'

'Yes,' she shrugged. 'He was afraid.'

'Well, he shouldn't have tried to move him on his own like that; bulls are very unpredictable. You need to be able to handle them properly. That's how people get hurt on farms. Livestock can be dangerous, even the cows an trample you, especially when they have their calves with them.'

'He asked the man to help him.'

'What?'

'He asked the man to help him.'

Jack's hands tightened on the steering wheel.

'What man?'

'The man with cuts.'

Jack knew straightaway who she was talking about: Danny Flood. His face was covered in scars from where he'd gone through a windscreen years ago. He'd been so badly injured that no one expected him to live, but Danny was too mean to die. Mean and the sort of man who might find it funny to make a kid feel like a fool badly enough to do something stupid.

'What did the man say?'

'I do not know. He knocked the boy's hat off.'

Jack's breathing grew shallow and he found he had to concentrate on the road ahead.

'Unpredictable, Emma, just you remember that. Animals are unpredictable.'

The year after the big snow had everybody twitchy in case they got a repeat event, but the following winter was mild and soggy, and on that November morning the main street of Killbragh was packed on either side with horseboxes and trucks and mud-splattered jeeps. Jack eventually found a spot to park the Ford in front of Lakelands Pub and crossed the street, with Emma and Anthony, still wearing their Sunday best, trailing along behind him, staring at the horses, cobs and ponies of every description being unloaded from trailers. More were hacked into the village from neighbouring farms. Foot followers and terrier men huddled under the eaves, smoking and having the craic.

'He's a hardheaded bastard is that one. Give him a belt there Gully, let the fucker know you mean business!'

Anthony turned his head in time to see Gully Donovan see-sawing the mouth of a dun-coloured horse. Gully was trying to turn him one way, though it was clear the dun had a different direction in mind already. Gully's father, Arthur Donovan, wearing his usual collection of rags – though rumour had it he wasn't short a few bob – waved a hawthorn stick about.

Anthony scowled and hurried after his father and sister. He hated Gully, who, at fourteen, was three years older than himself, but was so stupid he was still in Killbragh Primary school, which was ridiculous since he was a head and shoulders taller than anyone else and had the beginnings of a moustache on his upper lip. Gully bullied Anthony every chance he got, hitting him so hard one day that Anthony lost his hearing for the afternoon. But when Anthony had complained to Jack about him, his father had said that no man respected a tittle-tattler and Byrne men fought their own battles.

'For God's sake, Donovan!' Erica Delaney, sister of Sam Delaney, owner one of the largest arable farms around, wheeled her handsome chestnut out of striking range. 'Mind the bloody horse will you? Stop waving that stick around.'

'Mind your own fuckin' business!' Donovan roared back, bringing the stick down on the dun's hindquarters with a ferocious wallop. The dun sprang forward so fast Gully lost his stirrups and would have come off had he not dropped the reins and clung to the dun's mane, wide-eyed, baring his teeth like a madman.

'Bunch of yahoos,' Jack muttered under his breath as they entered the shop.

Larry Green was standing behind the counter smoking a cigarette, eyeing the chaos beyond his windows through bloodshot eyes. He was unshaven and his clothes looked as though he'd slept in them, which was as likely as not. Anthony remembered his grandmother saying that Larry lived in the pub and that he and his brother was 'a disgrace to their father, God rest him'. Anthony liked Larry well enough: he sometimes let him have bubble gum when he thought Jack wasn't looking.

'Morning Jack,' Larry said morosely. 'Not joining the cowboys?'

'Indeed and I'm not, no interest in haring around the country on a horse.'

Larry glanced at the children. Emma stiffened. Sometimes Larry cracked a joke or two with them, trying to make them laugh. The jokes were never funny and even though Anthony would happily fake a laugh, Emma would not.

'Up half the morning they have me, fecking hounds knocked over the bloody milk crates round the side. I told McGrath before not to have those bloody yokes running wild until they're ready to push off.'

'Ara he's no control over them at all,' Jack looked disgusted. 'Some of them ran through Pat's yard last year and caused ructions. They killed three of his good banties.'

'Go on?'

'Had to take pictures of the damage before the hunt would pay out. If he'd been there himself, I think he'd have shot them.'

While the two men talked, Emma drifted towards the door trying to get a better look at the horses and, after a moment, Anthony followed. More riders arrived. Anthony spotted someone he liked almost as little as Gully.

'There's Martin Harte. Look at his new horse.'

Emma followed Anthony's finger.

'See him? Look at the get-up of him, would you? Ponce.'

The horse was a showy bay with a deep chest, four white socks and a white blaze. Martin too was turned out to perfection, in cream jodhpurs and a bottle green velvet hunting jacket that somehow made him seem older than his fifteen years.

'He looks ridiculous in that get-up,' Anthony said, wishing his friend, Mark Bradshaw, was here to witness the scene. Mark was a funny fucker, and he hated Martin even more than Anthony did, ever since he'd had broken Mark's nose playing football the summer before. Mark had made a mistake – a good player, he had out-dribbled the older boy one time too many, so Martin used a sly elbow to the face, to even the score.

'The horse is beautiful.' Emma pressed her nose against the glass.

'Too good for the likes of him.'

Martin caught them looking and shot them the finger. Anthony scowled and pretended he hadn't seen the gesture.

'I fucking hate him, him and that gobshite Gully. I hope they fall and break their necks.'

Emma sighed. Anthony glanced at her, suspiciously. Martin Harte had a curious effect on girls; even he knew that, though why this was so escaped him.

'What?'

'I want a horse.'

'Oh, you always say that.'

'I always want one.'

Across the road, Gully managed to wedge the dun in between two bigger hunters. The dun's neck was streaked with sweat and foam, and Gully's face was red above his too-tight shirt.

'He looks like he's going to shit himself, doesn't he?' Anthony said, unable to keep the glee from his voice. 'Look at the face on him, on Gully, look.'

'Who's going to shit himself?'

Emma nearly jumped out of her skin and Anthony felt his own face go red. He hated it when she did that, when she acted like some kind of freak. It made him remember that she *was* different. He turned around and found himself facing Larry's niece, Lucy Green, one of the prettiest girls in Killbragh. One year older than him, she had the bluest eyes he had ever seen, her dark hair thick and bouncy and full of curls. She was friendly too – and smart – not like most of the other eejit girls around the place.

'Gully, he's riding a right mad yoke.'

Lucy looked past him to the street, the trace of a smile on her lips. Her lips were stained with some kind of gloss, and when she leaned closer to the glass to get a better look, Anthony could smell the scent of her shampoo on her dark hair, apple, like summer time, not like the rancid medicated shampoo his mother insisted they use ever since they got nits.

'Oh look. There's Martin too. That must be his new horse. He told me he was getting one.'

She lifted a hand, waggling three fingers, but if Martin saw her he never let on: he was too busy, Anthony thought savagely, acting the lord of the manor in his stupid get-up on his stupid fancy horse.

A hound bayed. Hearing it, the dun ripped the reins from Gully's hands and sidestepped, slamming into the grey hunter, pinning him against a trailer. The grey baulked, reared a little and leaped out onto the road, slipping and losing its footing on the slick surface. Sensing freedom, the Dun darted after the grey. Martin Harte threw back his head and laughed as Gully and the dun made their way up the street, travelling backwards at speed, with Gully, swearing and pink-faced, kicking the horse's sides as hard as he could to make him go forward again. But the dun didn't stop, and in seconds they vanished from view and stayed gone until Arthur Donovan and a number of other men ran up the road and beat the dun back to the rest of the field. Emma, who hated any kind of cruelty or violence, began to hum under her breath and rub her arms frantically.

Jack joined them, the Sunday papers under one arm and three Cornettos in his hand. He smiled at Lucy.

'Hello there young lady.'

'Hello Mr Byrne.'

Anthony felt like he was dying inside. His eyes shifted to Emma, who was starting to bounce from one foot to the other. Don't make a big deal of it, he silently pleaded. Just this one time, please don't make a big deal out of it.

'Emma?'

Beyond the glass, the dun, sides heaving, kicked out at a hound, sending it tumbling across the road. The hound gave an agonised screech, but managed to get up again and run off down the road, limping badly.

'Ara curse you, you fucking eejit!' Tommy McGrath slid his big hunter into Gully's horse and lashed Gully with his riding crop, catching him across the shoulders. 'Mind the hounds!'

Gully swore, and tried to steady the dun, who was starting to bunny hop.

'Pull his fucking head up!' Arthur Donovan roared from the side of the road.

Emma's hum grew louder, her nails raking into the fabric of her coat.

'Emma come on now, love, it's all right, it's all right–'

Shut up, Anthony pleaded silently; stop talking to her that way. You'll only make it worse.

'Emma–'

Horns sounded. The hounds began to mill forward, trotting out, tails up and wagging fiercely.

Gully gave the dun an unmerciful strike across the neck with his crop and the animal plunged forwards, frothing, fighting the bit with every stride. There was, Anthony noticed, blood in the foam on his neck.

'We should go.' Anthony grabbed the door and yanked it open too hard, so that he fell backwards and trod on Lucy, who yelped in pain.

'Anthony, here now, be careful where–'

Before his father could say another word Anthony was out the door and walking hard towards the car, head down, trying not to see or be seen. He was furious with Emma, with his father, with Lucy. Who cared if he'd hurt her stupid foot, she shouldn't have been standing half way up his arse in the first place.

'Watch out!'

A dark shape danced past, so close it almost brushed Anthony's nose.

'Fucking eejit, are you trying to get killed? Get out of the way.'

Anthony looked up into Martin Harte's furious face.

'Fuck off Harte, you don't own the road.'

He didn't know why he'd said what he did. He didn't mean anything by it at all, but as soon as the words left his mouth he knew it would cost him, he just didn't know how.

Martin Harte leaned down out of his saddle and said in a low, hard voice. 'Is that right, Byrne? We'll see about that.'

Martin spurred his horse and Anthony made it the rest of the way to the car unscathed.

CHAPTER 8

'I don't care what you have to say, have you seen the state of my son's arm? An animal wouldn't have done it. She nearly savaged him.'

'Please, Mrs Nolan, would you please calm down?' Mrs Pippet, the principal of Killbragh Primary, waved her hands ineffectually and proffered a chair for the second time. Elizabeth Nolan, who was in no mood to be placated, remained on her feet. She glared at Nuala Foyle, who was leaning against the radiator, unconsciously letting Mrs Pippet take the brunt of Mrs Nolan's considerable wrath.

'I don't want to sit down. Tell me this now and tell me no more, where were you, Miss Foyle, when that rip attacked my son?'

'As I said, I was writing on the blackboard. I had my back turned for a few seconds when I heard…when Gary started yelling.'

'He said she went for him like a dog. He said you couldn't even pull her off, she was that out of her mind.'

Nuala glanced involuntarily at her own legs. They were going to be black and blue when they finished swelling. Emma had kicked them to pieces.

'Please, Mrs Nolan, I understand you're upset–'

'Upset? I'm not upset, I'm livid, that's what I am, livid. It's not the first time she's gone for Gary is it? What are you going to do about that young one? What are you going to do to protect the children of this school?'

'Mrs Nolan–'

'She shouldn't even be here at all, and that's the truth of it. She's not right in the head. Everyone knows that.'

'Mrs Nolan, if you'll just give me a moment to–'

'I'll have to take Gary to the doctor and who's going to pay for that? It's not on; we don't leave our children here to be treated like this. She should be in a school for people…other people like her.'

Unaware that she was being discussed inside, Emma sat on a wooden bench in the school's concrete play-shelter. As always, she was alone, waiting for the dreaded bell to sound, which meant that she had to once more endure the small, pokey horror of the prefabricated classroom and the relentless attention of Miss Foyle.

There were only ten children in Emma's class, and that number included Anthony. It mattered little to Emma how many there were. Since her first day, she had been singled out and treated like a pariah. Not that Emma tried to break any ice with the other children anyway; she would not have known where to begin. She was bewildered by them and found the idea of forming friendships incomprehensible. Sometimes they made fun of her and called her names, but for the most part they left her alone and played amongst themselves.

But, on this day, everyone was whispering about her, about the fact that Gary Nolan's mother had arrived and was kicking up a storm while Gary sat on the bench in the hall, his arm in bits, his eyes red-rimmed from crying.

'There they go,' Mark Bradshaw said, ignoring the ball Anthony had kicked towards him. 'Jaysus, will you look at the state of him?'

Anthony glanced up in time to see Mrs Nolan striding out the school gate, head up in the air, with Gary trotting by her side, trying to keep up.

'She looks fierce cross.'

'Are we playing or not?'

'Why did Emma bite him like that? What did he do to her anyway?'

'How should I know?' Anthony said. He savagely kicked at the ball, slicing it with the outside of his foot so that it sailed over the back wall into the fields behind the playground. Mark stood with his hands on his hips, disgusted.

'Aw way to go, ya dipshit.'

'Relax the head. I'll go get it.'

Anthony ran past the shelter and scrambled up onto the wall. He was trying not to think about what had happened earlier in the classroom, though he was mortified by it. Since the first day they'd attended Killbragh Primary, Anthony had done his level best to distance himself from his twin and, for the most part, he had succeeded; but days like this tossed the salad and made people look at him funny, and he knew they were wondering if whatever madness Emma had tainted his flesh too.

He found the ball in the long grass, carried it back to the wall, tossed it over and climbed up again. As soon as he dropped down onto the school grass he knew something was up. Deirdre Cullen was grinning that malicious grin of hers – the one that suggested trouble was heading someone's way.

'What?'

Mark pointed. Anthony's heart sank when he saw his own mother enter the school gate and walk directly into the main building.

'Pippet must have called her in.'

Anthony shrugged and put his foot on the ball, pissed off that Mark sounded so delighted with the drama.

'Your mammy's here,' Deirdre Cullen said, twirling towards him with her friends, Alison and Colette, in tow. 'Bet you anything your stupid sister's going to get sent away now.'

'Shut up, pig nose.'

Mark tittered, but Deirdre wasn't finished.

'Bet they send her to that mad hospital. They'll put her in a straitjacket and feed her mashed foods. They'll open up her head with a drill and she'll be drooling like this…' She locked her arms around her sides and started rocking. 'Whooooo, oooooo, I'm mad, woooo.'

Other children were starting to laugh. Anthony's cheeks burned.

'I told you to shut up.'

'I bet they'll do experiments on her and–'

Anthony punched her straight in the chest. Deirdre when down hard. There was a moment of shocked silence, and then she started bawling loud enough to raise the dead.

'Oh shit,' Mark said, staring at him. 'Oh shit, now you've done it.'

'I hope you know this is all your fault,' Anthony said to Emma. They were sitting on the school wall, waiting for Evelyn to finish her meeting with Mrs Pippet.

Emma didn't reply, so Anthony bounced his heels against the pebbledash, puffing out his cheeks in temper.

Deirdre had told on him, as he had known she would the second he'd thrown the punch, and he'd had to go before Mrs Pippet, with his mother sitting on a chair in front of her desk, staring at him as though she didn't recognise him.

'She started it' was his only line of defence and it had sounded weak, even to his ears.

Emma picked at a scab on her hand. Now that she knew she was going home she was as relaxed as she could be in a public place.

'Why did you do it?'

Emma shrugged and went on picking.

'Tell me.'

'I do not want to tell you.'

'Why not?'

She sighed and looked away. Her dark brown eyes scanned everything until they focused on a small marmalade cat sitting on the wall of the house opposite the school: he was licking his paw and using that to wash his face.

'You have to tell anyway,' Anthony said, feeling crosser and more hard done-by as each second passed. 'Mam will want to know. I bet you anything you won't be allowed come to school anymore.'

'Good. I do not like school.'

'Yeah well, so, nobody does. You still have to go.'

'Why?'

'Because you have to.'

'Why?'

'It's the rules.'

Emma cocked her head and furrowed her brow.

'I do not understand the rules.'

'That's because you're a gobshite.'

She glanced at the side of his face. 'You are angry.'

'You bit Gary in front of everyone. Now everyone's laughing at you, at us.'

'People laugh at me every day.'

'So?' Anthony curled his hands into fists. 'That's your fault too.'

Evelyn came out the front door and stood on the top step. She smoothed her hair and plucked at her blouse, then walked towards them, fast, tight-lipped.

'Get your things.'

She climbed into the car and sat there. Anthony and Emma got into the back seat and sat as far away as possible from each other.

'Mam, listen I–'

'Be quiet Anthony. Don't say one word to me. And check your shoes. Did one of you step in something?'

'No,' they said in unison.

Evelyn rolled down the window, opened her handbag and extracted a packet of cigarettes and a box of matches. She lit one before she started the engine and took a really long drag on it before she pulled away from the school, spraying gravel in her wake.

As soon as they got home Emma went straight to her room and shut the door. Anthony hung around in the sitting room, half watching *Good Afternoon* until the cartoons began. Normally, he enjoyed having the television to himself, but that afternoon he could barely concentrate, not with the father-shaped sword of Damocles hanging over his head.

On screen, Thelma Mansfield smiled winningly at an old woman who looked uncomfortable and hot under the bright studio lights.

Time dragged; the carriage clock over the mantelpiece seemed louder than usual. Anthony picked at a thread on a sofa button until he worked it loose, then covered his crime with a cushion.

The door of the sitting room opened and his father filled the gap.

'Turn that off.'

Anthony slid off the sofa and turned the dial until it clunked. 'Well?'

'She bit Gary Nolan on the arm.'

'Was he messing with her?'

'No, I don't think so. She just bit him.'

'So then you thought it would be a good idea to beat up a girl?'

'I didn't beat her up. I hit her once and she fell over,' Anthony said, wondering why his father didn't ask if *she* had been messing with *him*.

Jack shook his head sourly. 'A girl, you big man, you hit a little girl. By Jesus, Anthony, have you no cop on at all?'

'She was going on about Emma.'

'Stick and stones.'

'I'm sorry.'

'Little good that does. Go upstairs and do some homework. I'm sick of the sight of you.'

Later that evening, Anthony watched from his window as his parents, dressed in their 'good' clothes, got into the car and drove off. Since leaving the farm mid-week was almost unheard of, as soon as the taillights disappeared down the lane, he hurried to the window on the landing so that he could see which direction they would take out on the road.

Left.

Emma was lying on her bed, reading an encyclopaedia.

'The folks are gone.'

'Yes.' Emma did not look up. 'I heard the car.'

'I bet they've gone to Nolan's house.'

'Is tomorrow a school day?'

'You know it is.'

'But I do not need to go now.'

'No, you've been expelled…kicked out.'

'Expelled. Yes. This is good.'

'It's not good you eejit, it's bad.'

'Why?'

Anthony sighed, suddenly bored stiff by the conversation. He looked at the stack of books on Emma's makeshift desk, books on animals mostly; *Exotic creatures of the Southern Hemisphere* read the one nearest to him. He picked it up and flicked through it: birds, monkeys, reptiles, weird creatures that looked like they'd been put together with the spare parts from other creatures. He put it back and wrinkled his nose.

'What stinks?'

'My school bag.'

He looked around and saw that she had thrown it in the bin. He reached in and lifted it out.

'Yerugh, it's…it's… is this shit?'

'Yes.'

Anthony flung down the bag. 'Did Gary Nolan do this?'

'Yes.'

'We have to tell Mam and Dad.'

'Why?'

'Because then they can… they'll know you didn't bite him for no reason. They can tell the school and they might let you back.'

'But I do not want to go to school.'

'You should bloody well tell them anyway. At least it would stop people going around talking about you like you're some kind of loony.'

'I do not care what people say.'

Anthony opened his mouth to argue, but stopped himself. What was he going to argue for? She was telling the truth. He thought about that for a moment. There were only a few weeks left before the summer holidays anyway. Emma-free weeks.

'You should burn the bag.'

'I will,' she said, turning the page. 'Did you know the largest tarantula is called a Goliath?'

Anthony hesitated, but there was nowhere for him to go except straight ahead and over the bridge. Unfortunately, the group he had to pass by to get to the other side contained Gully Donovan, Martin Harte and a number of other blockheads from around the area. Worse still, they'd already clocked him. To change course now would be a disaster. There was nothing for it but to maintain speed and course, a flesh-and-blood Titanic, head up, eyes in neutral. The closer he got, the more he imagined himself leaping over the hump-backed wall, letting the swirling water take him.

'How's it hangin' Bryne?'

Anthony recognised the minced-meat face of his addresser: Hacker Quinn, the most acned person to have ever walked the planet. Even his eyelids had spots. Nobody mentioned it anywhere near him though, not since he'd pushed Simon Kelly into the middle of a bonfire for jokingly calling him 'pus-chops.' It had taken many months for Simon's eyebrows to grow back and his hands had been so badly burned, they'd had to graft skin from his arse to fix them, resulting in some pretty spectacular nicknames of his own. Everyone who had been at the bonfire swore they could smell the stink of burning hair and flesh in their nostrils for weeks.

'Hello,' Anthony managed, trying hard to keep his voice steady. Should he stop or keep walking? Walking seemed the right thing to do, but what if it wasn't, what if that was some kind of silent insult? To cover all his options Anthony slowed to a crawl, but kicked a stone, hoping this action would give him enough cover to avoid any more of their attention. Alas…

'Where you going?'

'Table tennis.'

'Oh yeah? You any good?'

'I'm okay.'

'Got some free time on your hands to practise now though.' Martin Harte's sly eyes looked him over. 'Don't you?'

What he was implying was not lost on Anthony, though it was on Gully Donovan, who only laughed when everyone else had already started.

'Yeah, I heard you and your sister were booted out of the school,' Hacker said.

It wasn't a question, so there was nothing else to do but confirm it. 'Yeah…well no, I was suspended, only.'

'What you do?'

'I heard he nearly tore the Nolan kid's arm off,' one of the other blockheads said, passing a cigarette to Hacker.

'That wasn't him, that was his sister,' Martin replied, never taking his eyes off Anthony.

'Why was he shafted so?'

'He hit a girl,' Martin said, making 'girl' sound fruity.

'Hit girls do ya?' Hacker asked, taking a drag of the cigarette between three pinched fingers, the way tough guys always did on television. 'What the fuck's that about?'

Anthony's mouth was so dry he had to lick his lips before he spoke.

'She was talking shit, so I pushed her over.'

'Shouldn't hit girls,' Hacker said. 'Even if they deserve it.'

Anthony looked at his shoes. He wished he had stayed home, even if the atmosphere there was like Pompeii after the volcano had erupted.

'Fuckin' women though,' Hacker said. 'They would fucking drive you to it.'

'Yeah,' Gully said, too quickly. But it was understandable he'd feel that way. His own mother had run off years before with another man, back when Sean was still a baby and Gully barely old enough to keep a bed dry.

'Can't reason with them.'

'No,' a blockhead nodded sagely.

'Some of them don't want to reason, they keep pushing you to see what happens.' Hacker blew smoke through his nostrils. 'Like that one you were seeing Harte, the one that two-timed you with that four-eyed fucker in Arklow.'

Martin dug his hands into his pockets. 'I don't give a fuck about her anyway, he's welcome to her, she's only a hoor.'

'Should hear the shit my old lad has to listen to the second he gets in the door. Don't know how he doesn't fuckin' lose it some days. If I'd t'listen to that shit day after day…'

Nobody said anything this time; Hacker's eyes were backlit with thoughts that were too treacherous to dally with.

Anthony waited. He wanted to leave, but there were social rules to be observed here; he was the lowest rung on the ladder, the runt of the litter. He would stay here until the pack allowed him to leave. Fortunately, one of the blockheads solved his dilemma.

'I'm fucking starving.'

'Me too,' Gully said. 'I'm skint though.'

'Me as well,' Hacker said, after a moment of examining his many pockets.

Several eyes rolled towards Martin Harte.

'I would gladly pay you Tuesday,' Hacker said, doing a character's voice from Popeye, 'for a hamburger today.'

'What makes you think I've any money?'

Hacker laughed. A few others joined in. 'Don't be fucking daft, Moneybags.'

'I hardly get anything off the ould lad these days.'

'You don't need to *these days*, though, do ya?'

Martin scowled. He glanced at Anthony, who made sure to keep his expression neutral. Whatever they were talking about, it was *none* of his business.

'Come on Harte, the troops are dying in the trenches here.'

'Fine, but just chips.'

Almost as one they got to their feet.

'Enjoy your ping pong,' Hacker said, tapping one finger to his forehead in mock salute.

'Okay.'

'And don't be pushing no girls.'

'Okay.'

They moved off, hands in pockets, boots and tight jeans rolled at the bottom over their boots. Anthony watched them go, waiting until they were far enough ahead, so that he didn't have to walk on their heels. It seemed inconceivable to him that he might be one of them someday.

When they entered the chipper, he hurried on past to the Community Centre. He tried not to think of Martin Harte and why he might not need money *these days*.

None of your business, he told himself, heaving open the fire-proof door of the centre. Absolutely none.

CHAPTER 10

'There *are* other schools,' Evelyn said, peeling potatoes directly into a pot on the stove, splashing water everywhere.

'It's the only other primary for fifteen miles though.' Jack rubbed his eyes and picked up the newspaper he had hoped to read in peace before he had to go collect his mother and take her to town to get her bi-annual perm in one of the few hairdressers she did not despise.

'I can't believe they turned her down like that. So dismissive.'

'Her reputation precedes her.' Jack winked at Emma who paid him no attention at all and didn't get the joke anyway.

'She can't *not* go to school, Jack.'

'Evie, nobody is saying that. It's just–'

Evelyn's back stiffened. 'What? It's just what then?'

Anthony tried to concentrate on reading the back of the cereal box. Out of the corner of his eye he could see his father doing that thing he did with his leg when he felt cornered: jiggle jiggle tap, jiggle jiggle tap. Anthony spooned cornflakes into his mouth so fast the milk ran down his chin, but he didn't care, he just wanted to be finished so that he could leave. He was sick of his parents. For the last few weeks all they seemed to do was fight. He hated that no matter what *he* wanted to talk about every conversation turned back to Emma. Two whole weeks of it since the bite and he was sick to death of listening to them repeat the same boring things to one another. Worst of all, Gary Nolan was going around the whole place showing off his 'war wound' and telling anyone who would listen that Anthony's parents had gone grovelling to his house to apologise. Anthony wanted to beat his fat face until it broke, but he was afraid to touch him in case it caused more trouble. As it was, he was lucky not to have been suspended for giving Pig Nose Cullen a much-deserved wallop.

'There's no point getting angry about any of it,' Jack said finally. 'What's done is done.'

'I'm not angry.'

Anthony watched another splash of water and thought: I beg to differ.

'There's only a few weeks until the summer holidays anyway. She's not going to miss a whole lot is she? She'll be going to a different school next year anyway.'

'That is not the point.' Evelyn slammed the lid on the pot.

Emma, disturbed and irritated by the noise, drained the last of her milk and stood up.

'Where do you think you're going?' Evelyn said.

'Outside.'

'Sit down and finish your breakfast.'

'I am finished.'

'You didn't eat your toast.'

'There is butter on it.'

'So? A bit of butter is not going to kill you.'

'I do not eat butter.'

'Evelyn…' Jack said in a voice that made Anthony cringe.

'Oh go on then,' Evelyn said, snatching the plate with the buttered toast off the table with such ferocity that the toast went flying and landed, buttery side down, on the floor.

Emma made good her escape.

'No wonder there's not a pick on her,' Evelyn said, savagely hurling the toast into the scrap bucket they kept for the dogs. 'What's wrong with butter I ask you?'

Anthony lifted his bowl and drank the remainder of his cornflake-flavoured milk and wiped his mouth with the back of his hand.

'Can I go?'

Jack glanced at him.

'Go where?'

'Over to Mark's.'

'I need a hand moving the cattle at some stage today.'

Anthony glanced at the clock over the stove. During the week, Mark had told him about the greatest hideout spot he'd ever seen; they had made plans to investigate it and, if possible, build the greatest fort the world had ever seen.

'Emma will help you.'

'I know she will. So will you. You can go over for an hour or two, but I want you back before eleven.'

'*Eleven?*'

Anthony was outraged. This was not fair. He hadn't had a Saturday off in ages... it wasn't like he even wanted a *whole* Saturday. Just a few hours to himself.

'If you're finished, put your bowl in the sink,' Evelyn said. 'I'm not your maid, Anthony.'

Outside, Emma was sitting on the rockery wall, playing with one of the feral cats that roamed the yard. As Anthony approached, the cat leaped down and scurried away.

'How come they let you play with them?'

'They are not afraid of me.'

'How come?'

She shrugged.

'I'm going over to Mark's.'

She looked at him blankly.

'Mark? Mark Bradshaw – my best friend that we've known forever.'

'I know who he is.'

'Then why the hell are you looking at me like that?'

'Like what?'

Anthony pulled a dumb, bovine face. Emma frowned. 'Is that how my face is now?'

'I'm going.' Anthony stalked away, shaking his head. Honestly, she was so impossible sometimes he didn't even know why he bothered. If there really was a God, he'd have been an only child by now, like Mark.

He collected his bike from the shed and cycled down the lane, using the soles of his runners as brakes when he approached the road.

Mark was still in bed when he got there, but Mrs Bradshaw was nice, so he didn't mind waiting with her in the kitchen while Mark got dressed. Mrs Bradshaw was foreign, according to his grandmother, who made *that* sound like a bad thing, but Anthony couldn't tell if that was true or not, since she sounded exactly like everyone else in Killbragh to him. There was a Mr Bradshaw, but he worked in Dublin and was away from one end of the week to the other. A *queer* set-up, Anthony's grandmother said, but Mark and Mrs Bradshaw didn't seem to mind.

Mrs Bradshaw made him toast, which she cut into soldiers, and gave him a glass of Robinsons Barley Water. He ate the soldiers at the table, listening to her sing along to the radio.

Anthony loved the Bradshaw's kitchen: it was sunny and bright with double glass doors that overlooked the garden; not like the dark, pokey kitchen in his house. He liked Mrs Bradshaw too; she never shouted or gave out to Mark about stupid things. She let him eat mini pizzas and Angel Delight *and* let him choose his own clothes, something that made Anthony mad with jealousy.

'How's the craic?' Mark entered the kitchen, his face puffy from sleep.

'Good,' Anthony nodded, keeping his expression neutral. Mark was wearing new straight-legged jeans, Doc Marten boots and a black T-shirt. Anthony felt the toast he had been enjoying stick in his throat. Mark looked so grown-up, standing there in the sunlight, in his new clobber, his blonde hair tousled.

'What plan have you boys?' Mrs Bradshaw poured herself a cup of coffee – she never drank tea as far as Anthony knew. She smiled at Mark, who was helping himself to a slice of apple pie straight out of the fridge (he didn't even have to put it on a plate, Anthony noticed, just ate it standing up).

'Oh nothing much, we're going to go for a cycle.'

'Be careful on those roads.'

'We will,' Mark replied and winked at Anthony, who winked back when Mrs Bradshaw wasn't looking.

After breakfast, they took their bikes and cycled over towards Castle Douglas. It was a ruin of a place and hadn't been lived in for donkey's years. Some people said it was haunted – that on the night of the harvest moon, a strange woman in white walked through the grounds calling for her dead husband to come back to her. Anthony thought that was pure guff, but even so, he usually gave the place a wide berth.

'Ara, ghosts me hole,' Mark said, when he told him the story. 'I don't believe that, do you?'

'Course not, I'm only telling you.'

'Anyway, even if there was such a thing as ghosts, they wouldn't be there in broad daylight.'

'No, sure they only come out at night.'

'Exactly.'

They rode hard up Douglas Hill, standing up on the pedals, their upper bodies bent almost double over the handlebars, and soon they were cycling alongside the vast crumbling walls that surrounded the grounds.

'The wall near Sally's Bridge has collapsed,' Mark said, between gasps for air. 'We can stash the bikes and climb over.'

They freewheeled down the hill towards the bridge, laughing and yapping about nothing in particular. For the first time in ages, Anthony forgot about being angry.

They hid the bikes behind a ditch at the bridge and scrambled over the walls, using the branches of a tree as scaffolding. Mark went first and Anthony dropped down behind him seconds later.

'Whoa.'

'Yeah, I know,' Mark said proudly. 'This is the old orchard. I could see it the first day I climbed the wall.'

'Did you go up to the castle?'

'No…but only 'cause I hadn't any time. I wasn't afraid or anything.'

Anthony could tell without looking at him that he was spoofing, but he let it go. The truth that was even in the orchard the air felt a little different from the road: colder, older or something.

'Come on,' Mark said, taking off at a lope through the tangled undergrowth, 'let's go see our new headquarters!'

'Wait for me, ye big thick!'

Anthony raced after him, ducking branches and leaping briars, the words of his father all but forgotten.

CHAPTER 11

'Come quick!'

Anthony jumped down the last few steps and landed on cracked flagstone, in what had once probably been a pantry of some kind. It was dark: the windows were covered by ivy and other climbers.

'Where are you?' he asked into the gloom.

'Around here.'

Anthony peered around the corner.

'What is it?'

'I think there's another room back here. Give me hand with the door.'

They were down in the basement, in an annex of the castle proper. It was dank and musty, filled with shadows and vast cobwebs. Anthony preferred scouring the rooms upstairs. Some of those had been really cool, especially the round room at the end of the hallway on the upper floor, with its tiny, odd-shaped window covered in ivy. Anthony wanted to climb out onto the walkway between the round room and what remained of the ramparts to see if there were any old weapons still around, like a canon or something cool like that, but Mark had taken one look outside and declared the bricks dry and a little crumbly. He said he thought the walkway might collapse.

The bricks hadn't looked particularly dry or crumbly to Anthony, but he had followed Mark back downstairs anyway.

'It's stuck,' Mark said, hauling with all his might on a large rusted metal ring. 'Come on, pull.'

Anthony stepped in beside him and grabbed a hold of the ring too. He leaned back, bracing his foot against the wall. The door groaned and creaked and gave inch by inch, until they had a gap wide enough that they could fit through if they turned their bodies sideways.

Anthony wrinkled his nose.

'I'm not going in there.'

'What? Why not?'

'Er, it's pitch black, Mark, we might break our necks.'

'You're chicken.'

'I bet it's full of rats too.'

Mark tucked his arm into his armpits and flapped them.

'Bawk bawk bawk.'

'Stop that.'

'Bawk bawk.'

Anthony punched him on the arm, which only made Mark dance around and flap harder.

'Bawk!'

'All right, stop! I'll go with you, but don't blame me if we fall to our deaths.'

Mark grinned. 'Top man. We'll need sticks though, or something we can use as lights. I saw it on *MacGyver* last week. He's trapped in this abandoned coalmine, right, and there's no way to see, but he makes a torch using some sticks, some rags and some paraffin oil, or petrol or something.'

'We don't have any of those things.'

'Will you stop, *come on* help me look.'

After a thorough search, they managed prise off a panel from the wall upstairs. Mark set it against the steps and smashed it into kindling with the heel of his foot; they selected the longest piece and wrapped one end of it in a piece of oilskin they found in the parlour. The oilskin was so old and dry it cracked when they bent it, but it went up easy when Mark set a match to it (that was another thing about Mark, Anthony thought, feeling more inadequate as the day wore on: he always carried matches).

'Behold our torch!' Mark said, holding the wood aloft. He wiggled his eyebrows and put on a weird accent. 'Come on, my fellow explorer, let us enter the bowls of this ancient dwelling.'

'*Bowels*,' Anthony said, watching pieces of oilskins crackle and drop onto the floor.

'Wha'?'

'Ah Jaysus, forget it.'

Mark squeezed through the gap first, holding the makeshift torch in front of him. Anthony came next, trying not to gag on the rancid air.

'It's some kind of chamber,' Mark said, pointing the flame into the shadows. 'Look, benches and hooks! A torture chamber.'

'It's probably a cold room. I read about those before. They're for meat storage. Remember in history class? People used them before they invented fridges and shit.'

'Look, there's another door. I bet that's where they put the bodies when they took them down from the hooks.'

Something scurried across Anthony's foot. He shrieked and leaped sideways, crashing into Mark, who almost dropped the torch onto their heads.

'Here, be careful!'

'I think we should go, that thing's burning out fast.'

'Not until we check out that door, there could be skeletons or anything in there.'

The last thing Anthony wanted think about was a skeleton, but he clamped his jaw shut on his opinion, and stayed close to Mark as they tip-toed across the earthen floor. He tried to regulate his breathing, mad at himself for being afraid – mad at Mark for not.

The door was only half height, and it looked older in the flickering light than the one they'd opened first. It had strange ornate hinges and a weird insignia carved into the wood.

'Hey,' Mark said, sounding surprised, 'this has been opened already, look.'

He was right: Anthony saw that the door opened outwards and could see where it had dragged in the clay.

'Could have been years ago. Maybe by whoever did the torture.'

Anthony steadied Mark's hand and peered at the dirty clay floor.

'I don't think torturers wore runners though.'

'Oh shit, yeah, you're right. I can see the prints now.'

'We should go.'

'But what if there's a body in here?'

'Will you stop? Come on, that yoke's nearly out and the smoke off it is giving me a headache.'

'Here, one second. Hold it for me.'

Exasperated, Anthony took the sputtering torch and waited for Mark to open the door. It came easily enough, and both boys held their breaths as Anthony thrust the torch into the space beyond.

'What's all that stuff?'

Anthony looked closer and blinked.

'Machinery.'

'Torture machinery?'

'No you thick…soldering iron, that's a sander…shit, look, candlesticks…I bet this stuff is all stolen.'

'Oh.'

The torch flickered once, twice and dimmed as the last of the oilcloth smouldered to nothing.

'We need to go, now. Seriously, we need to get out of here.'

'But what about all this stuff, are we going to–'

Then they heard it: a dog barking. It sounded close.

It sounded right outside.

CHAPTER 12

'Run!'

Anthony dropped the torch and they ran. They squeezed back through the heavy door and hurtled this way and that, panicking. All thoughts of ghosts and ancient torture evaporated. Their fears were real now: afraid of being caught, afraid of getting into trouble.

There were two ways out of the castle, either straight through the broken front doors or climb out through the only ground floor window that wasn't boarded over, to the left of the main hall. But the barks came from that direction and they would surely been caught if they made a break for it.

'Quick,' Anthony said, keeping his voice low. 'Upstairs.'

They took the stone steps three at time, the soft soles of their runners soundless as they climbed – but where to hide? The rooms were virtually empty and offered nothing but cobwebs and flaking plaster to conceal them.

Mark's head jerked up.

'Shit, did you hear that?'

Anthony nodded. There were voices below.

'The round room,' Anthony said, and led Mark up another flight of steps and down to the end of the hall. 'We can get out onto the ledge.'

But at the small window something strange happened: Mark baulked.

'I don't think this is a good idea.'

'Are you mad or what? Come on, there's nowhere else.'

'We can't go out there… they'll see us.'

'No they won't, you'd have to be about a mile away to see us. Come on, quick, climb out.'

Mark shook his head and backed up a step. 'It's fierce narrow.'

'It's wide enough.'

'Not the window, the ledge.'

'It's grand, it will hold us if we keep close to the wall.'

'I don't like heights, Anthony.'

Anthony stared at him. MacGyver Mark, explorer, adventurer, bravest person he knew, standing there in jeans and Doc Martens – <u>he</u> was afraid of heights?

The voices were closer; at any moment they might be up there with them. Anthony felt his balls contract with fear.

'Get fucking out there before I throw you out.'

Something in Anthony's voice must have worked, because Mark blessed himself and slowly eased himself through the ivy and stepped gingerly out onto the narrow brick walkway. Anthony squeezed out behind him and rearranged the ivy to conceal the window as much as possible. As he did so, someone entered the round room. He ducked down and felt Mark's knees pressing in his back. He held his breath, offering God all manner of bribes if He would just, please, keep them from being discovered.

'I told you the dog was keen.'

Anthony cringed. He recognised the voice. It was Gully Donovan.

'Anything?'

Another voice this time, distorted but familiar. 'Nothing.'

'Did you search the other rooms?'

'Yeah, I told ya, there's nobody up here.'

'Well someone was fucking here, and they were here recently, that stick is still smouldering.'

'Martin Harte,' Mark whispered into Anthony's ear. Anthony elbowed him in the chest to warn him not to make a sound. The blood was pounding through his arteries so hard he was sure the older boys would hear it anyway.

'Maybe they ran off when they heard the dog.'

'We'd have seen them.'

Silence. Anthony could picture Martin's face: hard and sulky, his fat lower lip protruding, pouting like a baby.

'I don't like it. We'll need to move the gear out of here.'

'Today?'

'*Of course* today! Jesus Gull, are you fucking thick or what?'

'I told you to stop calling me that.'

'Stop acting it then.'

'Duggan is on the way though. Got no way of calling him off now.'

Martin swore.

Outside the dog started up again.

'That's probably him now.'

'Or the fucking cops.'

'Ah shite, is it?'

'I don't know, do I Gull? Fold that shotgun over your arm, for fuck's sake. If anyone asks, the dog flushed a fox in here and we just came to finish the job.'

Anthony's bladder tightened at the mention of the gun. He didn't risk a glance at Mark, but he knew from the way he was breathing he felt much the same way.

'Youse up there?'

'It's Duggan.'

'I know who it is,' Martin said. 'Right, say nothing about any visitors. We offload what he wants, and we move the rest today. Got it?'

'Yeah, but where are we going to take it? Can't go to mine.'

'We'll bring it up to the shed behind my Nana's house. She never uses it. We can leave it there for a day or two until we find somewhere better.'

'Hey, are youse coming down or are youse having a party?'

'Be right down Duggan,' Martin called, his voice steady as a rock. 'We're just looking at…cornicing.'

'At what?' Gully asked.

'Get the fuck down there, and watch where you're pointing that thing.'

Anthony's legs were starting to cramp. He tried to ease backwards, but Mark was wedged tightly against him.

'You need to move back,' he whispered.

'I can't.'

'Jesus, Mark will you move back a bit.'

'I'll fall.'

'You won't fall. Look, there's a good few inches between you and the ledge.'

'We're stuck here until they go, aren't we?'

'They'll be gone soon enough. Move back a bit.'

Mark inched back enough so that Anthony had room to turn and rest his back against the castle wall. He straightened his legs, letting them dangle over the ledge.

'Don't do that,' Mark said. His face was white as a sheet, and sweat beaded his forehead.

Anthony ignored him. He glanced at his watch and swore when he realised it was already close to ten o'clock. If he was late he'd never hear the end of it from his old man.

'We've got to get down from here, Mark. Slide over there and see if we can climb up onto the ramparts, there's got to be steps or something.'

Mark dug his nails into the brick.

'Fuck off, I'm not sliding anywhere.'

'They could be down there for ages. We've got to get out of here.'

'I can't.'

Anthony felt his head grow hot with temper. 'Fine, I'll go myself.'

'No!' Mark grabbed him, startling him badly. 'Don't leave me up here, Anthony, please.'

'Let go a me. You'll kill us both with that carry on.'

'Promise you won't leave me.'

'Shut up, okay. Just shut up. I won't leave you. Now, will you let go of me?'

Mark looked down at his hand and released him. He was trembling but at least he was quiet. Anthony rested his head against the wall and stared out over the tops of the trees to the purple hills in the distance. He realised he could see his house from there. He held out his hand and covered the farmhouse with his thumb.

'If they find us we're fucked. Do you know that?'

Mark closed his eyes, his lips pressed tightly together.

'Some fucking hideout,' Anthony said, watching a crow land on the ramparts and tilt his head in their direction. As he watched, it hopped a little closer, then launched itself into the air and flew away towards the village.

CHAPTER 13

Just before school broke for the summer holidays, Evelyn, in a somewhat desperate fit of madness, had decided she would throw a party for the twins. It was the first party ever to be held in the Byrne home in all the children's years at school, and Evelyn was taking it very seriously indeed. She baked sponges, cakes and buns, and bought bottles of KP lemonade and packets of crisps.

'Why are you doing this?' Anthony asked, watching her ice a cake. 'It's not our birthdays or anything.'

'I think after everything that's happened a party might be a good idea. Give everyone something to look forward to.'

'Who?'

'You, for one, and Emma.' Evelyn offered Anthony the spatula to lick. 'I really should have thought of this before now. We often had parties when I was growing up.'

Anthony raised his eyebrows. His mother rarely mentioned her childhood.

'This tastes really good.'

She smiled at him and ruffled his hair.

What Jack thought of the party Anthony had no idea, but he doubted his father relished the idea of his home being invaded by six children, of whom four were no relation.

Emma was also glum about the prospect. When pressed on the subject of who she might like to ask, she shot Evelyn a withering glance and went up the fields after Jack, a number of cats and dogs trailing in her wake.

'That young one.' Evelyn stood at the kitchen window, watching her go. 'I don't know what sort of girl she is at all. You'd think she'd be glad of a bit of company after the last few weeks.'

'She doesn't like people,' Anthony said. 'I don't know why you don't understand that.'

'There must be someone she'd like me to ask.'

'No,' Anthony said firmly. 'There isn't.'

'But surely she has to have one friend?'

Anthony rolled his eyes. 'Mam, she doesn't talk to anyone at school, not even the girls. She thinks they're stupid and they think she's weird.'

'Well I don't think that's a good thing,' Evelyn said, turning back to the stove. 'I don't think that's any way to carry on at all.'

Early that Saturday Jack ploughed the meadow, and planned to remove all the newly upturned rocks by hand before tilling. To this end, he had enlisted a number of local lads to help out. It was backbreaking labour, but quick enough to do with many hands. Normally, Emma and Anthony would be down there with him, but since it was the day of the party, he had given the children the day off. Emma protested loudly and said she was more than happy to work, but Jack insisted she take some time to 'have fun.'

Anthony was putting on a clean T-shirt in his bedroom when Emma slipped quietly in the door behind him. She wore blue shorts and a faded blue T-shirt with a cartoon lion on the front. Both her knees were covered in cuts and bruises, some old some new.

'Get out, I'm getting dressed.'

'Are you happy to have people coming here?'

'Not people, Emma, friends and family. Our cousins are coming too, you know.'

'Is this fun?'

'Of course it is, stupid. Don't you understand that?'

'No.'

'It's what people do. They have parties, play – they even talk to each other. Jesus, it's not that hard.' He scowled at her. 'You'd better not make a holy show of me.'

'I do not want people here.'

'Tough shit.'

The first of the children arrived not long afterwards. When they were all accounted for, Evelyn served up cake and lemonade and rice crispy buns in the kitchen, after which everyone was sent outside to play. As soon as she could, Emma slipped away and left them to it.

It felt weird showing people around the place, and Anthony wasn't entirely sure if he enjoyed the experience or not. The farm was home and most of the lads who were there came from farming stock themselves; but a few were not, and it was Gary Nolan who caused Anthony the most anxiety. He had been sure Gary would not be allowed to attend, but he had arrived with Mark Bradshaw and seemed in good spirits, his bite trauma shelved for the time being.

The boys played football for an hour in the yard, using Evelyn's flower planters as goalposts, careful not to make any sliding tackles on the gravelled surface. Tackling would surely mean a hell of a scraping, and none of them wanted to risk losing that much skin. Then they played three and in, laughing as Maurice Redmond, the bespectacled butcher's son, let in one goal after another.

'Come on lads, you don't have to *blast* them,' Maurice said, pushing his glasses up his nose for the umpteenth time, which made everyone roar laughing.

After a while they were exhausted and sweaty, and they trooped back to the house to refuel on lemonade and jellies.

'Where's Emma?' Evelyn asked.

'Dunno.'

There was still an hour to go before the first parent was due, so it was decided that they would head down to the meadow and see what the plough had turned up. They went, but found nothing more interesting than few pieces of broken blue glass. Their attention was soon turned, though, to the rather large number of frogs hopping about the place, disturbed by the overturned mud.

Laughing and chasing each other with the slippery amphibians, they collected as many as they could hold in their hands and carried them back to the yard. They threw them into the rain barrel Jack used to collect the runoff from the eaves, and started taking bets on whose frog could swim to the opposite side the fastest.

They were still racing frogs when they heard the sound of a car horn and galloped around the shed to see who was honking. It was Maurice's mother, a surprisingly glamorous woman who was at least twenty years her husband's junior (and a bit of a hussy, according to Anthony's grandmother).

Evelyn was leaning against a car door smoking a cigarette, and as the women chatted, the boys tore around, screaming and shouting, sensing that the end of their fun was near, hyped up on tiredness and sugar.

By the time the last boy had left, Anthony was cranky, tired and bordering on disagreeable.

'Did you have a good day, son?' Evelyn asked, waving at the final car.

'Yeah, it was okay.'

'Just okay?'

He shrugged. Truthfully, he was feeling a little sick from all the lemonade, but he would never admit that to a parent, *ever*.

'Did you see your sister?'

'Last time I saw her she was down the fields with Dad.'

'Oh. Did she say when she was coming up?'

'Not to me.'

He went inside and washed. He asked if he could watch television for a while and Evelyn said he could as long as he didn't put his feet on the sofa. Anthony switched on the monstrous set, settled back into the cushions and promptly fell asleep.

When he woke up it was nearly dark and Emma was standing over him. She was shivering.

'What's wrong?'

'You killed them.'

She lifted her right hand. Anthony saw the lifeless body of a frog, its pale yellow legs and webbed feet dangling down her wrist.

'I'm sorry I forgot–'

She flung the dead frog at him. It hit Anthony squarely in the face.

Anthony screamed; Emma flinched, and then struck him very hard across the cheek.

By the time Jack broke them up, Anthony had a swollen lip and Emma was bleeding from an enormous gash under her left eye where Anthony had kicked her off him.

'What the hell is going on here? Emma, stop it. Stop!'

'He killed them!' Emma screamed, wiggling free. 'He killed them. He let them drown.'

'Who? Who drowned?'

'The frogs!'

'What is going on?' Evelyn hurried into the room. 'Emma, *stop* screaming.'

Emma pointed her finger at Anthony. 'Why would you do that to them? They could not get out. They could not keep swimming. You let them drown. You did this!'

'They're just bloody frogs!' Anthony yelled.

'Yes, and you let them drown. You are like them. You are like *all of them*!'

'I'd rather be like them than you, you fucking weirdo.'

'Watch your mouth,' Jack said, grabbing him by the arm. 'There's no need for any of that, so there isn't.'

'Let go of me, talk to her, talk to her! She's the headcase, not me.'

'Anthony!'

Emma ran out of the room and upstairs. They heard her bedroom door slam.

'They're just frogs,' Anthony said, but Evelyn and Jack levelled him with such a look of disappointment that Anthony burst out crying and ran off to his own room.

CHAPTER 14

It was during breakfast on the second week of the summer holidays that Evelyn broke the news to Emma that she and Anthony were enrolled in a secondary school in Arklow, starting in September.

Emma, who had been nibbling dry toast while reading a book, took the news rather badly.

'I do not want to go to a new school.'

'Everybody has to go to school, Emma. Nobody *wants* to go.'

'I do not care about everyone else.'

Emma frowned, licked her finger and turned a page in her book.

'What are you reading about?'

'Animal husbandry.'

'You must have read those books a thousand times. Why don't you ever read any of the Judy Bloom books I got for you?'

'I do not want to go to that school. It is too far. How will I get there? How will I get home? Will you drive us?'

'You get picked up and dropped off by bus.'

'A *bus?*'

'Give it a chance. You never know, you might like it.'

'I will not.' Emma closed the book, put her plate in the sink and left without saying another word. Evelyn filled the kettle for a cup of tea, feeling relieved. It had gone easier than she had dared hope.

That afternoon, Emma pumped air into the tyres of her bike and cycled down the lane without telling anyone where she was going. She did not return for almost three hours. Evelyn was beginning to get worried when she appeared up the lane, a little sunburned and very thirsty.

'Where were you?'

'I do not want to go to the new school.'

'Oh not this again. You're going and that's final.'

Emma filled a glass of water from the kitchen tap and drank it in two swallows. She filled it a second time and aimed her eyes somewhere to the left of Evelyn's ear. 'With the correct curriculum I can study from home. You can apply to the Department of Education and–'

'No, no you can't.'

Emma set her jaw. For a moment, she reminded Evelyn of Margaret.

'Yes, it is possible. Mrs Pippet told me.'

'Mrs Pippet?'

'Yes.'

'When did you talk to her about this?'

'Today.'

'Where?'

'At her house. She has a very nice cat. His name is Edward.'

'I don't give a damn about her cat. Are you telling me you cycled all that way…to talk about staying home from school?'

'Yes, you can apply to the Department of Education for a special curriculum.'

'Okay, stop. I don't care what you can apply for. You're not staying at home.'

'Why?'

'Because you're not, that's why.'

'*That* is not a good reason.'

'Too bad. It's the only one I have.' Evelyn turned on her heel and went off to take the clothes in from the line.

That evening, Emma tried again as Evelyn prepared to dish up dinner: 'I would like to stay here and not attend that school.'

She threw this out over the table, not addressing anyone in particular. But Evelyn was on it in a flash.

'Emma, we've already discussed this.'

'There was no discussion. You did not discuss anything. You said, "Because you're not, that's why." That is not a discussion.'

Jack looked up from the pages of the *Irish Farmers Journal*. 'What's this?'

'Emma says she doesn't want to go to secondary school.'

Jack raised one eyebrow. 'Is that so?'

'Yes.' Emma used her fork to make sure none of her food touched the gold band that encircled the plate. This was a new concern of hers and it drove Evelyn up the walls.

'Everyone goes to school, pet.'

'That is not true. The children from the campsite do not go.'

'The *Tinkers*?' Evelyn snorted and drowned Anthony's mashed potato in gravy.

'Mam, that's too much gravy.'

She slapped the plate down before him hard enough for it to spill over onto the oilcloth covering the table. 'Is that who you *aspire* to be like?'

Emma wrinkled her forehead. 'Aspire?'

'You want to be like the Tinkers? Is that it?'

'I do not understand why I have to go there if I can do the curriculum from here.'

'Because you're *going*, and that's the end of it.'

Evelyn put Jack's plate in front of him. He folded the *Journal* and tucked it behind him on the chair.

'What curriculum are you on about?'

'Jack, don't encourage her.'

'I can apply to the Department of Education for a curriculum, and register to study from the family home. Mrs Pippet told me about it.'

'Well she needn't have bothered,' Evelyn said, with such a steely tone that Jack and Anthony both stared at her. 'You're not working from here. You're going to go to school like everyone else.'

'Dad, did you hear?' Anthony said, trying to change the subject. 'Someone broke into the Community Centre and stole the bathroom fittings and a load of the stackable chairs.'

'They did?' Jack chewed thoughtfully. 'Odd sort of thing to take, but sure I suppose if stuff isn't nailed down these days someone's bound to take it. Pat was telling me some crowd of cowboys robbed the six-bar gate from the bottom of the lane, and then didn't the feckers come along and try to sell it back to him.'

That evening, long after Emma and he had gone to bed, Anthony heard raised voices. He got up and crept across the floor, carefully avoiding the boards that creaked, and sat at the top of the stairs listening to his mother speak as she moved around the kitchen below.

'No Jack, you can see it as well as I can. If we let her leave what's next? She gets to withdraw from life itself?'

'Evelyn, there's no need to take that tone with me. I'm trying to look at it from her point of view too. She's frightened of crowds; she's frightened of new places and new people. This wouldn't be like a small village school where the students know her and teachers have endless patience and are happy to give her a bit of leeway. I don't see how she's going to cope with the upheaval. You saw her today, she's already stressed out to the eyeballs and she hasn't even started there yet.'

'There's plenty of things in life that will frighten her, Jack. She needs to *learn* how to cope. We'll be doing her no favours to cave in on this one.'

'Evie–'

'Don't Evie me.' A cupboard door slammed. 'I have fought with every single ounce of my being from the day that child was born to have her be treated like everyone else. I won't be the one to give up on her.'

'All right, all right,' Jack sighed. 'We'll find some kind of compromise. Tell her the first year is compulsory. Then we'll play it by ear after that.'

'For God's sake, we shouldn't need to compromise with our own child.' A chair scraped on the flagstones. 'This is exactly like it was with your mother. I knew you'd take her side. You take everyone's side but mine.'

'There *are* no sides. I'm trying to think what's best for her. You say you want her to be treated like everyone else, I understand that, but Evelyn...she's not *like* everyone else.'

'Do you think I don't know that?' Evelyn's voice cracked. 'I worry about her Jack. Sometimes I look at her and I'm afraid she's slipping away.'

Anthony crept back to his room and climbed under the covers. He thought about a school life without Emma: just him, no weirdo sister scratching and rocking and freaking out over nothing. The more he thought about it the more he vowed to help Emma realise her dream.

He would do it for her.

His altruism was a lie of course – he knew it was, deep down. But he could convince himself. He could pretend he was doing it for Emma, he could pretend he was putting her first.

He was okay with that.

CHAPTER 15

In the end, how to frame the compromise came to Jack in a stroke of near genius.

'How would you like to work with horses?'

'I would like that very much,' Emma said. She was feeding the calves milk from a bucket, and they were milling around her like large, knobbly-kneed dogs.

'If I set you up with a friend of Pat's, would you go?'

'Would I go where?'

Jack tried again.

'Pat's friend Pete owns a livery stable. Do you know what that is?'

'Yes, he keeps horses for other people.'

'Right, well this man, Pete, said he'd give you a job with him for the summer.'

Emma did not reply. One of the calves tried sucking the end of Emma's belt.

'There's a condition.'

Still nothing.

'You have to give the secondary school a go, for your mother's sake as well as your own.'

'I do not want to go to school anymore.'

'Well, I don't want to have to go dig up the weeds in the vegetable garden, but we need to eat.'

Emma emptied the last of the milk into the trough.

'What kind of horses does Pete have?'

'Oh now, all kinds I suppose, hunters mostly, a couple of ponies. He's got a fancy-looking horse of his own though. I've seen him out on it, a big black thing.' He held up his hand. 'Don't ask me what kind. I know as much about horses as I do about lions.'

The following Monday, Emma rose at dawn, dressed carefully in blue shorts and a blue T-shirt and went downstairs to make toast. She left the house without waking anyone, collected her bike from the shed and cycled to the stables. Jack had told her he would bring her, but she had the directions and she wanted to see how long it took her to get there by herself.

She arrived at the stables and found the gates locked, so she parked her bike in the knee-high weeds and climbed over the gates.

Her feet had barely touched down on the ground on the other side when a huge Rottweiler came charging out from the yard and bore down on her with terrible determination. Emma stood calmly. The dog stopped a few feet from her, barking, hackles up. Still Emma remained standing. She made no eye contact with the dog, nor any sound as it circled her, alternating between growls and barks.

By the time Pete Cartwright came running bare-chested from his tiny cottage, wearing only some faded denims and untied boots, the Rottweiler had given up barking and was sniffing the back of Emma's hand.

'What the flamin' hell is all this racket? Here, Ruby! Ruby, come away.'

'Ruby,' Emma said softly, and the dog wagged the nub of her tail.

Pete Cartwright was a skinny, chain-smoking horseman of mysterious origins. He was from somewhere in England – though he never confirmed where – and although he had been living in Ireland since the 1960s, he had never lost his English accent. No one knew his exact age (most people guessed him to be in his forties), nor did they know his marital status, political or religious views. He had little time for people, and less than little time for surprises, like the pale skinnymalinks standing in his yard at an ungodly hour.

'Has the cat got yer tongue? I asked who you are?'

'No, my tongue is in my mouth. I am Emma Byrne. I am going to work with horses.'

Pete blinked: 'Oh, yer early.'

'I was unsure of the distance. My father says it is better to be safe than sorry. I like being on time. I am not sure about being sorry.'

'I thought yer old man was going to drop y'off. I was planning to have a word with him.'

'My old man?'

'Yer father.'

'I do not think he is old. He is younger than you.'

'Don't pull any punches do yer?'

'Can I see the horses? I have read a lot about horses. They are one of our oldest domesticated creatures. Obviously, dogs are older, but that is understandable as dogs choose us.' She flicked out a hand and scratched Ruby under the chin. 'Horses would not choose us.'

'No, right enough.' Pete scratched his belly. 'Have y'ever ridden a horse?'

'No.'

'Have any experience with them at all?'

'No, but I have read a lot of books.'

'Flamin' hell. Right, well let me get dressed and I'll run through the rules with ye. Rule number one, by the way, is this is not a flamin' nursery. Yer to work.'

'Yes.'

'Rule number two, don't come 'ere before seven o'clock again. Rule number three, what I say goes.' Pete put his hands on his hips. 'Yer not afraid of dogs, are ye?'

'No.'

'Good.'

By half eight that morning Emma had helped feed and water twenty-two horses; by nine she was up to her eyes in horseshit and soiled straw. She had never been happier.

CHAPTER 16

By the end of Emma's first week it felt to Pete as though she had always been there. When Pat called to see how she was getting on, Pete told him she was 'daft as a brush but a champion worker'. Pat informed Jack and he informed Evelyn, who said, 'Well we already *know* that.'

Although unused to handling horses, it took Emma no time at all to study the animals at Pete's yard and learn their individual traits. They were a mixed bunch, but among her favourites were two good-natured hunters called Sober and Heppaworth, who, in Pete's opinion, should have been out on grass over the summer getting fat, not stuck in stables.

'Better to rest 'em,' Pete informed Emma, showing her how to tack Sober. 'Better for the mind and better for the body, they go sour otherwise. But some people,' Pete said, managing to make the word people sound like a swear word, 'think they know best.'

'Sour?'

'They get fed up. Horses get barn sour, some horses get work sour and some horses get herd sour – that's when they don't like being away from their friends.'

'Oh.'

Emma loved all the horses at the stables, but her favourite was Pete's personal horse, an eight-year old Friesian stallion named Claude.

'This boy,' Pete told Emma, 'is worth his weight in gold.'

'Really? That is a lot.' Emma said, gazing at Claude, wide-eyed. 'Is he dangerous?'

'He likes who he likes.'

'I saw a bull kill a boy once. My father says stallions are unpredictable, like bulls.'

'You treat 'em right, don't act stupid around them, they're no more unpredictable than any other animal.'

When he wasn't out in the paddocks, Claude was kept in a loose box at the end of the yard where he could watch the comings and goings, snickering at whatever caught his attention. Pete rode him out daily, no matter the weather, reining in his prancing elegance with light hands and a steady seat.

Emma thought Claude was the most beautiful animal she had ever seen, and she spent every spare moment she had hanging over his door, talking to him, patting his neck and feeding him polo mints. One morning, Claude surprised Pete by nickering to Emma when she cycled into the yard. When they stopped for a break after mucking out, Emma plied him with questions.

'Pete, why does Claude hate the Welsh pony?'

Pete lit a cigarette and crossed one leg over the other. He wore tattered corduroy trousers and a grandfather shirt that had been worn to threads. 'How do y'know he hates him?'

'He holds his ears flat and tries to bite him when he is close.'

'I reckon it's because the Welsh pony was late getting gelded.'

'Why does he hate the blacksmith?'

'Because the flamin' fool hit him one time, and once was enough for Claude.' Pete tapped his head. 'Claude don't forget.'

'Why does he hate the vet?'

'Because he's afraid of him.'

'He's not afraid of you.'

'No.'

'He does what you tell him.'

'He does.'

'But you do not hit horses.'

'That's right.'

Emma put her hands in her pockets and looked thoughtful. 'I am very happy about that. You are not mean.'

'I try not to be.'

'Why do people hate other people?'

'I…' Pete frowned, caught off guard. 'They have all sorts of reasons I suppose. Why y'asking, kid, do you hate someone?'

'No.'

'Did y'soak the beet like I asked?'

'Yes. He is not afraid of me either.'

'Who?'

'Claude.'

'No, I can see that. He likes you.'

'I like him.'

'I see that too.'

'I will not hit horses either.'

'That's probably for the best.'

'Will you teach me how to ride?'

'If you want.'

'But the way you do it, not like those people who were here at the weekend.'

'No?'

'No, the horses do not like that way.'

'You seem to notice a lot of shit other people don't,' Pete said. 'I'll show y'how to ride like me kid, but first finish that sandwich and let's get some work done. Eat the crusts n'all, they'll put hair on yer chest.'

Emma looked at her sandwich, horrified. 'Really?'

'No, not really, it's a flamin' expression.'

Pete was as good as his word. That afternoon he told Emma to go pick a riding hat that fitted her and come meet him in the arena. When she got there he was leading an older grey mare named Cara by her bridle.

'This old lady is bombproof,' Pete said, cinching the girth tighter. He bent down and offered Emma his cupped hand. Emma stared at it.

'You put yer foot in it,' Pete said after a moment, 'so I can give you a boost.'

'Oh.'

'Grab the pommel and when I say up, jump up.'

Emma put her foot into his hands and at his command scrambled on in an ungainly fashion. Cara stood patiently.

'I am very high up!'

'Put yer flamin' feet in the stirrups…now, how are they for length?'

'I do not know.'

'Stand up in them.'

Emma did as she was told, wobbling slightly.

'Good, now collect yer reins. No, not like that, like this. Turn yer hands the other way, no the other way! Okay…got it? Sit up straight, look through Cara's ears, not at the ground. Okay, yer feet… don't slide them the whole way through the stirrups, put yer heels down. Okay, ready? Give her a little tap with yer heel. No! Harder than that. Okay, now go.'

Emma learned fast, and within a few days she was riding like she had been in a saddle for years. She was fearless and followed every command Pete gave.

'She's a flamin' natural,' Pete told Jack when he saw him. 'You can't teach that kind of seat. You either have it or y'don't, and she does.'

'She's going all right then?'

'Pfft,' Pete said, jamming a Sweet Afton cigarette into his mouth. 'She's a grand kid, worth her weight in gold – but for God's sake don't tell her I said that!'

While Emma worked away the summer with Pete, Anthony landed a job scrubbing pots in the kitchen of a local hotel. It was tough work, and the pay was lousy, but Anthony liked it, and at least it kept him away from the farm.

'How are you getting on son?' Jack asked him one evening, as he was bagging up coins at the kitchen table.

'Fine.'

'Must be hot work in the kitchens.'

'I like it.'

'You're hair's getting long. Want me to make an appointment with the barber before school starts back up?'

'No, I like it this way.'

'It's hanging in your eyes. You'll go blind.'

Anthony bagged up the last of his coins and placed them in a cloth sack. 'I'm going upstairs.'

Jack watched him leave the room.

'That boy needs his hair cut,' he said to Evelyn.

'He'll get one before he goes back to school.'

'What's with all the black clothes all of a sudden?'

'I think he's trying to dress like some band he likes.'

'Emma seems happy working for Pete. He mentioned he'd be happy to offer her a full apprenticeship.'

'Jack, listen to me right now. She's going to school in September and that's that. She has brains to burn and she's not going to waste them fecking around in some stables.'

Jack lit his pipe. He waited for Evelyn to turn around, but she did not, and after a while he rose and went to watch television in the other room.

CHAPTER 17

The summer was short-lived, and before the Byrne children knew it, September was upon them and the new school year had begun.

Within a matter of weeks, Emma went from looking fit and relaxed to gaunt and miserable. She scratched at her arms, was clumsier than ever and her appetite waned to next to nothing. She hated her uniform, and no matter how many times Evelyn adjusted it, it hung awkwardly on her slender frame.

The nine-mile round-trip to school was the worst part of the whole experience: the bus was loud and bumpy, and it reeked of fumes and smoke from the furtively lit cigarettes in the back row.

Emma endured the journey to and from Killbragh wedged into the seat directly behind the bus driver. She spoke to no one and ignored the insults and paper missiles lobbed her way. Deirdre Cullen sometimes tried to provoke a response by tripping Emma on the steps or knocking her school bag out of her hands, but Emma did not respond. Anthony could see his sister was suffering and even felt a little sorry for her, but it would be social suicide if he got involved.

The school itself confused Emma. She got lost regularly and could not make sense of the timetable. She vanished one day after lunch-break, and Anthony was sent to look for her. He found her sitting on the wooden steps in the gym with a book open on her lap.

'You're supposed to be in science class. Mrs Campbell sent me to find you.'

She glanced up at him, almost making eye contact before sliding her gaze to his right side. It dawned on him that they had hardly spoken a word since the incident with the frogs.

'What's wrong, what is it?'

'I cannot keep doing this.'

'Doing what?' Anthony sat down beside her.

'This…I cannot go to the science lab. The light there hurts my eyes.'

'The light?'

'It flickers constantly.'

'You've got to go. You'll get in trouble if you don't.'

'I want to go home.'

'You can't. Anyway, the bus doesn't come until four.'

She closed her eyes and rested her forehead on her knees. Her hair swung down, exposing the back of her neck, pale and slender. Skin and bone, Anthony thought.

'Look, if you want I can tell Campbell I couldn't find you, okay?'

'Yes. I would like that.'

He stood up and waited for her to say something else, but she did not lift her head again, so he went back to class and lied about finding her.

That evening, Emma came home and refused to eat a thing. She retreated to her room and did not come out for the evening.

'What's going on with her?' Jack asked Anthony, who was struggling with his homework.

'I don't know. The usual.'

But it wasn't just the family who noticed things were amiss: Emma's teachers were concerned too. One Friday they sent a letter home with Anthony, and on the following Monday Evelyn and Jack found themselves fidgeting on hard-backed chairs outside the Principal's office.

The Principal, Mr Coffery was a kind, unassuming, slightly melancholic man in his late fifties. He was tall, but stooped –

he reminded Jack of an undertaker. That morning he looked gloomier than ever as he invited Jack and Evelyn into the office. They were soon to be joined by Mrs Howell, one of Anthony and Emma's teachers.

'Thank you both for taking the time to see me.'

He opened a file and placed it on the desk in front of him. He introduced them to Mrs Howell, who offered them a watery smile.

'Your letter said you have…concerns,' Evelyn started. She was clutching her handbag on her knees so hard her knuckles had turned white. 'Is something the matter?'

'I'm afraid so.' Mr Coffery inclined his head. 'Mrs Byrne, I imagine you already know that your daughter is struggling.'

'She…she does all her homework,' Evelyn said. 'I make them do their homework in the kitchen where I can keep an eye on them. Her Christmas results were good I thought – well she could probably do better in history, but–'

'Emma's marks are not why I called you in,' Mr Coffery interrupted. 'The truth, Mr and Mrs Byrne, is that we are rather concerned about Emma's well being. Her behaviour is becoming increasingly erratic and unpredictable.'

'How do you mean?' Jack asked.

'Well, there are her routines. She must be in the same seat for every class. If someone else takes it she get very upset. And she gets upset if assembly is called unexpectedly, or if we practise the fire drill. There's been a running battle to get her to participate in Physical Education. She won't go to the science lab anymore. She refuses to attend choir practice. She hasn't made any friends since she started. Indeed she fights with people–'

'She fights?'

'Well, fight might be too strong a word for what she does. She gets frustrated and lashes out. She reacts to normal, everyday behaviour with deep levels of stress.' He glanced at Mrs Howell before he continued. 'We think she is a very unhappy young woman.'

'I'll talk to her,' Evelyn said, 'I'll get her to behave. She's a good girl, really, it's just…she gets a little overwhelmed sometimes.'

Mr Coffery smiled. 'I am not sure, Mrs Byrne, if this is a simple case of poor behaviour. Emma is clearly suffering because of the environment she finds herself in. I'm wondering if perhaps our school is the right place for her.'

'You want to expel her?' Jack asked. Evelyn clutched her bag closer.

'No,' Mr Coffery told him. 'I want to *help* her, but I'm not sure this is the right environment for her. There are other schools, special schools for–'

Evelyn cut across him: 'My daughter is not handicapped.'

'A lot of troubled children are far from handicapped,' Mr Coffery replied. 'In fact, as far as I am aware, they can be remarkably intelligent.'

'So… what are you saying?'

'I'm saying, Mrs Byrne,' Mr Coffery said, 'that Emma needs help.'

'She needs,' Evelyn said, 'an education. That's what you do here isn't it?'

'Yes of course, but–'

'I'll talk to her. I'll make her understand how important it is for her to follow the rules. You have my word on that – there will be no more nonsense. Give her another chance, please.'

That night, Anthony heard his parent's arguing and crept from his room to listen.

'Jesus Christ, Evelyn!'

Anthony felt a quiver of excitement. His father rarely used the Lord's name in vain, unless he was really angry.

'Don't shout at me Jack, I've every right to question their motives–'

'Evelyn why are you getting so het up? They told you she could stay, didn't they?'

'Calling her handicapped like that, and she as bright as they come.'

'He never said she was handicapped.'

'I think she puts half of it on, sometimes.'

'*What?*'

'You said it yourself, when she's running around with Pete Cartwright there's not a bother on her.'

'Ah, would you give over. That's not what I said at all.'

'The way you act sometimes, it's like I'm a monster for wanting her to have an education.'

'Evelyn–'

'Maybe I'd have been better off letting her sit around here, humming to herself all these years. Maybe I should have let her run half wild. Maybe I shouldn't have *wasted* all that time and energy on her, is that it?'

'You're being fierce bloody stupid now.'

'Then what is it? What is it you want me to do here Jack? Give up?'

Silence. Then Anthony heard his mother sigh. 'What if they decide to put her out? What happens then? What school would take her? I don't want her to have to go somewhere…different. Jack I don't want that for her.'

'Evie,' Jack's voice was softer now. 'Stop worrying, she's not going to go anywhere.'

'Oh Jack. What are we going to do with her at all?'

Anthony edged back from the bannisters and retreated down the hall. He knocked once on Emma's door and slipped inside without waiting to be invited. It was impossible to see an inch in front of him because the room was pitch black (Emma had persuaded Evelyn to make up special blackout curtains for her, because she claimed even the faintest crack of light kept her awake).

'Are you asleep?'

'No.'

'I know why the school called Mam and Dad in today.'

She didn't reply.

'Emma.'

'Yes?'

'I said I know why Mam and Dad were called in to the school today.'

'I heard you.'

'Put on a lamp.'

He heard her sit up and seconds later a lamp clicked on. Anthony waited for his eyes to adjust, made his way across the room and sat on the end of her bed.

'They think there might be something *wrong* with you.'

'Who?'

'The *school* does. They told Mam and Dad they thought you might be handicapped.'

'Why?'

'Because of the way you act I suppose, why else?'

'I am not handicapped.'

'Well…okay, but here's the thing. The school is only barely letting you stay as it is. They told Mam they'd be happier if you didn't go there anymore. You don't *want* to go there anymore, right?'

'I think I am normal. I am normal for me. Pete says I am as normal as he likes to be around.'

'Never mind what Pete says. Emma, listen for a second, will you? If they think you're handicapped they won't want you there anymore, and then you can leave…maybe work down in the stables.'

'With Claude,' Emma said, so softly Anthony barely heard her.

'Okay, so here's the plan. You need to get them to kick you out. Make it impossible for Mam to talk them around this time.'

Emma plucked at the sleeve of her pyjamas. They were pale blue with white rabbits on them.

'You have science on Tuesday morning, double class, right?' he asked.

'Yes.'

'That's the time to do it.'

'Do what?'

'Get kicked out.'

'How?'

'Go mad, go absolutely ballistic.'

'Ballistic?'

'Like when people go crazy. Shout and yell and smash things up.'

'You told me not to do things like that in this school. You said it makes people angry and I will get you in trouble.'

'Yeah, well, now I think differently, now I think you should just—'

'Go ballistic.'

'Exactly. Anyway, I've got to go to bed. I wanted to let you know what was going on.'

'If I go…ballistic…I can go back to work with Claude?'

'Sure. Trust me, this is going to work, I promise.'

He waited for her to say something but she didn't. She just sat there fiddling with her sleeves until he went back to his own room.

CHAPTER 18

Jack was attaching lights to a trailer when he had a strange sense of foreboding. Looking up, he saw Evelyn running across the yard towards him – he knew before she had a chance to open her mouth it was bad news.

'What's happened?'

'Oh you're not going to believe this. The school phoned. I have to go in and collect our daughter, it seems she was involved in an incident this morning.'

'What kind of *incident*?'

'She apparently went berserk and wrecked the science lab.'

'*What?*'

'Tore the place apart, I'm told.' Evelyn's nostrils flared. 'She's in the office, they want me to come collect her straightaway.'

'I can't go anywhere now, Evie, I'm waiting on the vet to arrive.'

'I don't *need* you to come,' Evelyn replied. 'I doubt there's anything to be said at this point.'

She was right. The decision was unanimous: Emma Byrne was no longer welcome as a pupil of St Mark's, effective immediately.

Things didn't quite work out the way Anthony had promised. Initially, Emma was grounded while Evelyn figured out what she was going to do next, which quite suited her, as it meant she got to spend her days reading in her room, or helping Jack on the farm.

After a week of calling various schools and getting absolutely nowhere, Evelyn got up early one morning, before everyone else, went downstairs and made a cup of tea. She drank it standing at the window, staring out across the hills. She realised she had no idea what to do next. The truth was she was out of options. Later that same day she made contact with the Department of Education and asked for a curriculum so that Emma could study from home. She hung up, feeling strangely bested; it was an unsettling sensation.

'Would you not be worried about her, you know, missing out?' Margaret said, that afternoon over her tea when Evelyn informed her of their decision.

'Missing out on what?' Evelyn said, dully.

'On her friends and that.'

'Margaret, she has no friends.'

'That's not right. For a young one of her age.'

'Well, that's the way it is,' Evelyn replied, finally admitting the truth. 'She's happy the way she is.'

Unencumbered by a school timetable, Emma convinced her parents to allow her to work a few mornings a week at Pete's. Those few mornings became more frequent and the hours longer, until finally it could be said that she was working at the stables full time.

She flourished, growing more confident and competent as each week passed. Pete taught her how to 'start' a horse under saddle that summer, and by autumn she was better at it than he was.

'She can break in a horse better than most men I know,' Pete told Jack, when he came over one afternoon to give Emma a lift home because it was pouring out of the skies. 'She's got a way about her. They trust her.'

'Dangerous though, no? She's only fourteen, Pete, I wouldn't like to see her get hurt.'

'Not likely to get hurt the way she does it.' Pete lit a cigarette, and squinted through the smoke. 'I'm telling ye, she's a flamin' magician when it comes to breaking the young 'uns.'

'Breaking is a disgusting word,' Emma complained when Jack mentioned Pete's praise. 'Why would you "break" an animal? You don't "break" them – what does that mean? Back and break, back and break? If you broke them they would not work.'

'I suppose that's true,' Jack replied, trying to keep a straight face.

'You do not break them…you educate them. Young horses are very friendly and are quite willing to learn. They are very trusting. Talking about breaking them is ridiculous.'

'I think it's just an expression.'

'It is a stupid expression. People say stupid things.'

'Fair enough,' Jack said, pulling into their farmyard. 'Don't tell your mother you're…educating young horses. She'll be worried sick.'

The summer before she turned sixteen, Emma's reputation for being able to 'educate' young, skittish animals into 'bomb-proof' horses had spread so far that Pete began to receive regular calls from people wondering if she'd be interested in taking on a bit of extra work with their own difficult horses.

For the most part Emma shrugged and said yes, but she left it up to Pete to decide which jobs to take and which to avoid. So, it annoyed Pete a little to see Ivan Harte drive into the yard early one Tuesday morning as he was turning the horses out, since he had already refused the businessman's request over the phone.

'I'm looking for the young one.'

'She's out. Won't be back for an hour or more.'

'She never phoned me.' Ivan switched off the jeep's engine and looked at Pete, hard.

'Did you give her my message?'

'I did, and as I told you on the phone, she don't give riding lessons.'

'I'm not asking for much, Pete.' Ivan scowled and shrugged his massive shoulders, a man unused to seeking help. 'Fair enough if she doesn't give lessons, I just want that pony assessed. I'd send it to the knackers tomorrow if I could, but Grace, my daughter, is mad about the fucking thing.'

The filly Pete was leading pawed the ground impatiently and tossed her head.

'She doesn't usually do house calls neither. You'd have to bring the pony 'ere for an evaluation.'

'I'd appreciate it if she could make an exception.' Ivan looked past Pete to the horses in the paddock standing under the trees, swishing their tails at the flies. 'Tell her I'll make it worth her while.'

That Saturday Emma left the house, biked across the village and cycled up the gravelled driveway of Harte Manor. Half an hour later she found herself standing in the middle of a recently cleared scrub field, watching a chubby nine-year-old attempt to climb aboard an equally overweight palomino pony.

Every time the child stuck her foot into the stirrup, the pony sidestepped around in a circle, leaving the girl hopping after him on one foot. The girl, Grace, was getting worse tempered by the second.

'*Daddy*, I told you, you have to hold him!' she yelled after another unsuccessful attempt, which saw the pony ditch her fully and walk off to the gate. 'You have to make him stand still!'

Ivan rushed forward, grabbed the reins in one massive fist and gave them a vicious yank, which did nothing but cause the pony to partially rear. Martin Harte, who had turned up to watch the show, laughed unpleasantly from the railings.

'You should be able to get up yourself, round arse,' he called. 'How are you ever going to hunt if you can't even get on? Do you think Dad's going to be standing there to hold the reins for you then?'

'Martin,' Ivan said. 'Shut up and go find something useful to do.'

'Daddy! Hold him, he's trying to run away again.'

'You're Anthony's sister, aren't you?' Martin said to Emma, keeping his voice low, so that his father wouldn't hear him.

'Yes.'

'How come I don't see you around anywhere? Where do you go to school?'

Emma watched Grace scramble into the saddle, still complaining furiously to her father. She narrowed her eyes as Grace yanked the pony's mouth hard to the right, almost bringing its nose to her boot.

'You don't talk much, do you?' Martin said. 'That's all right; I don't mind a quiet bird myself. Are you really going to give Bessie Bunter lessons?'

'Who?'

'My sister.'

'Oh, it's possible. '

'You'll have your work cut out for you so. Doesn't like to be told what to do, the Princess doesn't.' He lit a cigarette and smoked for a second. 'Tell you what, why don't you–'

'Okay,' Emma said, moving away from Martin. 'I want you to walk him around me in a wide, loose circle, clockwise first. That means going right.'

'I'm not stupid, I know what it means,' Grace said. She booted the pony in the ribs and he strolled around, swishing his tail with absolutely no enthusiasm for the task at hand.

'This is boring,' Grace announced on her third revolution.

'Yes,' Emma agreed.

'You're supposed to be teaching me how to ride him.'

'I am.'

'No you're not. Anyone can walk around in a circle. This is stupid.'

'Grace…' Ivan said, but seemed to run out of ideas on what to suggest she do.

Grace jerked the pony's head again and booted him with both legs. The pony obligingly began to trot, gave a soft buck that almost unseated Grace, broke into a canter and took off for the gate.

'Grace!' Ivan ran after them.

A few inches from the gate, the pony slid to a halt, put his head down and Grace went sailing over it onto the ground.

'Oof!' Grace said.

'Grace! I'm coming!'

The pony, free from his burden, immediately began to crop grass under the fence in huge greedy mouthfuls.

'Typical pony, really. He is quite clever,' Emma said, side-eying Grace who, though unharmed, was bawling like she'd been shot. 'He knows she is off balance and he waits until she is loose in her seat to get rid of her.'

'Stop *saying* "she". I'm right *here*!' Grace yelled, forgetting about her tears momentarily. She shoved her father away. 'It's not my fault; it's this stupid pony. *He's mean.*'

'He is not mean,' Emma said, picking up the lunge line she had brought along. 'You are not a good rider.'

Grace's mouth dropped open. 'I'm a gold star member of the pony club.'

'You can ride, but very badly.'

'Daddy!'

'Emma doesn't mean that, love.'

'I do.'

Martin laughed.

Emma walked over to where the pony stood and looped the clip through the snaffle rings on his bridle. She removed the pony's saddle, rested it against the gate and walked the pony back to Grace.

'Get on please.'

'I don't like riding bareback. I'll fall off!'

'You already fall off.'

She pouted and looked at her father again.

'Give it a try, Princess.'

'Here,' Emma offered her hand for the girl to step into. 'Grab the withers, I will boost you.'

Grace allowed herself to be boosted and sat atop the pony with her arms crossed, still pouting.

'Oh good,' Emma said, glancing at the girl's arms, 'I do not want you to hold on to the reins either.'

'What?'

Emma stepped back, raised her right hand and flicked the ground behind the pony with the end of the line. Immediately, the pony moved off at a smart walk. Grace wobbled and snatched at his mane.

'Sit up straight. Look forward.'

'I am looking forward!'

'Also stop talking.'

For the next half hour, Emma made Grace focus on her position, specifically paying attention to her rounded lower legs, which she allowed to swing far too much. When she was certain Grace was more balanced, she got Ivan to place jump poles on the ground, spaced evenly apart. She walked and then trotted the pony back and forth across the poles. The pony, who Emma knew was not the slightest bit mean, followed her commands happily, now that Grace was no longer flopping about on his back like a sack of potatoes.

'When do I get to canter?' Grace asked at one point.

'When you can trot without bouncing,' Emma replied.

'When will that be?'

'I do not know. Stop talking.'

By the end of the session, Grace was so sore and tired she hadn't the energy to complain, but even Ivan could see she was much more secure in her seat.

'Did Pete mention I'd like you to give her some private lessons? Would you be willing to do that?'

'I don't need any lessons from her,' Grace whined.

'Love, Daddy is talking. Emma, can you do that?'

'Yes, I can do that,' Emma said, watching Grace dismount and shake out her aching legs. She unclipped the pony from the lunge line and let him nibble at her fingers.

'Great,' Ivan said. 'I'll set it up with Pete.' He offered his hand, which Emma pretended not to notice. She handed the reins to Grace, who snatched them from her sulkily and stormed off towards the stables.

Martin fell into step beside her as Emma walked back to the house to collect her bike.

'So, you really think Round Arse will be able to hunt this year?'

'Yes, it is possible.'

'You're a miracle worker, so.'

Emma picked up pace, but Martin matched her stride easily.

'Do you hunt yourself? I've never seen you out.'

'No.'

'Why not?'

'I do not kill animals for sport.'

Martin laughed, but stopped when she didn't join in. 'Are you serious?'

'Yes.'

'But you train horses for hunting.'

'Yes, I train horses.'

'Bit hypocritical, no?'

'Horses do not kill for sport either.'

'You're missing out. I go hunting all the time. I got a .22 for my birthday. You want to see it? It's up in my room.'

'No.'

They had reached the shed where Emma had left her bike. She bent down to unlock it, and when she rose again Martin was straddling the front wheel, his hands resting lightly on the handlebar.

'I've a crossbow too. Ever use a crossbow?'

'You are in my way.'

Colour rose in Martin's cheeks. 'I'm trying to be friendly here. You could try being a little friendly back.'

'Why?'

'Because…I like you that's why.'

'I do not like you.'

'You could get to like me.' He reached out and grabbed her by wrist. 'You could get to like me a lot.'

Emma wrenched her hand free. 'Do not touch me.'

'Oh I see, Miss Goody Two-Shoes, yeah? I know your sort. Fucking tease, is that it?'

Emma grabbed the handlebars and backed away, keeping the bike between them. She made it to the road, walking backwards all the while, got on her bike and cycled back across the village to the stables.

Pete was stacking bags in the feedroom when he heard Ruby yipping with excitement. He came out just as Emma was passing through the yard.

'How'd it go with the Squire of Killbragh?'

'She needs lessons, but I cannot teach her there.'

'He won't like that, will Ivan.'

'I will teach her here or not at all.'

Pete knew something was wrong so he tilted his head inquisitively. But either she didn't see him or she didn't want to talk about it, so he let her be.

When he went to look for her later, he found her sitting in the dark under the saddle rack in the tack room, with her legs drawn up under her chin.

'What are you doing in 'ere?'

'I have a headache.'

'Do y'want to go home?'

'No.'

Pete leaned against the wall and studied her. 'I know the perfect cure for a headache. What about a lesson then?'

'I do not need lessons.'

'You do if y'want to ride Claude.'

Emma unfolded her legs and raised her head. Her eyes flitted briefly across Pete's face. 'I can ride Claude?'

'Sure,' Pete said. 'I'll go tack him up.'

'Thank you,' Emma said and smiled. 'Thank you, Pete.'

'No problem, kid,' Pete said gruffly. 'Now cheer up, and for God's sake go give yer face a wash. Y'look like a flamin' tramp.'

CHAPTER 20

'I need you to do me a favour.'

Emma put down the hoof she had been scraping and stood up slowly, easing the muscles in her back. Harry Lynch, a local bigwig councillor and long-time friend of Pete's, was leaning on the stable door, looking at her.

Emma waited.

'I'm going up to look at a horse tomorrow afternoon. Pete was supposed to come with me, but now he says he can't. Will you come up and throw your eye over him?'

Emma blinked, and then furrowed her brow. 'Do you mean you want me to look at him?'

'Yeah, what did you think I meant?'

'Where is this horse?'

'He's one of Arthur Donovan's stock. Big bay. I've had my eye on him since he was a foal, so I have. Never thought he'd sell him, but here we are and he's selling him on this year.'

Emma rested her hand on the flank of the mare whose feet she had been cleaning. She knew of Arthur Donovan. He was trader and something of rogue, who toured the country buying and selling horses and anything else that took his fancy. Arthur lived in a run-down cottage high up in the hills near Sliabh Creen. He was also Gully Donovan's father – Emma had not forgotten *him* from her school days.

'I'll make it worth your while,' Harry said, mistaking her hesitation for something else.

'You want to buy this horse?'

'Oh he's a cracker. Big free-jumper, so he is. Vet's given him a clean bill, but I want another opinion. It won't take long. I'll run you up and back in no time.'

So it was the following day that Emma found herself shivering outside Arthur Donovan's dilapidated home, waiting for him to emerge.

When Arthur emerged from the cottage he did not look happy to see her there, and he barely grunted a response when Harry said she was coming to see the horse at his behest.

The stable yard was almost as unloved as the house: it was strewn with rubbish and as filthy as a yard could be. A pair of mangy-looking dogs lay in the weeds by the stables, alternatively nibbling or scratching at themselves in a vain attempt to find some comfort. There was, however, no doubting the quality of Donovan's stock, and the bay gelding that Donovan led from a dank stable was all class.

'Look at him, isn't he something?' Harry whispered, nudging Emma.

'Gully!' Donovan roared. 'Get your arse out here.'

Gully stepped out from a shed at the end of the stable line, cleaning a meat cleaver on a filthy, blood-stained apron.

'What?'

'Harry wants to see his horse.'

Emma recognised Gully immediately, though he had bulked up considerably since she had last laid eyes on him. But Gully had one of those faces that never really changed. Emma remembered the days he had harassed and intimidated her in school and stayed as close to Harry as she could. She wished Pete was there with them.

Gully stabbed the cleaver into a tree stump and walked to the yard, an unlit cigarette dangling from his lips. He took the halter rope from his father and trotted the bay up the yard and back down again.

'There's your hunter, Harry. There's not many will match stride with this boy,' Arthur said.

Emma glanced at him as he spoke, but his terrible face remained half hidden under the peak of his cap, and only the muscles moving in his jaw convinced her he was speaking at all.

'Bring him on there!' Donovan roared at Gully as he slogged past, puffing and blowing from the effort of running.

'What do you think?' Harry asked, 'He's a beaut isn't he?'

'Run 'em on!' Donovan roared again.

There was no denying the bay truly was a beauty. He was three, rising four, out of Arthur's own hunter mare, Avolane. He stood a fraction shy of seventeen hands, with an intelligent expression and kind eyes.

'He is very well put together,' Emma said as he was trotted towards them.

'Well?' Donovan spat and for the first time turned his head towards her. 'Of course he's put together well! I bred Avolane to Vincent Coor's Pan Handler, best point-to-point stallion you'll ever see around these parts, I can tell you.'

Emma said nothing. She narrowed her eyes and watched as Gully turned the colt to take another sally across the yard.

'What do you make of him?' Harry wasn't even looking at her; he was too busy grinning at the bay. Emma was surprised. Pete had told her often enough never to let anyone know what you were thinking when you were looking at a horse for sale.

'I'd like to see him jump a few fences.'

'Arthur, what about it?'

Some expression Emma did not understand flitted across Donovan's face.

'For Jaysus sake Harry, did you not see him jump the last time you were here? I've to be on the road in half an hour.'

'Let the lad show me, so.'

'Sure he's coming with me.'

Harry was not put off in the slightest.

'I know where you have the jumps set up. It won't take long.'

Donovan's expression was murderous, but he told Gully to take the bay to the field and set off after them, stalking across the mud in temper. Emma and Harry followed along with the mangy dogs.

The jumps were already set up in a rough field to the rear of the sheds. Gully set the bay loose inside the gate and waved him on using a lunge whip. Between him and his father they ran the bay over a small cross pole and a homemade cavaletti. The bay perked his ears forwards and hopped over a double with ease, but refused the last jump, spinning hard on his hocks and cantering away to the end of the field, his head and tail high.

Donovan was apoplectic with rage. 'Gully, you fucking gom, why'd you let him run out the side of that? Go get him and run him over them fences properly!'

Gully did as he was told, this time using the whip to beat the colt across the back of the legs before he even thought of refusing the third jump. The moment the knotted cord hit him the colt sort of bunny-hopped over the barrels, before racing to the rear of the field again, whinnying wildly.

'Well now,' Donovan turned to Harry, smiling unpleasantly, 'you've seen him jump for a third time, Harry. Is it business you want to do or don't you?'

Harry nudged Emma with his elbow.

'Big leap on him.'

Emma moved out of his elbow range.

'I do not think you should buy this horse.'

'Go way outta that,' Donovan said quickly, spitting a wad of tobacco beside her feet. 'Sure isn't he raring to go? Harry, I'll have this fella broke in no time. His mother would jump the house if you let her, and you know the father was a champion point-to-pointer. Not for you…and you riding that yoke from

Clancy's yard? I've never heard the like. Run him on there again, Gully, show Harry what a real horse looks like.'

'He does look a grand horse,' Harry said, watching the bay spin away from Gully's wild, flapping arms. In his mind he was tearing across the scrubby headlands, the wind on his face, the cry of hounds in his ears.

'Yes,' Emma said. 'He looks a *grand* horse. But this animal is injured.'

'He is in his shite,' Donovan snapped. 'What are you jawing about, girl? That horse has never been injured a day in his life. Harry, Harry don't listen to this guff. She's talking out of her arse.'

Harry held up a palm to silence him, and looked at Emma again. 'Why do you think he's injured?'

'It is in the way he moves.'

'Shite of the highest order,' Donovan said savagely. 'If you don't want him, there's plenty who will. By Jaysus Harry, I didn't think you'd be the sort of fella to fuck a man around like this. Wasting my time when I could have had him sold in Galway twice over last weekend. Turning down offers left and right I was on account of you.'

Harry's face was a picture of longing and trepidation.

'Are you sure? He doesn't look hurt to me and the vet passed him as sound only the other day.'

'It is your choice,' Emma said, uncomfortable under their gazes. 'I would not buy him.'

'No one's asking *you* to buy him,' Donovan said. 'Harry, look at me.' He spit on his hand and held it out. 'You made me a fine offer on him and I'm happy to take it, you won't get another like him if you travelled north to south.'

'I don't know Arthur.' Harry shook his head slowly. 'I...I think I need to think about it for another day or so.'

'Bring him back to the stable, Gully.' Donovan dropped his hand and wheeled away. 'Call up that other fellow who was asking about him. Tell him to come collect his horse. Tell him he's getting the finest hunter he'll ever sit his arse on. Go on now.'

'Arthur I'm sorry–'

'Aye, go on outta that,' Donovan said, swinging his arm in the direction of the lane. 'Go on, take that filthy-tongued tramp with you. I tell you, young one, you haven't heard the last of this. I'll be talking to Pete later and I'll be talking to your old lad.' He lunged towards her and raised a fist to her face. 'By God, you'll be sorry you crossed me. You'll be fucking sorry.'

Emma shrank away from Donovan and pressed against the fence. Harry grabbed Donovan and shoved him back

'There's no need for that. She was only doing me a favour.'

'That one did you no favours, Harry, only made a holy show of you and lost you the best horse you're ever likely to own. Go on. Go on now, we're finished.'

A few days later, Fintan Sheen, a farmer, bought the bay for his son, Colm. Barely a fortnight into the hunting season, the bay stumbled while jumping over a shallow dyke, landed badly and pulled up lame. Colm rested the horse, but he went lame again after a short hack and didn't recover as expected. Extensive veterinary tests revealed the bay had a damaged vertebra. The vet couldn't give a definitive answer, but surmised it was most likely the result of the bay being cast in his box at some point. He said there were no guarantees with back injuries, and he couldn't say if the handsome gelding would ever stay fully sound.

Sheen was incensed: he drove up to the mountain yard, bull-headed and demanding his money back. Donovan refused to accept any responsibility, saying the horse had been fine leaving his yard. When Sheen protested, Donovan set the dogs on him. The resulting bad blood did the rounds in horse circles in no time, as did the story that it was Emma Byrne who had saved Harry Lynch from making a four-thousand-pound mistake ('an'

Fintan Sheen supposed to be an experienced horseman,' scoffed Bennie Walsh, the blacksmith, to anyone who might listen). People couldn't stop talking about it.

'They say she has the gift,' Larry Green told Jack, when he stopped in to buy the papers that Sunday.

'Oh aye?'

'People are saying she sees things.'

'What kind of things?'

'I don't fully know,' Larry shrugged. 'Like she's some kind of animal mystic.'

'For God's sake, she's no mystic.'

'Right enough. I suppose though, anyone who can get one over on that fucker Donovan deserves a little respect.'

'Maybe so,' Jack said, but he wished Emma had nothing to do with the likes of Donovan at all.

CHAPTER 21

Less than two months after the incident in Donovan's yard, Emma was sitting outside the chipper eating a bag of chips with Anthony, when she heard her brother swear.

'Emma, quick, let's go.'

He slid off the wall but it was too late; they had already been spotted. Gully Donovan, with his younger brother Sean, rolled up to them on an ancient moped. It was early October and the day was cold, but despite that Gully wore only a T-shirt, jeans and a pair of work boots. Neither boy wore a helmet.

'Will you look who the fuck it is,' Gully said, getting off the bike and giving Anthony a none-too-playful punch in the arm.

'Gully,' Anthony said, trying to come across as nonchalant as possible. He was almost sixteen and tall, like his father, but Gully had twenty to thirty pounds on him. 'How's it going Sean?'

The younger Donovan said nothing, but his eyes glittered beneath his pimpled forehead. There were a number of old bruises healing on his face, and Anthony recalled the stories he'd heard of how Arthur Donovan could be quick with his fists, caring little who bore the brunt of them.

'What are you eating?'

'Chips.'

'Gives us one.'

Anthony offered the bag. Gully snatched it out of his hand and began to eat. He did not hand them back and stared at Emma while he chewed. Emma squirmed under his gaze and kept her eyes down, fixed on something to Gully's left, her food forgotten.

Gully took another chip and stuffed it in his mouth, his fingers shiny with grease. 'She doesn't say much, does she?'

Anthony shrugged. He wished Mark hadn't decided to head home early. Maybe with three of them...

'These are good,' Gully said. 'Salty.'

'Keep them, I've had enough.'

'I hear you're working in Lakelands these days,' Gully said, talking about the pub where Anthony worked part time on the weekends.

'Yeah.'

'What's it like?'

'It's grand. Quiet.'

'Yeah? How'd you land that?'

'I asked for it.'

'Didn't give old Flicky a reach around then, no? I hear he likes them lanky.'

Anthony flushed. His boss, Flicky Gillespie, was single and liked reading, which naturally made him suspect to Neanderthals like Gully. The fact that he also liked women didn't seem to matter at all.

'Is that it?' Gully said, leering. 'So are you Flicky's bum boy now?'

'Shut up.'

'Or what?'

Good question. Anthony glanced up the street, but there wasn't a sinner around. A chip bounced off his chest.

'Hey, fuckface, I'm talking to you. I said "or what?"'

'Nothing.'

'Yeah, that's what I thought. So, you're working and this one is working. That means you can afford to pay weekly.'

'Pay?' Anthony said. 'Pay for what?'

'For the money this bitch cost us.'

'She didn't cost you anything.'

Gully jerked his thumb towards Emma.

'I know this cunt can talk. She was quick enough to fleece me old lad out of his money from Harry Lynch. She can answer me a few question now, like who the fuck she thinks she is. Going around spreading lies about me father.'

'She didn't spread lies about anyone.' Anthony positioned himself between Emma and Gully. 'Every dog in the street knows that bay was banjaxed and you still sold him on. Your father was trying to pull a fast one and you know it. It's not her fault if he was found—'

Anthony never saw it coming. Gully flung the chips at him and when Anthony raised his hands to protect his face, Gully punched him as hard as he could in the guts. The pain didn't hit for a few seconds, but when it did, all he could do was lie on the ground, doubled-up and gasping desperately for air that wouldn't come. He felt his hair being ripped from his scalp and then Gully's ugly face was inches from his own.

'You owe me. Call it a cunt tax. As in I don't care which of you cunts pays it once it gets paid. Fifty quid a week, every week, until it's paid. You miss and I'll come looking for one or the both of you. I'm not fussy.'

Anthony rolled onto his knees and tried not to vomit. He heard the sound of the moped revving and pulling away.

'Anthony?'

He could do nothing but wave his hand at her. It took a few more minutes before he even managed to get to his feet, and he had to use the wall as leverage.

'You are hurt.'

'Give…give me a minute.'

He straightened slowly, feeling light-headed and nauseous. What little food he had eaten that day threatened to come straight back up; he wondered if that was a good or bad thing.

'Are you in pain?'

'I'm fine.'

'You do not look fine.'

'I think I'm more winded than hurt,' he lied.

'I do not understand why he struck you. You did not do anything to him.'

'He's a bully Emma. He always was and he always will be.'

'I do not want you to get hurt because of a bully who is angry with me.'

'It's not your fault.' Anthony pressed his hand against his stomach and winced as pain travelled through him. 'That prick doesn't need a reason to pick a fight. It's just an excuse with him.'

'We should tell our father.'

'No.'

'Why?'

'Emma, listen to me, don't tell Dad about this,' Anthony glanced at her. 'Or Mam – especially Mam. Remember what happened with Gary Nolan? If she hears this she'll freak out and make everything worse.'

'I will not tell if you do not want me to.' Emma walked away a few steps, then turned back. 'I do not want to give him my money. But I don't want him to hit you again.'

'Don't worry about Gully Donovan. I'll take care of it.'

Emma looked sceptical, but she said nothing. After a while Anthony felt strong enough to walk, so they went home.

They said nothing to anyone about what had happened.

CHAPTER 22

'Ah shit!'

Anthony braked and got off his bike. He stared at the tyre in dismay: it was as flat as a pancake. He spun the wheel and swore again. Glass. Now what was he going to do? He was three miles from Mark's house, two from the village; it was almost dark and threatening rain.

He glanced at his watch, thinking. If he walked back to Mark's house, Mrs Bradshaw would quite happily put the bike in the boot of the car and give him a lift, but on the other hand it would be pitch black by then. In the end he decided might as well carry on towards the village and call his mother or father from the phone box and ask them to come and pick him up.

He was pushing the bike along by the ditch when he heard a familiar voice from behind:

'Hey Byrne. Where you going?'

He did not turn around or slow his pace; outwardly he wanted to give no sign that he was worried, even as his heart pounded in his chest.

Why, why now?

Gully drew alongside him on a nice-looking racing bike with silver tape on the handles. He wore a filthy tracksuit and a denim jacket with the sleeves cut out. His hands were covered in oil.

'Got a puncture?'

'Yes.'

'Where's your repair kit?'

'At home.'

'Fucking stupid place for it,' Gully said, taking a packet of Rothmans out of his pocket with one hand and shuffling one free. 'Want one?'

'I don't smoke.'

'Go on, take one.'

It wasn't really an offer, so Anthony reached over and took one. He put it between his lips and waited as Gully popped one between his own lips and lit both with a Zippo from his other pocket.

Anthony sucked the smoke into his mouth and held it behind his teeth. It tasted dry and bitter on his tongue. He wondered how long he should hold it in his mouth without it looking weird.

'So where were you? Over with your friend?'

'Yes.'

'Yiz are always hanging out. What do you two do together?'

Anthony belched out the smoke and glanced at him suspiciously. Gully was affecting an air of breezy camaraderie that was making Anthony very nervous. 'Nothing.'

'You must do *something*.'

'I dunno, we watch films, listen to music, that sort of thing.'

'Yeah? What music d'ylike?'

Anthony wished he had turned back and walked to Mark's house, to ask his mother for a lift. He didn't like the way Gully was looking at him. Didn't like his smile, or the curiously excited, faux-friendly voice he was putting on. Everything about this encounter told Anthony that he should remain on high alert.

'What the fuck way are you smoking that?'

'I…'

'You suck it in, not whatever the fuck you're doing. Pull it in.'

Anthony took a breath and attempted to swallow the smoke. It went down and got caught at the back of his throat, and in a panic he coughed; he felt he was choking, and kept coughing until his eyes were streaming, and he was full sure he was going to vomit.

'There you go!' Gully said, laughing, slapping him on the back. 'Now you're sucking diesel.'

Anthony got his spluttering under control and wiped his eyes with his sleeve.

'Haven't see much of you lately. Thought you might be avoiding me.'

'I've been busy.'

'Oh yeah?'

'Yes.'

'With your job'

Anthony didn't answer: again it wasn't a question.

'So how come you've got to go to school and your sister doesn't? I thought you two were twins. That means you're the same age, right?'

'She studies at home.'

'Oh yeah? I didn't know you could do that. I don't go to school myself either. Started as an apprentice in a garage on the main road.'

He looked at Anthony. Anthony realised he was waiting for him so say something, and as much as he desperately wanted to remain silent, Anthony said, 'A garage. You're going to be a mechanic?'

'No. I'm going to be a fucking dentist,' Gully laughed. 'Of course I'm going to be a fucking mechanic. Shit, and you're the smart one.'

Anthony turned his head away. He hated this. He hated feeling afraid and stupid.

They carried along the road a bit further, Anthony walking his bike, Gully smoking and freewheeling back and forth along the road. A car passed by with its lights on; Anthony watched the red taillights disappear around the bend. What do we look like, he thought. What did they see? Two buddies or something, two pals out walking along enjoying a dry, cold stroll in November?

'Your sister's not a bad-looking woman. Bit skinny like, but more than a handful's a waste. She ever go out with anyone?'

'No.'

'But she could though, right? I mean all her bits work don't they?'

Anthony didn't respond to that, couldn't respond to it.

'How 'bout you? You seeing someone?'

'No.'

'You got no girlfriend?'

'No.'

'How come?'

'I just don't.'

The tip of Gully's cigarette glowed red. He peddled backwards on his bike, swerving in close to Anthony. 'I think we need to talk about a payment schedule.'

Anthony gripped his handlebars a little tighter. 'I'm not going to pay you, Gully.'

'No?'

They had reached the bottom of one little hill and were about to climb another. Anthony felt a little bit better: it wasn't far to the village now. Once they crested, he'd be able to see the lights. He'd be safe then.

'Thing is though, either *you* pay me, or *she* does. Maybe she can offer something better than money.'

Gully swerved into him again, closer this time. Anthony could smell sweat and petrol on him, and something else, something rancid, cloying.

Please, Anthony thought, a car, another person out walking, anyone.

Halfway up the hill, Gully swerved into him a third time and clipped his back wheel, the bike slewing onto the grass verge. Caught off balance, Anthony tripped over it, got tangled in the frame and fell.

Before he knew what was going on, Gully jumped off his own bike and threw it into the drainage ditch that ran the length of the road. He grabbed Anthony by the back of his jacket and dragged backwards into the ditch.

'Stop, Gully! Stop!'

Anthony grabbed at his bike, missed; aimed instead for the grass, the weeds. Clumps of soil came up in his fingers. He got his feet under him, but only for a second before he was swung like a rag doll through a gap in the hedge.

'*Gully, what the fuck are you doing?*'

'Shut the fuck up,' Gully's voice said hard in his ear.

He pitched forward and fell onto wet grass, got up again and tried to run. A leg swept his own out from under him, taking him from behind the knees, followed by a punch to the kidneys. No time to put his hands out to protect his face, his face bounced of the grass and left him dazed. Gully flipped him over onto his back.

Barely able to see, Anthony swung a fist at Gully's face; it was a wild, glancing blow that didn't make a blind bit of difference. Gully laughed and straddled his chest.

No matter how much he kicked or struggled, Anthony couldn't dislodge him. It was useless. Outweighed and outmuscled, what chance did he have?

'Gully, listen to me—'

Gully ripped up handfuls of grass and rammed them into his mouth so hard Anthony's gums would bleed for the rest of the week every time he brushed them. He scratched and clawed, but Gully belted him so hard he saw stars. He screamed, inhaled clay and coughed until he retched, panicking that he might choke.

Gully thumped him again, grabbed one of his arms and pinned it under his knee. With his free hand he yanked down Anthony's black jeans, his favourite new pair.

Shock as the cold air hit his bare skin. Anthony felt Gully's hand snake under the band of his underpants. He kicked and writhed. Gully fingers closed around his genitals, tightened and twisted left. The pain hit hard – Anthony stopped moving instantly.

'Now, I want you to imagine…'

Gully twisted his genitals to the right this time. Burning pain.

'I want you to imagine how your sister would enjoy something like this. Although, maybe she'll like it, maybe it will make her wet, maybe she'll be all "fuck the money Gull, take me!"'

Anthony's fingers clawed at the grass; he squeezed his eyes shut.

This is not happening. Things like this can't happen to people.

Another twist.

'Be easy to get her, she cycles the same way every day.'

Anthony's ears were ringing from the relentless beating and his balls were on fire.

'But I won't need to do that, will I? 'Cause you're going to pay me what's owed, right?'

Anthony nodded.

'You get paid on Sunday?'

Nod.

'I'll be waiting. Make sure you don't miss me.'

Nod.

Gully tightened his grip a little more. Anthony moaned.

'You can tell people about this if you want.' Gully's voice held some mocking note; Anthony could hear it chime over his pain. 'But I've got your cock in my hand, and I know, deep down, you're enjoying this.'

Tears ran down Anthony's cheeks, into his ears.

'See, I think you're as bent as a two-pound note. You and your friend Mark going around in your queer clothes, with your queer hair. I'll say you offered to suck my cock.'

One more tweak.

'So keep your fucking mouth shut and make sure you look for me on Sunday. Do *not* piss me off.'

He released him. Anthony rolled onto his side, cupped himself and tried to curl his feet up to his chest to lessen the pain.

There was no single moment when he knew he was alone again – Gully was there and then he was gone. Gradually, the heat subsided, if not the pain, and he was able to ease into sitting up. He cleaned the grass out of his mouth with his fingers and pulled his jeans up over his legs. He tried to fasten them but his hand was shaking too much to work the zip.

Standing was hard; walking was worse.

'Look at the cut of you,' Evelyn said, when he finally made it home. 'Where were you until this hour? I was worried sick, I rang Mark's mother and she said you left there ages ago.'

'I got a puncture.'

'You're filthy dirty.' Evelyn looked down at his legs. 'And you've got grass stains all over your new jeans. Why did you wear them if you knew you were going to be horsing around? Honestly, you've no respect for anything. You needn't ask me to wash them for you especially. They'll have to wait for a dark wash.'

'It's okay,' said Anthony, dully, 'I'll wait. I don't mind waiting.'

CHAPTER 23

In late March, not long after the twins had turned sixteen, Margaret Byrne walked down to the bottom of her garden to put out some washing on the clothes line and slipped on a patch of black ice, breaking her wrist and knocking herself unconscious. She lay there undiscovered until her neighbour came home from doing her shopping and spotted her from an upstairs window. By the time the ambulance arrived, Margaret was conscious, but in pain and more than a little confused.

Jack and Evelyn drove to the hospital as soon as they heard what had happened. They found Margaret lying on a trolley in a packed corridor. She looked frightened and she had clearly been crying, which Jack later told Evelyn he couldn't ever remember seeing his mother do before, not even on the day they buried his father.

'I'm worried about her,' he said the following evening, as Evelyn was making brown bread. "That house is too much for her to manage.'

'She's pretty fit for her age, Jack.' Evelyn shook some flour onto the chopping board and rolled the dough expertly between her fingers.

'Anything could have happened to her. Fierce cold it was too. What if Nancy hadn't come home when she did? She might have died lying out there in the garden.'

'But she didn't.'

'She's not steady on her feet anymore. I noticed that in town the other week.'

Evelyn stopped kneading and wiped her brow with the back of her hand. She looked at him squarely.

'Jack, what are you getting at?'

'I'm not getting at anything. I'm stating the facts as I see them.'

'Which are?'

'She is too old to be living on her own.'

'I see. And what do you suggest?'

'We could have her here, maybe. For a while, anyway. At least until her wrist heals.'

'Here? Where? We don't have any room for her here, and anyway, she'd never agree to it!'

'You saw her yesterday, you saw how she was. She was shook up. I've never seen her like that before.'

'I can't have that woman living in my house, Jack. What about your sisters?'

'That woman is my mother, and my sisters live in Sligo and Cork.'

'Yes. They had to travel that far to get away from her!'

No sooner had the words left her mouth than she regretted them.

'Jack, I'm sorry.'

He wouldn't look at her.

'My mother,' he said, with a tremor in his voice, 'put food on the table and clothes on our backs with no help from anyone else. She asks for no help now – it's not her way, it's not the woman she is. But you saw her yesterday and you saw the state she was in. You tell *me* what's the right thing to do?'

'All right Jack, all right. For a little while, until she's back on her feet.'

'Thank you.'

'But you'll need to talk to the children.'

The following morning Jack broached the subject over breakfast with the twins.

'How would you two feel about Granny moving in with us for a while?'

Neither twin responded. Anthony, who had just sat down, looked pale and uninterested. Emma was poking at her scrambled eggs with the edge of her fork and didn't even look up.

'Emma, did you hear what I said? She's all alone in that house, and I feel, we both feel, it's too much for her at the moment. We're thinking it might be nice if she came and stayed here for a bit when she gets out of hospital.'

Anthony poured cereal into a bowl and splashed milk over it. Jack noticed he was wearing black nail varnish. He started to say something, but managed to stop himself. It was too early in the morning for another row. He was sick and tired of fighting with the boy.

'What do you think, Anthony?'

'Do what you want.'

'But what do you–'

'I don't care.'

'You should care.' Jack said, feeling his temper rise despite his best efforts. 'She's our flesh and blood.'

'I do not understand,' Emma said. 'She has a house.'

'I know she does, but she's all alone and she's not able to look after herself as well as she used to do.'

'Yes, but she already has a house. We have our house and she has her house.'

Emma gave up on her eggs. She stood up and scraped them into the plastic bucket used to feed the collies at the end of the day. 'Now I need to make more eggs and I will probably be very late. I do not like to be late.'

'Your father's trying to talk to you.' Evelyn rolled her eyes. 'Will you sit down for a minute?'

'Where will she sleep? What room will she use?' Emma suddenly jolted. 'She cannot have my room.'

'Well, of course not. She can have the utility room, we'll fix it up.'

'The washing machine is in there, and other things: it is not a bedroom.'

'I can move the washing machine into the kitchen. It can easily be made into a bedroom.'

'But she has a good bedroom.' Emma removed two eggs from the pack and cracked them into a frying pan. 'It is in her house.'

'Emma,' Jack said. 'It's not about houses. Your grandmother is hurt and she needs her family around her… will you leave the eggs for a minute and listen to me when I'm *talking to you?*'

Emma turned off the heat and moved the frying pan to one side.

'I am going to work.'

'You haven't eaten anything,' Evelyn said, pouring a cup of tea from the pot.

'I am not hungry and I do *not* like shouting.'

She turned on her heel and left the room. Anthony stood up and carried his cereal bowl to the sink.

'Where are you going?'

'Work, Flicky's got a delivery coming in.'

'What do you think?' Jack asked. 'About your granny–'

'I already told you, do what you like.'

He followed in his sister's wake.

'Well,' Evelyn said, blowing on her tea, 'that went well.'

Anthony collected his bike and caught up to Emma who had stopped at the end of the lane to tie her laces.

'You okay?'

'I do not know why he shouts.'

'*Fuck* him.'

'You are angry. Are you angry with me?'

'No. Come on, let's go together.'

'I am currently,' Emma said, coasting along beside him on her bike, 'educating a horse called Stanley. He is what Pete calls "an honest sort". Harry Lynch bought him for his wife, as she is taking up riding. I think Harry's wife will be able to hack him out quite shortly. He is easy to train, which will make him ideal for a beginner. Quite unusual for his age I would have said. The sort of horse Pete also calls "bomb proof", but I do not know if that is true or not. I imagine a bomb *would* scare Stanley. He is afraid of JCBs. Yesterday I put the lunge rope on him and walked him to the garage and back, and he saw a JCB parked near the phone box and he stood staring at it, snorting through his nose. I had to…'

Anthony let her talk, content to listen. He drew some relief from knowing that she was happy doing whatever the hell it was she did. Sometimes it seemed to him she was the only happy person he knew, and that frightened him so badly it made him want to curl up and die.

He had missed his payment the week before. Gully had been waiting for him on the road after work the next night, primed and stinking of cheap beer and sweat. Anthony had managed to land one blow and it had been a doozy, a real haymaker of a swing that caught Gully on the ear and made him swear. After that, there hadn't been much to be smug about except that he hadn't cried when Gully had knocked him down. That was power, wasn't it?

Beneath his T-shirt, bruises covered his ribs and his kidneys. He had pissed blood earlier that week and had almost fainted in the bathroom. Whatever else you might say about him, Gully was a clever bastard that way – he left no wounds visible to those who did not know where to look.

Gully. Anthony leaned to one side and spat; even thinking his name left a bad taste in his mouth.

Anthony lifted his face to the morning sun, and let hatred fill him as Emma nattered on. Hate would keep him going: hate would be his fuel.

CHAPTER 24

It was barely light when Emma and Pete set out on their way to Harrowfield Horse Market. Someone had told Pete there was a trader coming from Galway that day, a man who did a fine line in cobs, and Pete was eager to have a look at what was on offer.

Emma yawned and pulled up the collar of her blue fleece.

'Tired kid?' Pete glanced over at her.

'Yes.'

'We'll grab a coffee when we get there.'

'Useful animals, cobs,' Pete told Emma as they drove through a series of villages, grinding down through the gears as they slowed down. 'Not as smart-arsed as ponies if you ask me, more honest.'

'What will you do with them?'

'I got a buyer in mind, don't I?'

Emma furrowed her brow. 'Who?'

'Remember that woman with them hairy dogs?'

'Do you mean the lurchers?'

'Yeah, last time she was over she asked me to keep an eye out. She says she wants two to drive in harness.'

'Does she have stables?'

'No.'

'She would keep the animals with you?'

'Well, that would make sense wouldn't it? Someone has to train them t'drive.'

'Win-win.'

Pete rolled his eyes. 'Win-win' was her latest expression.

'When you say it like that it sounds like I'm pulling t'wool over her eyes.'

Emma looked at him blankly.

'Tricking her into buying two cobs she don't want.'

'But she does want them,' Emma said.

'Right.'

'And you want them to stay with you so that you can get more money.'

Pete lit a cigarette and puffed on it for a while, wondering if it was even worth bothering to answer. 'Right.'

'So it *is* win-win.'

'If yer going to be pedantic about it, yeah.'

'Am I pedantic?'

Pete laughed. 'If y'looked up that word in a dictionary, yer picture would be there beside it.'

'Really?'

'No. *Not really*. Flamin' heck, that's exactly what I'm talking about.'

They reached the horse fair shortly before nine, and, as Pete had guessed, the place was packed. They parked in the field allocated for cars and walked back towards the action.

'It is very noisy,' Emma said, stepping up onto the ditch as two young lads jockeyed past, riding bareback on small, nondescript ponies.

'Come on then, lets go find them cobs.'

Pete hustled them along, much to Emma's annoyance. She wanted to see everything, not just some cobs, but he was relentless.

'You take a gander *after* business. Come on, he'll have 'em sold before I can get 'em.'

They passed thoroughbreds, hunters, cobs and ponies of every description, as well as dogs and a few grumpy-looking goats. Beyond a stall selling homemade jams and chutneys Pete spotted the Galway dealer and hurried over. He took a long look at his stock – a group of burly young cobs, with feathered feet and thick, stocky legs. Two caught his eye immediately: a pair of sooty palominos, just under fifteen hands, with excellent conformation. The dealer untied them and pulled them out. Pete watched them being trotted back and forth. Emma studied Pete's face and knew straightaway he was impressed. They had natural reach and movement and would, she knew, be superb under harness.

'Well?' the dealer asked.

Pete shrugged. 'If I'd known y'were bringing the dregs down, Paddy, I'd have stayed in me flamin' bed!'

'Dregs is it? Sure I suppose I can't expect better from an Englishman, sure what would you know about quality?'

While Pete and the trader insulted each other's intelligence and intentions, Emma's attention was drawn to a sleek black thoroughbred, ridden by a girl not much older than herself. The girl was trotting him up and down, showing him to prospective buyers.

Emma could see the buyers were green: middle aged, well dressed – probably well heeled too, if their clothes were anything to go by. A husband and wife, she guessed, open-faced and enthusiastic, all of which equalled disaster at a market.

The horse was well turned out, compared to most of the horses there. Groomed to perfection, his coat gleamed and his mane had been plaited with care and consideration. From the shine on his nostrils, it was obvious to Emma that a liberal coat of Vaseline had been applied. In fact, he was so well turned out that Emma became curious. She drifted closer towards them and watched the horse turn and trot back and forth. He was collected and calm – the girl rode him with light hands, but his ribs and chest revealed a different story.

'He's some boy to go, no bold in him, like,' the girl was saying. 'This is your lucky day, sir – a horse like this fella wouldn't normally be here at all. I wouldn't be selling him if I wasn't moving abroad. Breaks me heart it does, sir, breaks it.'

'He's beautiful. How old is he?' the man asked, peering into the horse's mouth to check his teeth, with no clue what he was looking for. 'I mean, I don't want too young a horse, or too old for that matter. It's for our daughter you see. She's been riding a couple of years now.'

'Oh this fellow is rising nine, experienced in the field. Easy to clip and box. Honest as the day is long, sir. Watch this.'

She turned him smartly and rode him across the road to the bank, then popped him over a low stone wall, turned him, and did the same on return.

'D'you see, sir? He's a gentleman of a horse.'

Emma watched as she reined the horse. He arched his neck beautifully and sidestepped over towards her.

'He's yours for three,' the girl said. 'I'll even throw in this bridle…for luck.'

The man smiled and glanced at his wife. 'We'd need a few minutes to talk it over…'

'Don't take too long, sir,' the girl said, smiling: she knew she had them. 'This fella will be gone before the hour's out.'

'Oh, really?'

'Look,' the girl tossed her head at Emma, 'there's another lady likes the look of him. That right love?'

'He is beautiful.'

'Oh he is that. He's the whole package this one.'

Emma laid her hand on the gelding's muzzle. His nostrils flared as he in sucked the air

'What is wrong with him?'

'Wrong?' the girl said, narrowing her eyes. 'Not a thing.'

'He is breathing very heavily, but he is not sweating or hot. Does he have heaves?'

'Heaves?' the man said, frowning slightly.

'Indeed and he does not!' the girl snapped. 'Fuck away off with you now.'

'What are heaves?' asked the man's wife.

'An allergy. It can be to dust or bedding, sometimes to food. It can be treated of course, but it is an on-going treatment. And–'

'Are you a vet?' the girl said, leaning half out of her saddle.

'No.'

'Then get your fucking hand off me horse, stop talking shite and go somewhere else before I knock your fucking teeth in.'

Emma flinched and backed away.

The girl fixed a smile on her face, but it was too late; the damage was done. The couple were peering intently at the gelding's sides.

'He *is* breathing rather heavily.'

'Excited, that's all. Crowds'll do that.' She gave a laugh that didn't sound convincing to anyone.

'Well, I think we should–'

'Two seven, after that you'd be robbing me.'

The man glanced at his watch. 'I'll tell you what, we'll go have a chat about it okay?'

'Two and a half, and that's the best I can give you!' the girl said, a ring of desperation to her voice.

The couple carried on walking. As they reached the burger and chip van a few yards down the field, both of them looked back, and it was clear from their faces that they had already made up their minds.

Emma inched closer to the horse and bent down. Even his hooves had been oiled. Something whirled past her face. Emma yelped and jumped back just in time to avoid being struck across the face by a riding crop.

'And you, *you* can go fuck yourself!'

The girl kicked the black in the ribs so hard he semi-reared before springing forward and disappearing into a crowd of people, scattering them like ninepins.

Emma retreated to where Pete and the dealer from Galway were mauling the two cobs as though they were prized jewels.

'Is he buying them cobs?'

Martin Harte was standing by her elbow, so close that Emma was forced to edge away from him.

'Yes.'

'You look nice. Let me buy you a coffee.'

Emma was thinking of how to reply to that when Pete and the trader finally settled on a figure, spat in their hands and shook on the deal.

Pete put his own head collars on the two cobs and turned to Emma. He eyed Martin with little or no measure of friendliness.

'How you getting on Martin?'

'Fine Pete, never better.'

'You buying or selling today?'

'Oh just admiring what's on offer.' Martin winked at Emma, put his hands in his pockets and walked away.

Pete handed her one of the lead ropes. 'Was he bothering you?'

'No.'

'If he bothers you again tell me and I'll—'

'*There*, that's her. That's the stupid bitch right there.'

The girl was back, this time on foot, and she had Arthur Donovan with her.

'Her? I might have fucking known.' Donovan rushed forward and shoved Emma in the chest. He hit her so hard she went flying backwards into the line of startled cobs. 'I warned ya. I warned ya to keep that fucking nose of yours out of my business.'

'Hold on there, hold on!' the trader yelled – the cobs had panicked and shied, and were tangling lines and snapping knots.

Pete grabbed Donovan by the shoulder, spun him around and punched him in the side of the head so hard he sent him sprawling on his back.

'Don't be hitting *him*. It's that stupid bitch there that cost us a sale!' the girl yelled, jabbing her finger towards Emma, who was now in a panic and desperately trying to dodge the hooves of frightened animals.

'Give over.'

'She told people the horse I was riding had heaves.'

'It's a vendetta!' Donovan spluttered, outraged. The girl ran to him, but he waved her off and sat up rubbing his jaw, already bright red and swelling. 'That's what it is, a vendetta. You all heard. Fuck's sake, mouthin' out of her like that.'

'I did not know it was your horse!' Emma said. 'I am sorry if I did something wrong.'

The Galway dealer stepped in beside Pete. 'Go'wan with yourself Arthur, if hitting girls is all you're good for.'

'Something needs to be done about her,' Donovan said. He got to his feet, picked up his cap and clamped it on his head. 'She's not right in the fucking head.'

He stomped off, swearing and snarling at anyone who got in his way.

'It's all right now,' Pete said to Emma. 'Don't mind that git. Come on, give me a 'and getting these two loaded. Come on now, kid, yer all right.'

They led the cobs along the road to the truck, with Emma rubbing her chest and talking ninety to the dozen. Pete knew she was completely freaked out by what had happened.

'I asked the girl why the horse was breathing so hard. He was not sweating. I said I thought he had heaves. I did not know she was connected to Mr Donovan.'

'Everyone knows Arthur at these meets, so she's probably a ringer.'

'I do not know what that means.'

'He's uses other people to sell horses for him and then it's buyer beware. They can't come back on him you see?' Pete shook his head. 'Shitty carry on, but hardly surprising for that flamin' git.'

They reached the truck. Pete loaded the cobs into the truck and closed up the ramp.

'Still, we got what we came for, yeah?'

'Win-win,' Emma said, dully. She climbed into the cab and shut the door. She didn't say one word during the long drive home. When they eventually arrived back at the stables, she helped Pete get the cobs settled, then headed straight for the tack room and closed the door.

CHAPTER 25

The following morning, Jack was hosing down the floor of the milking parlour when the collies started barking their heads off. He walked outside in time to see Pete's truck turn into the yard.

'Morning Pete. You've missed her.'

Pete shut off the engine and climbed down from the cab. 'I wanted to call in person and say sorry about yesterday. I should've kept my eye on 'er better than I did.'

'You'll have to run that by me again, Pete.'

'Yesterday,' Pete said. 'Did Emma not tell y'what happened at market?'

'Tell me about what now?'

Pete sighed and pinched the bridge of his nose. He patted his top pocket for his cigarettes and lit one before he spoke.

'She'd a run in yesterday with Arthur Donovan at the market. The bastard shoved her 'cause he was pissed off over some ringer of 'is losing a sale. I thought she might've mentioned it. She were right upset yesterday.'

Jack took his pipe out of his back pocket and filled it from the bag of loose tobacco he carried with him at all times. After a couple of attempts, he got it to light and stood puffing, gazing down the hillside towards the grazing cattle.

'Well, she never said a word, about any of it. So I appreciate you coming here to tell me this Pete. But if what you say is true, it was hardly your fault.'

'Thing is, I don't like seeing her frightened like that though. It sets her back.'

'Best thing ever happened to that girl was taking up with yourself Pete. Evelyn and I are very grateful for everything you've done for her.'

'If only it was just the horses she had to deal with.' Pete stuck one foot up on the bumper of the truck. 'Speaking of horses, you'll never guess who I ran into.'

'Who?'

'Dody Molloy. Remember him?

'Oh aye? I thought he was out in Japan?'

'He's back and he's only gone and bought the flamin' stud over on Sliabh Rua.'

'Oh, is that who bought it?' Jack looked mildly surprised. 'By God, he'll have his work cut out for him so. Sure that place is a ruin.'

'I told him. But you know Dody, plenty of money and not a lick of sense. Anyway Jack, I'd better push on.'

They shook hands and Pete left.

That evening, Evelyn asked Emma to give her a hand rounding up the chickens for the night.

'Your father tells me you had a run-in with Arthur Donovan.'

Emma shrugged. 'He was angry. It was my fault. I ruined a sale.'

'He shouldn't have laid a hand on you. He had no right to do that. Emma, listen, don't let anyone ever hurt you.'

Emma cornered the cockerel and grabbed him before he had a chance to duck under her and make his escape.

'If anyone goes near you again, you're to tell me. All right? Me or your father.'

Emma lifted the squirming bird and held him close to her chest.

'Emma, did you hear what I said?'

'Yes, but we fight our own battles.'

'What?'

'That is what we do. We fight our own battles.'

'Who told you that?'

'Anthony.'
'What battles is he fighting?'

Emma would not be drawn on the subject any further. She put the cockerel in the coop, shut the door and went inside to bed.

CHAPTER 26

The twins sat their Leaving Certificate exam over a two scorching hot weeks in June. Anthony told Evelyn and Jack that he found most of the papers pretty easy (except for French, which he was never very good at, but overall he was happy enough with how it went). Emma, who attended the same exam hall without protest, said her papers were 'unremarkable'.

On the day of the last exam, Anthony cleaned out his locker and made one final pass along the corridors, walking with his hands in his pockets, studying framed photographs of the winning football and hurley teams over the years. It was hard to believe school was finished; that he was free to go wherever he wanted to go, and to be whoever he wanted to be.

But even as he crossed the grounds and walked towards the gates, he knew his pleasure at freedom would be short lived. Lately, Jack had been putting him under increased pressure to involve himself more in the farm, but the more Jack talked the more Anthony resisted. It was a bone of contention between them that was steadily eroding what was left of their relationship.

'So, what *do* you want to do?' Jack demanded one night. 'Sit around daydreaming about music? Slopping around in a bar?'

'What?'

'If you don't want to farm, you're going to need a trade, or a something to fall back on. It's a cold world out there, Anthony, no place for dreamers.'

'I know that,' Anthony said, sneering, 'believe me.'

'Ah, you know nothing,' Jack said, picking up his newspaper and then putting it down again. 'You're away with the fairies half the time.'

Muscles in Anthony's jaw bunched. He'd be turning eighteen later that year and he hated been spoken to as though he was a child – as though his life was one of roses and rainbows. He wanted to grab his father and scream that it was *he* who had no idea what the world was actually like, what darkness lingered beyond the farm gates. Instead he said:

'I'm sorry you feel that way.'

'Divil a bit you are, Anthony,' Jack said, picking up his newspaper again. 'Mé féin – that's you lad, a mé féiner.'

That had been three weeks ago, and they had hardly spoken a word since.

For Emma, the exams marked the end of the whole wretched 'school experience', as she now called it, and she was eager to forget all about it, which was pretty easy to do since she was busier than ever. She now split her time between Pete's stables and the Sliabh Rua Stud, where Dody Molloy had convinced her to take on a few days riding for him.

'I think I would like to write a book,' Emma told Jack a few days after her final exam. It was Saturday evening and she was helping him clean the gutters of debris.

'What kind of a book?'

'A book for people, so that they can understand horses.'

'Oh aye? Do you think you could do that?'

'Yes.'

'Would you not need some kind of a typewriter?'

'Dody said I could have a word processor.'

Jack glanced at her. 'Dody?'

'That is his name.'

'You told him about it?'

'Yes.

'You'd have to learn to type.'

'Yes.'

'At least one of them is showing some gumption,' Jack said to Evelyn later that evening. 'A bit of drive.'

Evelyn, who was darning socks on the sofa, put them to one side and looked Jack squarely in the face: 'You are too hard on that boy, Jack.'

'Every other man I know has sons to help him out. There's plenty for him to be doing around here, instead of wasting his life away down in that bloody pub. Listening to the likes of Flicky Gillespie filling his head with notions.'

'What did you tell me about Emma, all those years ago?'

'That's different.'

'You said she'd find her own way. I listened; I trusted in her. Why can't you let your son do the same?'

Jack made a dismissive gesture with his hands and got up out of his chair. 'I'm going to bed.'

Evelyn thought to stop him, but decided against it. She watched him cross the room. Old, she thought, he'd gotten old and cranky somewhere along the way, and if that was so, what did it make her?

She sighed and picked up her sewing again, repairing what she could.

CHAPTER 27

The interior of Lakelands pub was old-fashioned and ramshackle, a place of mismatched furniture, tasselled lamps and blackened wooden beams. The main bar was connected to the lounge by swinging saloon doors, which opened onto a set of snugs that hardly anyone used anymore. A turf fire blazed in the hearth throughout both the winter and summer months, and Ned, Flicky's wall-eyed Labrador, slept before it, bloated on a diet of crisps and roasted peanuts (which Flicky strictly forbade customers to feed him due to his noxious flatulence), snoring contentedly on a rug of indeterminate colour.

Anthony liked Lakelands. He liked that it had not changed in all the time he'd known it. He liked standing behind the bar on a summer's evening, listening to the chat, and he felt more at ease among the gnarled, seasoned drinkers than he did with anyone of his own age. The regulars, a core group of old wags, liked him well enough too – he could tell from the way they slagged him mercilessly.

'What sort of music is that you're listening to at all?' they asked whenever he came in for a shift wearing his Walkman.

'Sisters of Mercy.'

'Nuns is it? Never took you for the religious sort. You want to get yourself some Big Tom. Now, there's a man who can hold a tune.'

When Anthony got one of his ears pierced, the ould fellas spoke of nothing else for weeks.

'You want to get yourself a nice pair of dangly earrings like yer woman from *Coronation Street*,' they said. 'Flicky, are you sure you hired a young man to help you out? Did you take a look at the chassis or just at the bonnet'

More than anything, Anthony liked that Flicky treated him as a man, a colleague – a friend even. Flicky didn't judge him, or put pressure on him to be anything other than on time. He listened when Anthony spoke and laughed at his jokes. A surprisingly educated man Flicky could discuss an array of topics and subjects. Compared to Jack, Flicky was a revelation.

Every so often, Anthony would consider telling Flicky what was going on, that he'd been paying Gully Donovan practically since he'd been working there, but then he would think of Emma, of Gully's threat, and the words died in his throat.

'Ho ho,' Flicky said, one Friday evening in late June, 'look lively Anthony. It's the Squire of Killbragh, come to visit the humble peasants.'

Anthony grinned as Larry Green strolled into the bar, resplendent in a crumpled linen suit and a cream fedora, beneath which a shiny red face and glassy eyes spoke of an afternoon well spent.

'Gentlemen,' Larry bowed at the waist in mock salute, slurring only a little. 'I have seen the future, and the future is…'

'Is?'

'D'you know, I've bloody forgotten.'

'What can I get you, Squire?' Flicky asked.

'I'll have a pint please.'

Flicky leaned imperceptibly closer. 'A pint you say?'

Larry squinted his eyes, taking time and care over his next decision. 'Perhaps a small one to chase.'

Flicky beamed and Anthony wandered to the other end of the bar to leave him fleece his neighbour in peace. On nights like this, there was really only one outcome. Larry would stay until closing, discover his car keys were missing – Flicky always stole them at some point during the evening – and either sleep in the small storeroom over the newsagents or get Flicky to phone Clodagh, Larry's long-suffering wife, to come and collect him.

But that night, someone else pushed open the pub doors.

Anthony had been aware of Lucy's existence in much the same way he was aware of everyone who lived within a thirty-mile radius. But they had not shared a class in primary school and Lucy had gone to boarding school at the age of twelve. It was with some shock that Anthony discovered the girl he vaguely remembered from childhood had somehow been transformed into a stunning young woman.

She was tall, almost Anthony's height, curvy, with the same lustrous hair and amazing blue eyes; and when she smiled, as she did now, she lit up the room around her.

'Hi Anthony. I'd heard you were working here.'

'Lucy…I'm, yes…I am.'

I'm here to pick up Uncle Lar.'

'Oh.' Anthony jerked his head towards the main bar. 'He's asleep inside. Can I give you a hand helping him out to the car?'

'Thank you, but I think I can manage,' she smiled. 'Good to see you.'

She walked through the swing doors, Anthony followed from behind the bar.

He watched her collect the car keys from Flicky and exchange a few words with the assortment of wags that clearly had no homes to go to. She appeared cool and unflappable as she gently woke her uncle and helped him to his feet. She even had the good grace to say goodnight to everyone before she led him out to the waiting car.

A class act, Anthony thought.

'Close your gob Anthony, you're catching flies,' one of the wags said, laughing when they noticed him standing in the nook.

Anthony flushed. 'I don't know what you're talking about.'

'See now, Flicky,' another one started almost immediately, 'that's what this place needs. A bit o' romance, the peal o' wedding bells.'

'Might as well stake your balls to the ground as get married,' Flicky said, with a genuine shudder. 'Why in the name of all that's holy would any man want to tie his wagon to one woman for the rest of his days?'

'Ara, wouldn't you like to settle down some day? Maybe have a few childer?'

'Children?' Flicky looked around his bar with wild-eyed horror, as though imagining teams of burly toddlers abseiling through the windows. 'Come on now gentlemen, have you no homes to go to?'

But as they were cleaning up later, Flicky, stacking the ashtrays, casually said: 'She's a nice wee girl, is Lucy. I suppose you know she's seeing Martin Harte.'

'No,' Anthony replied, 'I didn't.'

'Plenty more fish in the sea, lad.'

'I wasn't fishing,' Anthony said, closing the dishwasher door with a thump.

CHAPTER 28

The first week in July, Pete took delivery of a flashy, eight-year-old liver-chestnut mare called Rouge Velvet, or Red, as she became known. Red, an on-the-rise show jumper of impressive talent, had recently been bought by Catherine O'Gorman, a hard-nosed businesswoman from Templerainy.

Catherine was an accomplished rider long before she got into jumping, and was well used to hunting and point-to-pointing. But, from the moment she entered a show jumping competition and won a rosette, she was hooked. Pete had sourced her last horse for her, a deep-chested bay named Acova, and together he and Catherine were a formidable team for a spell. But Acova was close to retirement age and Catherine had bought Red as his replacement, having watched her jump six months before at a show in Slane. She had ridden Red only three times since buying her, and had been thrown on each occasion. On the last, Red had reared straight up and over with Catherine on her back. Catherine was lucky to have had escaped without serious injury, and she knew it.

'You've never seen anything like this Pete,' she told him over the phone, 'no warning at all. Straight up and over.'

'Dangerous.'

'I couldn't keep her feet on the ground. And the time before that she ran me straight into a fence. I'm telling you Pete, every time I ride her it gets worse…I don't know what else to do with her. I'd be hard pressed to sell her on at this stage. I don't think I could live with the guilt if she killed somebody.'

Pete had known Catherine for a good number of years and liked her well enough. She was brassy and a bit of a show-off, but under the bluff she had a good heart, and he felt bad that her confidence had taken such a bashing.

'Catherine, if y'really want to sell her on I can put feelers out, but why don't you leave her with me for a few weeks first? Y'know young Emma who works for me, right?'

'I've heard of her.'

'She's extremely good with problem horses. Why don't y'let her have a crack at Red?'

'Oh I don't know Pete. She's too much horse for most people,' Catherine said, sounding close to tears. 'No exaggeration, I've had her on full livery in Dermot's place for three months, and honestly, every day I'm waiting for him to call and ask me to remove her. She attacks his staff when they enter the stable to feed her; she bites if they groom her, she bit the vet, the blacksmith, even Dermot. They can't even turn her out because she's such a holy terror with the mares. The last vet who examined her thought it might even be neurological.'

'Best bring 'er over. Give us a chance to do an assessment and we'll take it from there.'

Emma was sitting on an upturned bucket in the sunshine, cleaning tack, when Catherine O'Gorman's Mercedes, horsebox in tow, pulled into the yard. Catherine got out and pushed her sunglasses up on her head.

'I'm looking for Pete, is he here?'

'He is gone for feed. He should be back shortly.'

'What about Emma Byrne? Is she around?'

'I am Emma Byrne.'

'*You're* Emma Byrne?'

'Yes, that is my name,' Emma said, carefully soaping a martingale.

Catherine looked at her for a long moment. 'Did Pete mention I would be stopping by?'

'I do not know. Who are you?'

'I'm Catherine O'Gorman. I've got…well my horse is having trouble.'

Emma cleaned off the soap with a dry cloth and set the bridle aside. 'You are the owner of the rearer.'

'Yes, I suppose you could call her that.'

'I have a stable ready. I will unload her.'

'You might want to wait until Pete gets back.'

'Why?'

'She can be a bit aggressive with strangers.'

'Pete is a stranger.'

Catherine wondered if the girl was being smartarsed, but Emma gave no indication that she was.

Together they walked to the rear of the horsebox. Catherine undid the locks and lowered the ramp. Red swung her hindquarters around, blocking their access immediately.

'Stop that.'

'You should go through the front door,' Emma observed.

'Did I mention that she bites?'

'No.'

'Well, she bites. Trust me, we're better off letting her out this way. She's not tied, she doesn't like to be tied.'

Catherine lifted the safety bar and Emma watched as two heels lashed out, narrowly missing Catherine, who leaped backwards.

'Shit! God damn it.'

Catherine fetched a lead rope from the boot of her car and tossed it to Emma. 'Red is extremely highly strung. She bites, she rears – she kicks too. You can't put her in with other horses because she bites them. She hates dogs, so you'll probably need to keep that one,' she pointed at Ruby, 'away when you take her out of the stable. That's if you *can* take her out.'

Red stamped her feet in the box, then kicked the side.

'If you *do* get her out – listen to me, this is important – if you do get her out, be careful with her. She charges, she bucks and she kicks on the ground. If you ride her, you need to know that she has a very hard mouth, so I've been using a hackamore. I would urge you to do likewise or else she bolts. She's an excellent jumper, until she starts bloody rearing. Oh, and if you're turning her out, don't bother…did I mention this all ready? She is very hostile to other horses. Also, you'll need to use a twitch if you want to go near her feet. She is very bad about having them picked up… she will bite.'

Emma stared wordlessly.

'Are you sure you're getting all this?' Catherine said, narrowing her eye.

'Yes.'

'Okay, now. She's also touch sensitive, so you cannot use a currycomb at all – you need to be aware of that. Oh, and she bites when you feed her in the stable, so the best thing to do is…'

Emma let Catherine run her mouth until she was done. She wasn't really interested in the woman's observations because they belonged to Catherine, and one person's experiences were just that. But Emma had learned it was always best to let owners feel they were imparting information she could not figure out for herself. Why – or how – this made people feel better was beyond her understanding.

What did interest Emma was Red's reaction when she came steaming down the ramp. When in a new yard most horses checked out their surroundings immediately: they lifted their heads high, snorted and scented the air; they whinnied or answered other whinnies. Claude had screeched a greeting twice, but Red acted as though she had heard nothing. She did none of the things Emma would have expected. She remained where she stood, stock still, tense and quivering, with her tail pressed tight to her body. Her eyes were fixed and her ears lay close to her head. To Emma she looked positively terrified. When Pete's truck came into the yard, Red turned one ear towards the sound and went rigid again.

'She is very fearful,' Emma said to Pete after they had managed to coax Red into a stable and Catherine O'Gorman had driven away. 'I have not seen fear like this before.'

'I noticed that myself.'

'Of course, the owner is afraid too. Both of them have nervous energy. They are feeding off each other.'

'How do you figure Catherine is afraid?'

'Nervous dogs bark a lot,' Emma shrugged. 'She talks a lot'

Emma looked over the top of the stable door. Red stood facing into the corner, her hind legs aimed towards them.

'So what's the plan of action?'

'I do not know.'

'You don't?' Pete smiled. 'That's a new one on me.'

'I think something happened to this horse. She is afraid for a reason.'

'I can find out when it started.'

'That is a good idea. I am going to have to take her back to the very start again, and rebuild her confidence. Hopefully, it will become a win-win situation.'

'Win-win?'

'Yes, she will be not afraid and the woman will be not afraid either. Win-win.'

'Well kid,' said Pete as he turned away from the stable door and headed for the house, 'I reckon you've got your work cut out for you with this one.'

Emma left the mare alone to settle that night and went to the yard early the following day to begin Red's assessment. As Catherine had mentioned, even feeding was difficult. Red tried to chase Emma out of the stable repeatedly, baring her teeth and striking with her front hooves. Each time Red attacked, Emma waited until she retreated; she would then re-enter and chase the mare backwards, keeping the feed bucket down by her side. She knew the mare was hungry, yet it took over thirty minutes for Red to realise that there was no food forthcoming if she didn't stop trying to attack Emma every time she walked into the stable. Eventually, Red flattened herself against the back wall, ready to spin if necessary and show a pair of heels. Emma upended her food into the trough and left her to it.

After breakfast, Emma re-entered the stable again and began to work on some ground rules. She made Red back up, and then moved the mare from corner to corner, front to rear, always calmly demanding her own space. Red tried to swing her hind around, but Emma nimbly kept to her shoulder. She finished the session and stood waiting at the door. As expected, Red approached her, ears forward.

Emma took a hand full of nuts from her pocket and hand fed her with them.

'Very tough going, I know.'

She stroked the mare on the neck with her free hand. Red raised her left hind hoof and kicked the air, but did not pin her ears and did not try to take a chunk out of Emma.

When Red was finished play-acting, Emma attached a lead rope to her halter and opened the stable door. Immediately, Red became pushy and aggressive, almost walking over her, yanking her this way and that. She snapped at the other horses as she passed the doors of their stables. It was clear to Emma that she was used to getting her own way and very used to pushing people around.

Emma led Red to the barn, cross-tied her and then stepped back to observe her for a few minutes. One of the first things she noticed was that the mare was unbelievably sensitive to touch. She shuddered and flinched at everything. A fly landing on her withers sent her into spasms. She made no attempt to escape or pull back on the lead; but neither did she make any attempt to interact with Emma and she scraped the ground constantly with her front hooves.

After ten minutes, Emma left her and came back with a grooming kit and a soft cotton rag. She was working on Red when Pete walked past leading Zebbie, a goofy big grey he was hoping to sell before the hunting season. Emma had ridden him for the first time only a few weeks before, but the horse was already proving to be a calm soul.'

'I'm going to the arena.' Pete said.

'Okay.'

'Are you giving that horse a massage?'

'Yes.'

'Why?'

'I am overloading her senses. She needs to desensitise and she needs to know that I am not her enemy.'

'Better watch those hooves of hers.'

'I am.'

'I mean it. That one will kick you if she gets the chance.'

Emma kept her hand moving, sidestepping easily out of the way whenever the mare snaked her head around. 'She has a scar over her ocular bone. I think somebody hit her.'

'Doubt it was the fellow Catherine bought her from. I know him, and he's an all right sort of bloke.'

'Tomorrow I am going bring her out to the arena and use the "tickler".'

Red's head whipped around again, her teeth snapping the air where just a moment before Emma's shoulder had been.

'Vicious. She really means business.'

'She does not want to hurt me. If she did, she would. She only wants for me to leave her alone.'

'If you say so.' Pete shook his head, mounted Zebbie and rode out.

CHAPTER 30

Margaret moved in permanently over the August bank holiday weekend. She had spent two months staying with her daughter in Sligo while Evelyn and Jack readied her new lodgings, and this was her first time seeing the room.

'Well what do you think? Evelyn asked, opening the door and ushering her mother-in-law inside.

'Oh...' Margaret said, stepping in and doing a slow turn. She put down her handbag and patted the bedspread. 'You made a grand job of it.'

'Your chest of drawers is over there and I put your reading chair right beside the window.

It's a bit small I know, but I think it'll be very comfortable.'

'You shouldn't have gone to so much trouble.'

'It was no trouble. I told you Jack and I, we're delighted you've agreed to stay.'

Margaret nodded. She had tears in her eyes and Evelyn could see she was struggling to keep her emotions in check.

'You know, I think I'll go put the kettle on. I've been dying for a cup of tea all morning. Will you have one yourself?'

Over the next few days, Evelyn and Jack went out of their way to make Margaret feel at home. Anthony bought her a plant for her room, and Jack asked her opinion on the herb garden, noting that she had a far greener fingers then he had been blessed with. Emma, however, avoided her grandmother as much as possible until Evelyn caught her at the front door one morning, putting on her riding boots, and pulled her up on her behaviour.

'You're being a bit of a cow to your grandmother.'

'I do not know what you mean.'

'You haven't said anything to her about moving in here. She's very upset about leaving her home at her age. It's horrible and you're making it worse by avoiding her.'

'I do not want to upset her.' Emma frowned. 'I do not want her to live here.'

'Well that's too bloody bad. Do you think Margaret wanted this? It's not about what you want. It's not about what any of us want. It's about doing what is right.'

Emma stood. 'I have to go to work now.'

'You should talk to her this evening.'

'About what?'

'For heaven's sake, I don't know, something… *anything*. Use that big brain of yours.'

Late that evening after dinner, Margaret was in her bedroom reading when she heard a sharp knock on the door.

'Can I come in?'

'If you like,' Margaret said, putting down her book and peering at Emma over the top of her glasses as she entered the room, 'I hardly see you these days you're so busy.'

'Yes, I am very busy.' Emma stopped just inside the door and glanced around. 'Your things look wrong here.'

'They do don't they.'

'Your chest of drawers is too large for that wall and the bed is in the wrong place.'

'Your mother thought it would be better that way.'

'But you sleep on the other side, and now it is by the wall.'

'How did you know that?'

'I remember from your old house. This way, you will have to climb out on the wrong side.'

'I don't mind.' Margaret looked down at her hands. 'I suppose I should be grateful I have any bed at all.'

'I would mind.' Emma moved about the room picking up thing and putting them back down again. When she came to a stack of magazines she paused. 'What are these?'

'It's called the *Ireland's Own*.'

'You collect them?'

'Yes, I like the stories.'

Emma opened one and flicked through it. 'Interesting. There are no boring things about makeup and fashion.'

'Oh no, I'm too old to worry about that sort of thing.'

'It is very boring.' Emma put the magazine down, cleared her throat and stood to attention. 'Granny. I did not mean to upset you or act like a cow. I am very sorry about that. I did not realise I was being wrong.'

'You... who said you were acting like a cow?'

'My mother. Although I must say I find that to be a strange expression. She means I am not being very nice, but cows are usually quite nice, so it seems odd to say "acting like a cow" to mean not being nice. Either way, I am sorry for not being nice to you.'

'Oh Emma,' Margaret put her hand to her mouth and started to laugh, 'you're not being anything other than yourself and to be perfectly honest I think I prefer it.'

'My mother says I should talk to you about something.' Emma sat on the edge of the bed and folded her arms stiffly. 'Is there a particular subject you would like to discuss?'

'Well, why don't you tell me about the horse you're working with at the moment? I hear it's a handful.'

'Red?' Emma said, suddenly looking cheerier. 'You want to hear about Red?'

'Yes, I think I'd like that.'

'Well.' Emma crossed her legs and hooked her hands over her knees. 'Red is a mare. You can call her she, not it. She came in two weeks ago. I think someone hit her in the head and it scared her quite badly. Of course, I cannot prove that. It is only an assumption. Pete tells me I assume too many things, but actually I think you must make assumptions according to what you see. Then, if what you base your assumptions on makes perfect sense, you can also assume you are correct. That is what animals do. They make a decision based on how they perceive something, which in a way is an assumption. If a horse assumes something is dangerous, even though it might not be dangerous at all, it will act as though it *is* dangerous. And to me that is acting on an assumption. Not on a fact. But there is a fact at work here. For example, Red is head shy, and she has a scar…'

'I hope Emma's not bothering you,' Evelyn said a few days later. She and Margaret were folding clothes in the kitchen. A late evening sun filtered through the windows. 'You know you can tell her to stop wittering on about horses anytime you like. In fact, you *have* to tell her to do so, or she'd talk the legs off you.'

'She's no trouble,' Margaret said, shrugging one shoulder. 'I like our little evening chats.'

'Oh?' Evelyn raised a sceptical eyebrow.

'Her views…the way she thinks…it's odd, but it's refreshing.'

'Tell that to Harry Lynch.'

'The councillor?'

'Emma called him fat the other day.'

'She *did not*.'

'She said something along the lines that he ought to lose his summer belly before the hunting season begins. Because he's a hunter and that's what the hunters do. I don't think Harry was too impressed.'

Margaret said nothing for a moment, and then pronounced 'Well, he could probably stand to lose a *few* pounds.'

'Yep, 'Evelyn said, snorting a laugh. 'And the rest.'

'She's very keen on Dody Molloy.'

'Mmm,' Evelyn said. 'I've noticed.'

'She says he talks a lot but he is not mean.'

'High praise indeed.' Evelyn shook her head. 'It's good she talks to you then. To be honest, I worry more about Anthony these days than I do about Emma. He's so ...rootless ...I wish he and Jack would stop butting heads over every little thing.'

'He's a young man. He needs to see a bit more of the world in order to appreciate what he has right under his nose.'

'He's not going to see much of the world if he insists on being holed up in Lakelands for most of his waking hours now is he?'

Margaret glanced at her daughter-in-law. 'People often surprise you, Evelyn.'

'That's what I'm afraid of,' Evelyn said, smoothing her hands over the last of the clothes.

'What do you mean you haven't even ridden her?' Catherine O'Gorman said, incredulously. 'She's been here for *weeks*.'

'She is not ready to be under the saddle yet.'

'What are you talking about?'

Emma furrowed her brow. It was a ridiculous question. 'I mean she is not ready to be ridden.'

They were standing outside a pasture watching Red rolling with delight in the soil. As the two women talked, Red got up and shook herself vigorously, sending clouds of dust high into the summer air.

'Pete promised me you could fix her rearing problem. How can you fix her if you don't even ride her?'

'I do not need to ride her to know what is wrong.'

'Well what's wrong with her then? Why does she keep rearing?'

'She rears to get you off her back.'

'I *know* that. I want to know *why*?'

'She does not trust you. She is afraid.'

'Oh for God's sake.' Catherine snorted. 'Her? Afraid? Afraid of what?'

'Everything.'

'Now *you* listen to me. I've a competition coming up in September, so she had better get bloody over her *fear* before that.'

After Catherine had driven off, Emma headed to the tack room, to sit for a while with the door closed and the lights off. Although she had long since learned to control her own fears,

Catherine O'Gorman never failed to give her a full-blown anxiety attack. Emma was beginning to understood how Red felt.

Twenty minutes later, Pete stuck his head in the door of the tack room. 'Rough, huh?'

'That woman is very loud. She makes my brain hurt.'

'She's just frustrated. She wants you to wave a magic wand over Red and fix her.'

'I do not do magic.'

'I know that, kid. But that's people, innit? Are y'coming out of there any time soon?'

'In a few minutes.'

But magic or not, Red was slowly beginning to respond. She no longer shied away from Emma's touch, and sometimes actively looked for it. She stopped trying to bite the other horses when Emma led her past them. One morning, she even stuck her head over the stable door and whinnied to Emma as she cycled into the yard.

'I'm going to put Red out in the front pasture,' Emma informed Pete, later that day.

'Okay.'

'With Zebbie, and maybe a few of the cobs.'

'You think she's ready.'

'She is a horse, a herd animal. She needs to act and think like a horse.'

'Don't put her with the mares.'

'I am not stupid.'

After lunch, Emma took Red to the outdoor arena, where she had set up a serious of small, easy jumps. The first few times she had attempted this previously, Red would shake and try to turn tail and gallop back to her stable. Now, however, Red no longer viewed the arena as a gladiatorial battleground.

Emma lunged her on a long line, letting her warm up, grow supple and engage her hindquarters. Red trotted, then cantered calmly in whatever direction Emma sent her, and stopped at a single gesture, always happy to return to Emma for quick rub under the chin,

That day, Emma untied Red, and set up a few small jumps, nothing spectacular, just a double and two singles. Pushing Red out, Emma let her negotiate the jumps at liberty and she smiled broadly when Red sailed over them, kicking up her heels with the sheer delight of jumping.

Anxious to finish on a high note, she caught Red and led her from the arena, walked her past the stable block and on towards the front paddocks It was a beautiful afternoon. Most of the horses had been turned out early that morning and were now grazing quietly or sprawled on the grass in the sunlight. A few snickered to Red as she pranced past, with her head high and her nostrils flared.

Emma walked her past the main paddock and down to where Zebbie and the cobs had a small field to themselves. She opened the gate, led Red inside and unclipped her head collar.

Red quivered and refused to leave her side. She stared at the horses, swishing her tail. Zebbie lifted his head from grazing and immediately pranced up to Emma. Red squealed and snapped at him, her ears flat to her head, but Zebbie, who simply hadn't a bad bone in his body, sprang out of range easily, snorting, looking amazed that any horse might not wish to share his company.

Red turned her head and looked at Emma, who stood where she was, the lead rope dangling from her hand. Red whinnied high in her throat and took a few cautious steps closer to her, but Emma sent her away with a flick of her hand.

'Go on.'

Red did not need to be told twice; she sprang forwards and cantered off, bucking and kicking. Zebbie followed, and even the cobs gave chase. Red slid to a halt under the trees, dropped and rolled. When she got to her feet she stretched her neck out as far as it would go until her nose touched Zebbie's. Red squealed again and took off at a gallop.

Emma closed the gate and walked back to the yard.

Red had learned another invaluable lesson: horses were not the enemy.

CHAPTER 32

Jack used his toes to ease off his muddy wellingtons before entering the kitchen. He was so tired he could barely keep his eyes open and every muscle in his body seemed to be at war with the one next to it.

'Something smells good.'

Evelyn smiled. 'I made a leg of lamb and roast potatoes.'

'Are we having visitors?'

He washed his hands at the kitchen sink, drying them on a hand towel Evelyn passed to him.

'No, but you need to eat more than tea and sandwiches. You're on your last legs. Sit down there now and it won't be long before it's ready.'

Evelyn steered him towards his chair and made him sit down. She couldn't recall a time she had ever seen Jack look as exhausted as he did now. She lifted the lamb out of the oven and let it rest for a few moments while she gathered the plates and the cutlery.

'We lost another calf,' Jack said, after a few moments. 'Nothing to be done.'

She stopped with the dinner things for a moment. 'Oh Jack I'm sorry.'

'Don't know what it is about this year at all, I don't know if it's because the calves are bigger or what. Nearly lost the cow too. You should have heard the cries out of her. If it hadn't been for Pat, she'd be gone.'

'Where is Pat? I thought he might stop in for a bite to eat.'

'He's gone on home. Poor devil's been up half the night with one of his own sure.'

He yawned as Emma arrived in to the kitchen and slid wordlessly into her chair. Her hair was wet and tied loosely in a ponytail; she wore clean jeans and a brushed cotton shirt that was practically falling apart at the seams. She popped a book onto the table and was about to open it, when she remembered her manners.

'Hello,' she addressed both her parents.

'Howya chicken?' Jack smiled wearily. 'You in long?'

'No.'

'Haven't seen much of you lately. You must be fierce busy.'

'Yes.' Emma glanced at him briefly. 'I have taken on another two horses.'

'Be careful you don't wear yourself too thin.'

'I will not become thin. Do I have time to read?'

'You have a minute and then I'm dishing up the food and I want that book off the table,' Evelyn replied.

Jack glanced at the clock over the stove.

'Where the hell's that other fella?'

'He's on his way.'

'He had a day off today, didn't he? The least he could've done is give me a hand. I don't like him staying out all night like that.'

'He was probably working late, Jack.'

'My eye! It's only a few miles away and he could have walked home if he'd wanted to. He treats this house like a hotel.'

'Jack!'

'Well he does. Never looks up or down at the place. I suppose you have plans this evening too?' Jack said to Emma.

'I *plan* to go to Dody's house and play chess. He is teaching me the moves. Some of them are very complicated.'

'Teaching you the moves?' Jack muttered under his breath, 'just make sure that's all he's teaching you.'

Emma looked at him. 'What do you mean?'

'Jack,' Evelyn put a plate down before him. 'I'm sure we don't need to have that conversation right now.'

'Chess is very complex,' Emma said, trying to separate her peas from her sweetcorn.

'Complex,' Jack snorted. 'Make sure he drops you home at a reasonable hour. You've got work tomorrow.'

'I have work every day.'

'Emma, call your grandmother and tell her dinner is ready,' Evelyn said.

'Chess,' Jack muttered again, shaking his head.

It was almost midnight, when Jack, who had been dozing in his chair by the fire, heard the front door open and close. He rose stiffly and walked out to the hall and saw Anthony attempting to lock it. Jack could smell the booze off his son from where he stood.

'Leave it. Your sister is not back yet.'

'Where is she?' Anthony turned and looked at him blearily. 'She shouldn't be out this late.'

'She's over in Dody Molloy's…playing chess.'

'Chess?' Anthony leaned one hand on the doorjamb and grinned. 'At this hour?'

'Where were you 'til now?'

'Out with Mark.' Anthony shrugged off his jacket and flung it at the coat stand. It missed and settled on the floor. He stared at it, picked it up and jammed it on with deliberate care.

'How come you didn't come home last night?'

'It was late when we were closing up, so I stayed over at Flicky's.'

'I could have done with a hand here today. We lost another calf.'

'Sorry,' Anthony shrugged. 'You should have said.'

'I shouldn't *have* to say. I shouldn't *have* to say what work needs to be done on a farm… Anthony, you look at me when I'm talking to you.'

'Dad, I'm going to bed.'

'For God's sake, will you look at the cut of you? Is this the way you want to spend your life, is it? Falling home here at all hours, reeking of booze and those filthy cigarettes. I don't know what the hell is wrong with you. With everything you have, all the opportunities, and this is how you carry on. Even your sister's making more of her life than you are, and she's had to overcome–'

'Oh here we go,' Anthony shook his head.

'What do you mean?' Jack grabbed him by the upper arm, suddenly furious. 'What do you mean by that?'

'Get off me.' Anthony shoved Jack backwards. 'I don't want to row with you Dad, okay? I'm going to bed.'

'You'd want to buck up your ideas,' Jack said. 'You're a disgrace, that's what you are. An absolute disgrace.'

'Yeah, I get it. I'm a disgrace. No need to tell me twice, Daddio.'

Anthony made his way upstairs, leaving Jack standing in the hall, watching him go.

CHAPTER 33

The air was muggy as Emma put her bike in the shed; pewter-coloured clouds had rolled in across the hills overnight, bringing with them the threat of rain. The horses were restless. Claude snaked his head back and forth over his stable door and scraped his front hoof on the concrete. He snickered to Emma when she walked past, but refused to let her rub his muzzle, which surprised her a little.

'I wish it would flamin' rain,' Pete said, wiping his forehead with the hem of his shirt. 'Break the back of this cursed heat. I've never felt anything like it for September.'

Emma accepted a cup of coffee from him and sat down at the table. Pete glanced at her, puzzled. There was something different about her that he couldn't quite put his finger on. She wore a blue vest, navy jodhpurs and short riding boots, pretty much as always, her hair tied in a ponytail…

'Since when do you wear makeup?'

'Since yesterday.' She reached for a battered copy of *Horse and Hound* and flipped it open.

'Why?'

'Women wear makeup.'

'They do, right enough, but…well I suppose I never really thought you would be bothered with it.'

'Dody likes it.'

'Right,' Pete said, feeling odd and uncomfortable all of a sudden. 'Tell me, how are we are we fixed for feed?'

'Eight bales of hay left after this morning.'

'Beet?'

'Two bags.'

'Oats?'

'Two bags.'

'Nuts?'

'None.'

'Right. You turn 'em out and I'll go over and stock up on feed. You riding?'

'Yes.'

'Don't forget Catherine…Red's owner–'

'I know.'

'–Is coming to pick her up tomorrow, so make sure you've all her gear ready.'

Emma nodded. Catherine had ridden Red that weekend and had expressed her delight and her gratitude in what she called 'Emma's miracle' by hugging Emma, smothering her in a perfumed embrace, which Emma endured, rigid and unmoving, her arms pinned to her side. For that reason, and that reason alone, Emma vowed to be out somewhere riding when Catherine and Red departed from the yard.

That afternoon, Emma groomed and tacked Red in her stable, led her outside and mounted her quickly. She rode her around the indoor arena a few times, asking nothing of her other than that she engage her hindquarters and bend a little to her leg as they warmed up. The little mare responded to every cue, holding a perfect frame each circle. Over the course of the previous weeks, Emma had added a lot of gymnastic movements to Red's daily exercise, building not just confidence, but muscle, fitness and grace.

Emma did one more loop before she aimed Red at one of the small cross-poles. The mare leaped over it, tucking everything under her. Emma turned her and, before she could think about it, set her up over a double. Red took the first one a stride too far out, but she popped the second one with a magnificent swish of her tail. Emma patted her on the neck and the mare collected herself and cantered out the gates.

She met Pete walking across the yard towards the truck.

'How'd she go?'

'Very well, I'm going to ride her out now. I want to finish her last day on a good note. She will enjoy an outing. Something different.'

'Where you thinking of heading?'

'Crilly Woods. I will do the four-mile loop.'

'Don't be out too long,' Pete eyed the sky. 'It's going to flamin' lash down any minute.'

Pete drove the truck over to the feed yard and bought what they needed, had a quick chat about nothing of any great importance with the owner and drove back to the stables. He unloaded the feed, checked on the horses, filled Claude's water bucket with fresh water and went into the cottage to grab a cup of coffee and glance through the paper.

Shortly before four o'clock, he abandoned the paper and stepped outside, surprised to see no sign of Emma. Muttering under his breath, he walked out onto the road, looked both ways and checked his watch.

At four-thirty, Pete got into his truck and drove up towards the woods, following the logging tracks, pausing every now and then to climb out and take a look around. He found no sign of Emma; the long dry spell had left the ground hard and compacted, so it was impossible for him to distinguish fresh hoof marks from the many others.

He glanced at the sky again and drove back to the yard. When she still wasn't back by five-thirty, he drove over to the Byrne's farm.

CHAPTER 34

Jack was working on his tractor when Pete clattered over the cattle grid and drove into the yard. He grabbed his shirt from the seat, and put it on, aware that he was sweaty and smeared with oil.

'All right, Jack?'

'Pete. Fierce close isn't it? I reckon we're in for a bit of thunder.'

'No doubt. Listen you haven't seen Emma have you?'

'No,' Jack shook his head, puzzled. 'I thought she was over with you.'

'She was there earlier all right. She took the chestnut mare out. Said she was going up to do the loop in Crilly, but she hasn't come back.'

'What time did she head out at?'

'A couple of hours ago.

'Maybe she went down along the river. I know she likes it down that way.'

'Maybe, but she said she was going to Crilly and she normally sticks with the routes she says she's taking.'

'You sound worried.'

'I don't know that I'd say I were *worried*…' Pete hesitated. 'But it's not like her not be back when she said she would.'

Jack closed the bonnet and wiped his hands on a rag.

'I'll tell you what. You head on back to the stables in case she's there. I'll go get my car and follow you over.'

Pete left and Jack went into the house to get his keys and change into a clean T-shirt.

'What was Pete doing here?' Evelyn asked, as he came back downstairs.

'Looking for Emma.'

'Why would he be looking for her here? Isn't she supposed to be at his place?'

'It's probably nothing, Evelyn. She went out for a quick ride earlier and he's a bit worried because she hasn't come back yet.'

'Oh, but what time did–?'

'She's probably over in the stables now. I'm going to swing by and see…no don't come out it's about to bucketing down out there.'

Jack kissed her on the forehead and left before she could ask any more questions. Minutes later, he was on the road. Pete was standing by the main gate when he got to the stables, with Ruby at his heels.

Jack pulled in and rolled down the window.

'Well?'

'No sign of her.'

'Right. You hang on here and I'll drive up the woods. If I come across her, I'll drop back this way and let you know she's all right.'

Pete nodded, sucking furiously on a cigarette. He didn't need to say a word: his thoughts were etched all over his face.

Jack did a U-turn and drove up to Crilly Woods. By the time he'd turned onto the first of the tracks, fat drops of rain were splattering against his windscreen. In seconds, it became a deluge. Visibility reduced to next to nothing, even with the windscreen wipers going full speed. His tyres spun as the rutted track quickly turned to mud. The deeper into the woods he drove, the harder he found it to keep calm. He was sweating heavily, and cold fear was making a mockery of his ability to reason.

In the end, he almost missed her, as she stumbled along the tree line. A few seconds later, he would have reached a fork in the road and he *would* have missed her. He braked and leaped out of the car, leaving the door hanging open.

'Emma!'

She stopped walking and looked at him – no, not at him, through him.

'Emma, what happened?'

He ran towards her, but she held up both her hands to ward him off. She was soaked to the bone and her face was streaked in blood. There was blood in her nostrils and her jodhpurs were torn and filthy with mud and grass stains.

'Emma, it's me. It's Dad.'

She blinked and continued walking. He moved in front of her but did not touch her. 'It's me, Emma, look at me, it's Dad.'

'Daddy?'

Thunder rumbled overhead. The rain intensified, beating down on them, bouncing against them like pebbles.

'Where is all this blood coming from?'

Emma raised one hand to the back of her head. Her fingers came away streaked with blood that the rain turned to ribbons of pink in seconds.

'Red was frightened, we…we fell down a bank and… I think she's hurt.' Emma turned in the direction from which she had come, weaving on her feet slightly. 'I need to find her, I need to find Red.'

'No, you're coming with me now.' Jack reached for her, but again she moved away from him and stood in the mud swaying like a drunk.

'I need to find–'

Her legs buckled underneath her and she collapsed into a dead faint. Jack lifted her up and carried her to the car. He laid her across the back seat and reversed down the steep hill until he found a section of path wide enough to turn the car. Praying she would be all right, he put his foot down and headed for home.

CHAPTER 35

Evelyn was out of the house and running across the yard before Jack had a chance to turn off the engine.

'I have her. She's been in an accident.'

'Oh my God. Is she all right?'

'I don't know. Open the door for me.'

Jack carried Emma into the house and laid her down on the sofa in the sitting room. He put a cushion under her head, lifted her wrist and felt her pulse. It was weak, but steady.

'What's going on?' Margaret said, as she entered the room. 'What's happened to her?'

'We don't know,' Evelyn said. She knelt and gently cupped Emma's chin in her two hands.

'Emma, come on now. Open your eyes. Oh God, Jack, where is all the blood coming from?'

'Her head I think.'

'Emma love, it's Mam. Can you open your eyes?'

Emma's eyes fluttered open. Closed again.

'Emma?'

They opened, a little glazed and unfocused, but this time they stayed open.

'Granny?' 'You're at home,' Margaret clutched her chest. 'Emma, it's okay now.'

'My head hurts.' Emma pushed Evelyn's hands away and touched her fingers to her head. 'Hurts.'

'Don't,' Evelyn said. 'I'll need to look at that cut and clean that out. Emma, do you remember what happened? Can you tell me?'

'I…I don't know…'

'The bloody horse bolted.' Jack said.

'No,' Emma closed her eyes and winced. She looked like a frail, bloodied ghost. Even her lips were bloodless. 'No, she was frightened…someone was shooting.'

'What?'

'Shooting. I heard shots.'

'Those fucking jackasses and their guns,' Jack said furiously. 'How many times do people have to be told not to go shooting like cowboys up there? It's a wonder more people aren't killed.'

Emma pushed herself onto her elbows. She tried to get up, but Evelyn wouldn't let her. 'What are you doing? You can't go anywhere. You need to keep still now.'

'I need to find Red.'

'Never mind the damned horse.' Jack said.

'She's hurt.'

'We need to get you fixed up. You've got a head injury. You might need a few stitches. Mother, call Dr Williams there and see if the surgery is still open. If it's not, ask him if he can come here, I don't think–'

'I need to find Red.'

'Listen to me, you're–'

'I have to find her.'

'– not in a fit state to –'

'Stop touching me!'

Evelyn recoiled as if physically slapped.

'Look,' Jack said, after a moment of stunned silence. 'Listen to me now, you stay here. I'll go find the horse.'

He left the room and phoned Pete to explain the situation. They had a brief conversation before Jack got into the car again. This time, he drove straight to Lakelands.

When he got there, the place was half empty and Flicky was sitting behind the bar, his chin in his hand doing a crossword puzzle. He was wearing a pair of what looked like ladies reading glasses, complete with a fine gold chain.

'Jack! Long time no see. Filthy evening for it. What can I get you?'

'I was looking for Anthony.'

Flicky sat up straight, realising immediately something was wrong. 'He's in the stockroom. Hold on. I'll get him for you.'

Anthony appeared a few seconds later wearing a leather apron and a scowl which Jack was beginning to think might become permanent.'

'What are you doing here?'

'I need your help. Can you come home?'

'What is it? What's going on?'

'Emma's been in an accident.'

'She's what?'

'She's all right. I mean I think she is, but I need…I just need you to come with me.'

When Anthony glanced at Flicky for permission, Jack felt something tighten in his chest.

'Go, *go*. I hope she's all right. Phone me later and let me know how she is.'

'I'll have to drop you off,' Jack said, stalling the car on the first try.

'Where are you going?'

'I told Emma I'd find that fecking horse. She's distraught over it.'

'I can help you.'

'Anthony,' Jack said, trying the engine again. 'If you want to help me, you can keep Emma from doing something stupid until I find that bloody horse.'

By the time they reached the farm, the rain had eased a little. Jack put on the handbrake, but left the engine running.

'Is she sure about hearing shooting?' Anthony asked as he opened the car door.

'I don't know. She's confused. Maybe.'

'How long will you be?'

'As long as it takes to find that horse.'

Evelyn was hanging up the phone in hall when Anthony opened the door. She had a livid red mark on one of her cheeks and, the moment she saw him, she started to cry. Shocked, and a little unsure what to do, he wrapped his arms around her.

'Oh Anthony,' she said, between sobs. 'Talk to her will you? She won't listen to damn thing I say.'

'What happened to your face? Did she do that?'

Evelyn stepped out of his embrace and dashed at her eyes furiously with the heels of her hands. 'It's not her fault…she's very upset.'

'Where is she?'

'Up in her room.'

'I'll go talk to her.'

Evelyn gripped his wrist. 'Try and talk some sense into her. I think she has concussion, but she says she won't go to the hospital and she won't let me call the doctor to come here.'

'Call the doctor. I'll sort her out.'

Anthony took the stairs two at a time. He knocked on Emma's door and let himself in without waiting for an answer. It took his eyes a few moments to adjust to the gloom. Emma lay on her bed in filthy, blood-stained clothes, holding an ice pack to her head.

'I hear you've been in the wars?'

She didn't answer and her chest rose and fell in exaggerated jerks. There were tear tracks streaked across her face.

'She won't let me go out.'

'She's worried, that's all. You look bad.'

'I need to find Red.'

'Dad and Pete are out looking for her.' He walked across the room and sat on the edge of the bed, like he used to do when they were children. 'What happened?'

She closed her eyes.

'Talk to me.'

She was silent for so long he began to wonder of she had fallen asleep, but then she took a breath and began to speak: 'I heard dogs barking, then a shot. I...' the fingers on her free hand fluttered up towards her face. 'I do not remember. Everything is jumbled in my head. All the pictures are mixed up with different things and I...I do not know...what are the right pictures. I heard Red screaming...I knew she was afraid. I tried to get her to go left, but there was another bang, nearer the second time, and then we fell.' She opened her eyes. Anthony could see the fear and confusion in them. 'We fell.'

'Okay, then what happened?'

'I do not know.' She shook her head. 'I do not remember. Dad...Dad was there. He was there in the trees.'

'You need to go to the doctor and get that head looked at.'

'I do not want to go to a doctor.' She said it loudly, agitated. 'I want to find Red before dark. She is bleeding. She is hurt.'

'So are you. You need to get your head checked out.'

'No, I need–'

She pressed her hand against her mouth and sat up. Anthony grabbed the bin from under her desk and managed to get it to her before she retched.

'Jesus, Emma.'

She wiped her mouth with the back of her hand. Her eyes were huge and beads of sweat stood out on her pale skin. She took a breath, leaned forward and vomited again.

'Emma, you're going to a doctor. No arguments,' Anthony said. 'I'll go with you. I'll stay with you. I won't let them do anything bad to you, I swear. You've got to trust me.'

'Anthony – I am scared.' Tears filled her eyes. 'I do not know what happened. All the pictures…but I heard her scream.'

'Come on, sit up. Okay, look at me.' Anthony put the bin out of view. 'We're going to get you out of those clothes. Then I'm going to take you to the doctor's or he can come here, whichever. Okay? Logically, if you want to help Red you've got to help yourself first.'

'Logically,' Emma said softly.

'Yes, logically. Now let me help you.'

While Emma submitted herself to her brother's ministrations, Pete and Jack separately scoured Crilly Woods for the missing horse. They drove their vehicles for miles up and down tracks and roads, but there was no sign of Red anywhere.

'This is hopeless,' Jack muttered under his breath, driving slowly back down the muddied track where he had found Emma. It was dark and his tyres were getting more and more stuck as fresh rain churned months of dust into a sucking bog. He turned left at the fork and followed a smaller track, not much more than a path, all the way to the summit of a rocky outcrop. He was not surprised to find Pete there already, standing on the roof of his truck scanning the darkening woods and surrounding land with a small set of binoculars.

'Anything?'

'Nothing. She could have gone anywhere.' Pete climbed down from the roof. 'Look Jack, if y'want to go back home I understand, mate.'

'I *want* to find that blasted horse. Where have we not checked? God dammit Pete, you know horses, where would she go?'

'I don't know,' Pete said. 'Back to the stables maybe… if she was able.'

'Right,' Jack said, 'let's go again, I'll take north and head over towards the Sliabh Rua. I'll meet you back at the gates in an hour.'

They climbed into their separate vehicles and spent another hour combing the woods; by midnight they were still none the wiser.

Jack's headlights washed over Emma as he drove into the yard. She was sitting on the stone steps, wearing a long flannel shirt over pyjama bottoms. On her head she sported a large bandage, which glowed white in the darkness.

'Did you find Red?'

'No,' Jack shook his head, wearily. 'I'll head out early tomorrow morning. Pete's gone back to the stables. Says he's going to make a few phone calls and put the word out for her.'

Without a flicker of acknowledgement, Emma turned on her heel and went back into the house.

'No luck?' Evelyn said when she saw him. She was sitting at the kitchen table, a cup of hot cocoa between her hands.

'No. What happened to your face?'

'It's nothing. Sit down, let me make you something to eat.'

'Did she do that to you?'

'Jack, it's all right. She didn't mean it. Come and sit down. You need to eat. You look shattered'

'Where's Anthony?'

'He's gone to bed.'

Evelyn made Jack a ham sandwich and a mug of tea. While she flitted around the kitchen, she filled Jack in on the events of the evening.

'I don't know what I would have done if Anthony hadn't been there. She wouldn't let me near her. I've *never* seen her like that before. Well, not since she was very small. She was so…upset, and angry. She barely let the doctor touch her head, let alone any other part of her, and she was bleeding from her legs somewhere. She absolutely *refused* to have stitches and she nearly lost her reason when he tried to take her pulse.' Evelyn put the plate with Jack's sandwich down in front of him and sank into the chair on the opposite side of the table. 'I still don't know what to make of it all.'

'What did the doctor say?'

'He said we should keep an eye on her tonight. And if there is any more vomiting to take her to the hospital.'

Jack rubbed his eyes with the heels of his hands. 'Well, hopefully, we'll find the mare tomorrow and we can put this day behind us.'

But there would be no putting that day behind them. Not for any of them.

CHAPTER 37

Shortly after dawn, Pete was woken from a fitful sleep by the unpleasant sound of the hall phone jangling. Ruby jumped down as he got out of bed, and he followed after her, feeling old and stiff.

It was Sam Delaney, a local farmer, on the line. He apologised for the hour, but said he calling to say there was a horse on some scrubland behind his farm in Ballinatone. He said he knew Pete was missing one of his.

'I am, Sam. A little red mare. She's still tacked.'

'Aye. That's her all right.'

'Let me get dressed and I'll be over there shortly to pick her up.'

'Pete–'

Something in Sam's voice made Pete's stomach contract.

'I might as well tell you that she's not looking too good. I'll see if can get the trailer and bring her in. But it looks to me like she might have got tangled up in the reins and taken a fall or two. The two front knees are cut off her and, Pete, to be honest with you, this animal looks in a bad way.'

'I'll be there in a little while.'

'Grand. See you then.'

Pete hung up and stood with his hands on his hips, thinking. By rights, he should probably phone Catherine and let her know that Red had been found. But, on the other hand, there was no point in talking to her until he knew what condition the horse was in. Then there was the question of Emma. What was he going to do about that? She would want to know the minute he had any definite news

Unsure if he was doing the right thing or not, he drove over to Byrnes farm and was not entirely surprised to find Emma already up and dressed, stalking back and forth across the yard like a caged tiger.

'Pete,' Emma said, hurrying to meet him. 'I wanted to come over to the stables earlier, but Dad would not let me leave. Have you found her?'

Pete lit a cigarette and squinted at her through the smoke. Her face was a mess of cuts and mottled bruises and she had a bandage on her head. But what absolutely gutted him was what he read in her eyes: trust and hope.

'How you doing, kid? You look a bit beat up.'

'Yes. Have you found Red?'

'Sam Delaney called me earlier. She's up in his place now.'

Emma looked at him blankly.

'He's a farmer. Red wandered onto his land.'

'Then we should collect her.'

'I'll go get her myself, Emma. I only stopped by…I wanted to let you know she'd been found.'

'No, I will go with you. She will be frightened and will need to be reassured.'

'I don't think–'

'She trusts me, Pete. I will go with you.'

'All right then. Go get some shoes on.' Pete glanced towards the house, wishing to God there was something he could do or say that would change her mind. He noticed Jack standing at a window, watching them, and raised his hand in greeting.

'Emma, wait. There's something I've got to tell you. From what Sam says, Red's not in good shape.'

Emma looked at his neck, expressionless. 'Oh?'

'He thinks she might have got tangled up in her reins or something.'

'Then we should go immediately. She will be very tired and probably hungry. We must go right away.'

Jack came out of the house and walked down the yard towards them. He nodded to Pete. 'You found her then?'

'I got a phone call to say she's up in Delaney's, I just called in to let Emma know.'

'I will get my boots,' Emma said. 'Wait here.'

She ran straight past Jack without saying a word and disappeared into the house. Jack leaned a hand on the roof of the truck. He was unshaven and looked as exhausted as Pete felt.

'How is she?'

Jack shrugged. 'Up since all hours pacing around the yard. Won't eat. Won't talk to us. You know how she gets when she's worked up.'

'I'm thinking it were a mistake coming 'ere.'

'How so?'

'Sam says the mare's in a bad way. Not sure I want the kid seeing that.'

'Too late now. If you don't bring her she'll follow you. I won't be able to stop her.'

'Any more word on what happened?'

'She's not sure. She's still got concussion, so everything's a bit mixed up. But she says it was definitely shots. Two shots.'

'It don't make any sense. It's off-season and a lot of folk ride up that way. I don't know who'd be stupid enough to go discharging in Crilly Woods during the day.'

'Someone poaching maybe?' Jack replied. He might have said more, but he caught sight of Emma tearing towards them, trying to jam her feet into her boots as she ran. She hopped around to the passenger side, got in and slammed the door.

'We should go now.'

'See you later,' Jack said and slapped the door of the truck.

Neither Emma nor Pete spoke much as they drove to Delaney's. At a hand-painted sign, Pete hung a left, dropped a gear and the truck chugged up a smooth driveway, lined with apple trees. A wire-haired terrier met them halfway and raced alongside the truck, barking his head off, until Pete stopped and parked to the side of a neat, modern bungalow.

Sam must have been watching out for them, because he emerged from a side door almost immediately. He called off the dog with a single word and sent it inside the house.

'Howya Pete?'

'Sam.'

Pete knew Sam to be a good-humoured sort of chap with a ready smile: he was not smiling that day. He looked anything but cheery.

Emma got out and slammed the door.

'We are here for Red.'

Sam and Pete shook hands.

'My daughter, Gillian, managed to catch her in the end and we brought her down there a few minutes ago. I took off the tack and put out a bit of grub for her, but she won't eat at all. Wouldn't take any water neither.'

'She's probably in shock,' Pete said, acutely aware that Emma was now bouncing impatiently on her feet, her hands twitching. 'Where is she?'

'I put her in one of the calving sheds out the back, away from all the noise. Come on, it's back around this way.'

They followed Sam to the back of the bungalow and across a spotlessly clean yard to a cluster of sheds.

'There's the gear there,' Sam pointed to a bridle and a saddle. Pete was shocked to see how badly damaged it was. The pommel was split, which meant it was likely that Red had landed hard and heavy on her back at some point.

'She's in here, but, like I said to you on the phone... I don't know a whole lot about horses, but this one looks like she's in a right bad way altogether.'

Emma opened the door and peered inside.

'It is very dark.'

Sam flicked on the lights.

'Jesus,' Pete said under his breath.

Red stood to the rear of the shed, facing them. Her body was filthy, covered in scratches and cuts, but it was her front legs that made Emma stop dead in her tracks: they were massively swollen and the right knee looked as though it had been cored out with a knife.

'She is very badly hurt.' Emma said, sounding surprised and Pete wondered if she'd heard a single word he'd said to her earlier.

At the sound of Emma's voice, Red lifted her head and grunted softly. She attempted to take a step, but did not attempt another, so Emma walked slowly to her. Red tucked her head into the crook of Emma's arm and tried to distribute her weight onto her hind legs as much as possible. She moaned, a terrible sound; Pete knew she was in agony.

'We need to take her home,' Emma said. 'We need to bring her home and help her. We need to make her better.'

'She can't really walk much,' Sam said. 'It was one hell of a job getting her this far.'

'I'm going to go get the truck,' Pete said. 'That all right with you Sam?'

'Work away.'

Pete got the truck and backed it up as close as possible to the door. He stepped out of the cab carrying a head collar and a length of rope, which he handed to Emma. Red lowered her head, but when Emma tried to lead her to the door, she refused to take a single step, and stood panting and rolling her eyes.

'I'm going to get a length of rope from the truck,' Pete said, 'we can loop it behind her back legs.'

Between the two men, with Emma providing encouragement from the front, they managed to get Red to take one small, juddering step and then another. Slowly, inch by painful inch, they coaxed her outside. In the daylight, the full extent of the damage was staggering to behold: apart from Red's mangled front legs, her flank and rump was covered in blood, her skin peppered with tiny holes and tears.

'She's been shot,' Pete said with disgust.

'Looks that way,' Sam agreed, shaking his head.

'Who the bloody fuck – pardon my French – but who the bloody fuck would shoot a flamin' horse?'

'Ah, there's plenty of eejits up in them woods. They might have thought she was a deer.'

'But Emma was riding her!'

Pete ran his hand over Red's shoulders and down to her legs; he carefully lifted each one, testing flexibility and motion as gently as he could. Red didn't move a muscle. When Pete was finished his examination, he stepped back and shook his head. 'Her tendons are torn to pieces.'

Sam looked at him. 'Is that bad?'

'Can be.'

Emma stood silently, her hand resting on Red's neck. Pete glanced at her, wishing he had left her back at her house.

'Let's bring her back to the yard.'

It took nearly an hour and all their strength to load Red. Pete was so concerned about her falling on the journey back to the yard that he borrowed a few bales of straw from Sam and wedged them on either side of her for support.

Once they were on the road, Pete tried to get Emma to open up a little. He promised her they would do whatever they could for Red, but he wanted her to understand that sometimes horses could not be saved.

Emma kept her eyes firmly on the road, unblinking.

They could see Catherine O'Gorman's Mercedes parked in the yard as they turned in the gate. She was sitting in the driver's seat with the door open, listening to the radio. For a moment, Emma didn't recognise her and was confused when Pete said her name: she realised she had never seen the woman without her makeup before. She looked older in the morning light.

Pete parked the truck as close as he could to the biggest of the loose boxes and jumped out of the cab. Claude watched them, his ears flicking back and forth. Catherine got out and walked to the rear of the truck.

'You have her?'

'She's in the trailer,' Pete said. 'Catherine, before you see her, I'd like a word.'

He took her to one side. 'She's hurt. Hurt bad. Looks like she's got a lot of damage to her front and–'

'Oh God.'

'Look, why don't you let me handle this? I've McCoy on the way,' Pete said, referring to the equine specialist vet. 'We'll know more when he sees her. Right now, we should probably let her be.'

'I want to see her,' Catherine said, straightening her spine, physically pulling herself together before Pete's eyes. 'She's my horse, I want to see her.'

Pete could see there was little point in arguing with her. He lowered the ramp and together they entered the truck. Emma sat on the low wall and heard, rather than saw, Catherine's reaction. Ruby joined her and laid her head on Emma's lap, looking for rubs, so Emma rubbed her until Catherine, white-faced and tight-lipped came back down the ramp and stopped before her.

The slap nearly knocked Emma off the wall. Ruby started barking furiously.

'I trusted you.'

'Yes,' said Emma, holding her hand to her burning cheek, 'so did Red.'

'Stop it Catherine!' Pete jumped down, grabbed her arm and yanked her away. 'None of this was Emma's fault.'

'Of course it wasn't. My beautiful Red is a walking piece of shredded meat. How could I even think it might be this weirdo's fault? It's my fucking fault, my own stupid fault for leaving her in this *godforsaken* yard in the first place.'

'Catherine, calm down. Come on now. Let's go into the house. McCoy will be here any minute now.'

Catherine allowed Pete to lead her away. She was crying again.

Emma rose shakily to her feet. She walked up the ramp and stood by Red's shoulder. The mare's body was trembling from the effort to remain upright, so Emma removed the bales and watched as Red sank to the floor. Emma joined her there, her head resting against Red's side, listening to her laboured breathing, talking to her quietly.

She did not leave Red's side. Not when McCoy arrived, not when the decision was made to release Red from her misery, not when the vet pressed the bolt gun against Red's beautiful head, not when Red collapsed over onto her side and was still.

For the next hour or so, Emma would not budge, ignoring Pete's coaxing entreaties. Eventually, exhaustion and exasperation got the better of him and he lifted her, kicking and screaming, and plonked her on the ground outside. Within seconds of finding her balance, she was off. She didn't stop running, until she reached home. On arriving there, she tore through the cottage, slammed her bedroom door behind her and refused to come out.

CHAPTER 38

The next day and the one following that, Evelyn tried everything she could to coax Emma into talking, but she refused point blank. She barely ate a thing and spent long hours in her room, with the door locked.

'She's broken-hearted, Pete,' Evelyn said over the phone. 'I've often seen her bad, but I don't think I've ever seen her like this before.'

'It's my fault, this. I should never have let her stay in the truck when the vet put Red down. I should've known, I should have flamin' known it were too much for her.'

'Well, what's done is done,' Evelyn said, trying to be kind, though she agreed with Pete, and felt he should have been more responsible at the time. 'Look, she would have been cut up over it one way or the other Pete.'

'Will you say I called? And tell her that Claude and Ruby missed 'er today.'

'I'll tell her.'

On day four Emma finally made an appearance at breakfast. She came downstairs in her pyjamas and allowed Evelyn to make her some toast. But she would not talk to Pete on the phone when he called and she told Evelyn she had no interest in getting dressed. She said it in such a dead tone that Evelyn wanted to pick her up and hug her.

'But what about work? What about the horses?'

'I am not going.'

'Emma, you have got to work.'

'I do not *have* to do anything,' Emma replied in a dull voice.

'Emma, listen to me. I'm sorry about Red. Honest to God I am, but accidents happen, especially with animals. None of this was your fault.'

Emma did not respond. She took her toast and wandered into the sitting room to Margaret's rocking chair, where she remained for most of the morning, staring into space.

Evelyn was worried sick. She put on her wellingtons and went across the yard in search of Jack. She found him in the adjoining field, chopping down the huge elm that threatened to fall every time a gale swept down from the hills. Jack dropped the axe and wiped the sweat from his brow when he saw her approach.

'Is she up?'

'She's up, but Jack, I don't know what to do. I really don't. She says she's not going to work. I… think she means *ever*.'

'She's had a shock. She'll be all right.'

'How can you be so sure? It's been three days now. If we don't do something she might… it might get worse.'

'Where's Anthony?'

'He didn't come back last night.'

'Evelyn, what do you want me to do? She doesn't want to talk to me either.'

'I don't know,' Evelyn said, twisting the corner of her apron anxiously.

At lunchtime, Evelyn insisted that Emma join her and Margaret in the kitchen to eat some soup. Emma's hands were shaking so badly, her spoon rattled audibly inside the bowl. The moment she finished eating, she disappeared to the rocking chair in the sitting room. When Margaret, prompted by Evelyn, followed her and asked if she would like something to read, Emma stood up, headed soundlessly to her room and firmly shut the door.

CHAPTER 39

A week passed, and then another – each day characterised by a heavy, impenetrable silence that had a profound effect on those living in the small house. To cope – and sometimes in an attempt to escape the atmosphere – Evelyn often retreated to folding clothes or cleaning the house unnecessarily. On the really bad days, she found herself crying with the stress of it all

Pete rang every day asking after Emma, passing on his thoughts and well wishes. Dody Molloy called to the house in person and seemed genuinely hurt when Emma told her mother she didn't want to see him.

'Tell her I miss her,' he told Evelyn, 'and tell her that her job will be here waiting for her whenever she feels better.'

The only person who seemed unperturbed by events was Anthony, who went about his routine as normal. At least, that is, until he arrived home one afternoon, pale and hollow-eyed from a night God knows where, and Evelyn turned on him with such ferocity she scared the bejaysus out of both of them.

'Where the hell have you been?'

'Out. Work. Places,' Anthony said, flicking his fringe out of his eyes.

'How can you act like nothing's going on? What kind of son did I rear at all?'

'One who knows that flapping around this place isn't going to make any difference. Anyway, I came back for a change of clothes, not an argument.'

He went upstairs and changed, leaving his clothes on the floor. He noticed that someone had given the room a once-over. The stack of plates and half-filled glasses was gone. His mother, of course, he reckoned. She was always snooping around looking for information. Let her look; she'd find nothing that he didn't want found.

On the landing, he paused outside Emma's door, and briefly rested his hand on the handle. Suddenly, a great wave of exhaustion washed over him and he decided he couldn't bear the thought of a discussion – *any* discussion – with her. It was too much; she was too much of a burden to carry any longer.

Without saying goodbye to anyone, Anthony existed the house and walked across the yard. At the cattle grate, his scalp prickled and he looked over his shoulder. Emma was standing at her bedroom window, watching him. He raised a hand. She let the curtain drop without indicating that she had seen his gesture.

A third week passed. Emma retreated further and further from everyone. She no longer worked on her book and showed no interest whatsoever in the farm. She hardly ate or spoke and rarely dressed. She was tired, she said, and it was true: she seemed to spend a lot of time asleep, curled up on her side on her bed, or dozing in Margaret's rocking chair under a blanket.

'Head injuries,' Margaret said, when Jack suggested they talk to someone about it. 'A lot of people go a bit queer after a head injury.'

'It was a minor concussion,' Evelyn said, wishing her mother-in-law's arrows didn't always manage to land so close to the mark.

Pete cornered Anthony in Lakelands one Saturday night in October

'Is she ever coming back to work?'

'I don't know Pete. You'll have to ask her.'

'I would. But she won't talk to me.'

'I don't know what to tell you Pete. She's…' Anthony shrugged, tired of people demanding answers he did not have, tired of searching for the right words. He wished people would stop bothering him about Emma. What answers could he give Pete when he had no more insight into his sister's motivations than anyone else? He did not know what was wrong with her, only that she was obviously struggling with something, something he had no idea how to bridge.

'This is my flamin' fault,' Pete said softly. 'She won't say what it is that I've done. But *I* know. *I know* I should never have let her see Red die like that. I put too much on her shoulders. I see that now.'

Anthony leaned across the counter. 'Give her time Pete. I'm sure she'll come round.'

But she didn't come round; the following week, Evelyn decided it was time, and called an emergency family meeting around the kitchen table.

'We're going to have to get her some professional help. We can't go on like this. We have to do something…even if it's a little drastic.'

'What are you suggesting?' Anthony looked at his watch; he was supposed to be meeting his friend, Mark Bradshaw,

'Maybe we can sign her in somewhere, just for a few weeks, to help her deal with whatever she's going through.'

'Mam, if you put her in one of those places, she'll never come back out.'

'How can you sit there and say that, Anthony? How can you even *think* it?'

'People don't come out of nut houses.'

'Anthony!'

'What?'

'It's little you know about such things.' Margaret narrowed her eyes at him and Evelyn was absurdly grateful to her for taking her side.

'I'm only saying.'

'Well *don't*.'

'There has to be more to it than that horse,' Evelyn pressed both hands on the table with her fingers splayed. 'Did she say anything at all about what happened? Apart from the stuff about the noise and the gunshots?'

'I've told you everything she told me. She heard gunshots. The mare reared up and hit her in the face with her neck, they fell and she blacked out.'

'But what's happening to her? I don't understand,' Evelyn said, her voice cracking. She took a moment to compose herself and then looked across the table at Jack.

'Well, we can't go on like this, we just can't. She needs help, professional help. I'm calling Dr Williams tomorrow and we'll set up an appointment.'

Jack stood up.

'Are you leaving?'

'I've got work to do.'

Evelyn shook her head disbelievingly, angry even.

'Can't it wait?'

'For what? You don't need me. Sure you seem to have all the answers.'

'Oh no Jack. I have no answers at all, but I'm not going to sit around here any longer with my head in the sand and pretend that everything is normal.'

'Is *that* what I've been doing?'

Anthony waited until Jack left, then he stood too.

'I'll see you later.'

'Where are you going?'

'Out.'

'Anthony please, we need to talk about this.'

'What do we need to talk about. He's right, you've made up your mind.'

He left and grabbed his jacket off the coat stand in the hall. Outside he paused to zip it up and noticed his father sitting on the wall off the rockery, trying to get his pipe lit.

Anthony began to walk towards the lane, when he heard his father's voice.

'I think it was that fucker Donovan.'

Anthony stopped walking and turned around. 'That fucker Donovan what?'

'I've been thinking about it. Arthur's always up in those woods. Wouldn't put it past him to do a rotten stinking thing like that. Sure hasn't he had it in for her ever since she bolloxed Harry Lynch's sale? He told Pete didn't he? He told Pete she'd be sorry after the horse market. He's the sort that would do that.'

Something flared hot in Anthony's his chest. 'Donovan? Arthur Donovan?'

'Wouldn't put it past him.'

'We need to do something about that.'

'Sure what can we do?' Jack shook his head. 'What can anyone do with the likes of them? Sure even if we went to the guards they'd hardly believe us.'

'What happened to fighting our own battles?'

'What?'

'That's what you always told me and Emma when we were growing up.'

'I don't remember saying that.'

Anthony stared at his father as if he didn't recognise him. He tried to speak but no words would come out. So, he turned and walked down the lane sleepwalker, thinking of all the money he'd spent in order to keep his sister safe, all the beatings he'd endured, the mockery, the constant, relentlessly sickening fear he laboured under. He thought of all this and something inside him began to stir.

CHAPTER 40

'So, what do you think?'

Jack shifted over on the sofa to accommodate Ruby's considerable bulk. He had moved twice already, yet despite this, the dog's head massive head remained inches from his face, her hot breath on his skin. Two days had passed since he'd told Anthony about his suspicions and less than two hours since a great idea had struck him like a thunderbolt from the sky.

'I don't know…' Pete lit a cigarette from the butt of the one he had ground out in the ashtray. 'I'd be happy to do it, but what did she have to say about the idea?'

'She's not saying much of anything these days,' Jack said, hooking his hands together on the table. 'Look, I don't know if she'd go for it, but we've got to try something Pete.'

'The thing is,' Pete said, filling his and Jack's glasses with a liberal splash of Jameson, 'the thing is, there'd probably be no shortage of takers. The accident notwithstanding, the kid's got a reputation around these parts, plenty willing to use her and her expertise,' he said, thinking. 'Course with the winter coming you'd need to be able to house them.'

'I know that.' Jack took a sip of his drink and tried not to grimace. 'I'm thinking of dividing up the barn. I reckon I could fit four or five stalls in there easy enough. They wouldn't be big now, but they'd do.'

'It's a gamble. What if after all that work she don't bite?'

'Then I'll try something else,' Jack replied with determination. 'Her mother's talking about sending her off to some place… a psychiatric hospital.'

Pete looked at him aghast.

'No!'

'Aye. I don't mind admitting it, but, for a while there, I thought she might be right, but…but now I don't know. Horses are all she's ever cared about. There's got to be a way.'

Pete glanced out the window at the rain-sodden yard. 'It's funny, I miss having that flamin' kid knocking about the place. Never thought a man of my years would get attached to a kid, especially one like Emma.' Realising what he had just said, he coloured slightly. 'Do whatever you decide, Jack. I'll lend a hand any way I can.'

That weekend, with Pat's help, Jack cleared the machinery and every piece of scrap metal and junk he'd collected over the years out of the barn.

It took them a few hours, but, finally, the barn was empty. Using chalk and masking tape, Jack outlined the areas that needed to be cordoned off, while Pat cut timber planks down to size and bolted them onto joists. Evelyn pitched in too, scrubbing out buckets and screwing in hooks to the walls. By Sunday evening they had themselves a rudimentary set of stables.

'We're some team when we get going,' Jack said, surveying their work proudly. He was tired and sore and in need of a long hot soak in a bath.

'Yep,' Evelyn said, looping an arm behind his back. She rested her head against his shoulder. 'So now what?'

'Pete says he has four horses lined up to go. He'll be here with them in the morning.'

'I really hope this works Jack.'

'It has to work.' Jack said, giving her a squeeze. 'It has to.'

Monday morning, on the dot of eight, Pete's truck chugged up the lane and into the yard. Jack went out to meet him.

'Morning Pete.'

'Jack.'

'What have you got for me?'

'I've brought Zebbie and Garryowen from my place, and there's two new Irish Draft mares owned by a pal of mine. He'll want them fit for hunting later in the season. They're as green as grass, so they are, and the bigger one, Dora, is a flamin' nightmare. She'd be a prime candidate for Emma.'

'Right, let's unload them and get them settled in.'

'Does she know?'

'We haven't spoken about it, but I know she was down giving the whole set-up the once over last night.'

They unloaded Zebbie first; then the draft mares, leaving Garryowen to last.

'Not a bad looking set-up. I like the Yank-style doors,' Pete said, shaking the links of chains that Jack had strung across the opening of each stall.

'I didn't have enough wood to make doors,' Jack admitted. 'They'll do as a temporary measure but if this scheme works, I'll look into building something more permanent.'

Zebbie arched his head and whinnied; Garryowen, further down the row responded.

'Right,' Pete said, 'I've got blankets and tack in the back of the truck. I brought two bags of nuts too, which will tide them over for a few days. But if you have anywhere for a spot of grazing, that would be ideal.'

'I can use the meadow out the back.'

Pete patted Jack on the upper arm. 'Good luck mate, I hope this works, for all our sakes.'

Lunchtime came and went with no sign of Emma. That afternoon, as the daylight was disappearing, Jack wondered if his plan would do anything other than burden himself with more work. But then, as he was putting the hens into the coop, she appeared from the shadows like a ghost.

'There are horses in the storage barn.'

'Are there?' he said, wiggling his eyebrows.

'Yes.'

'Well there you go now. You learn something new every day.'

'They are Pete's horses. Why are they here?'

Jack abandoned trying to be funny. 'Pete's taken in more hunters this year. He hasn't time to work the young ones now that you've stopped going over.'

Emma aimed her dark eyes at her father's shoulder.

'So they will be staying here?'

'I guess so.'

'They will need hay nets.'

'I'll get some.'

'Zebbie prefers to be beside Garryowen. They are friends.'

'Which one is Zebbie?'

'The grey with the short mane.'

'Why don't you move him so?'

Emma walked away without replying.

Jack locked in the last of the hens, checked the wire and walked back to the yard. He paused by the pump to clean the muck off his boots. From where he stood, he could see directly into the barn. Emma had moved the grey into a different stall and now his big head was nestled in the crook of her arm while Emma spoke softly to him.

Jack shook the water from his boots and went inside to leave, smiling to himself.

The next morning Emma was up before anyone in the house. By the time Jack had finished his breakfast, she had filled the water buckets, put the horses out to graze in the meadow, and was already mucking out. When Jack asked her if everything was all right, she handed him a list of things she said she needed and he took it without comment.

CHAPTER 41

During October, nature stayed kind to the inhabitants of Kill-bragh. The skies remained blue, and it was a warm southeasterly wind that stripped the remainder of the leaves from the trees on the Byrne farm.

Tuesday morning started peacefully enough. Jack had gone to milk the cows, and Emma was still in bed. Anthony was at home and, despite a mild hangover, was in fine form, munching cornflakes and listening with something close to contentment as Evelyn chatted to Margaret about some seniors club that had been set up in the area recently. Evelyn was trying to convince Margaret to join, but, from the look on his grandmother's face, this idea was a non-runner. The reason for Anthony's cheer was upstairs under his mattress upstairs. The day before a letter from the Australian Embassy had arrived at Flicky's place, informing him that his application for a visa had been accepted. All he had to do was find some way of breaking the news gently to Emma and his parents.

The second Emma entered the kitchen he knew immediately that something was wrong. She looked paler than he'd ever seen her.

'What's the matter? Are you sick?'

'No…yes.'

Evelyn pressed her hand on Emma's forehead, but Emma recoiled from her touch and went to sit in her usual chair.

'She's a white a sheet.' Margaret said, peering at her grand-daughter over the tops of her glasses. 'What ails you?'

'I cannot explain. I feel odd, and my stomach is rolling.'

Evelyn rose and opened the cupboard over the fridge where she kept medicines and painkillers. She took down a bottle of Milk of Magnesia and rummaged for a tablespoon in the cutlery drawer. 'Here, take a spoonful of this. It will help settle your stomach.'

Emma blanched. 'I do not like that medicine. It tastes like chalk.'

'One spoon,' Evelyn said in a voice that brooked no argument.

Emma poured and swallowed a mouthful of the medicine with her eyes squeezed shut.

'Now,' Evelyn said, 'I know you're going to tell me you're not hungry, but–'

Before she could finish the sentence, Emma vomited violently, spewing white liquid all over herself, the kitchen table and the floor.

'Oh that's disgusting,' Anthony said, grabbing his cereal bowl and leaping up from the table.

'I am sorry,' Emma replied. She ran to the sink and vomited again.

Anthony bolted from the kitchen and went upstairs to dress. By the time he came back down, Emma was in the sitting room, stretched out on the sofa, with a damp tea towel on her forehead. Evelyn was in Margaret's rocking chair, looking as pale as Emma.

'What's wrong with her?'

'Just go on about your business.' Evelyn got up and practically shoved him out the door.

'But–'

'Feed the horses will you? Emma's sick.'

'But what's wrong with her?' he repeated.

'Anthony. For once in your life will you *just do as you're bid?*'

She slammed the door in his face.

CHAPTER 42

Anthony fed the horses and turned them out into the meadow. He rinsed out their water buckets and was untying the hay nets when he heard a car door slam. As he looked out the barn door, he caught sight of his mother driving out of the yard at considerable speed, his sister Emma, pale and wan, lolling in the passenger seat beside her.

Curious, he thought.

They had only gone ten minutes when Jack drove into the yard on his tractor, cut the engine and climbed down from the cab.

'How come you're doing this? Where's Emma?'

'She's sick?'

'What's wrong with her?'

'I don't know. She threw up all over the place. Then she and Mam went somewhere.'

'Did she say where they were going?'

'Not to me.'

Anthony leaned on the pitchfork as Jack took out his pipe out and filled it. He replaced his tobacco pouch and lit it, taking a few deep draws to get it going.

'Not a bad day, Thank God,' Jack said eventually.

'Yeah, warm.'

'Right, well I'd better get back to it.' He looked as though he might say something else, but then changed his mind and walked off, tendrils of smoke drifting along in his wake.

Anthony scattered fresh straw over the last stall, heard a car drive up the lane and went outside. He was surprised to see a small silver Toyota Starlet enter the yard, driven by Lucy Green.

'Hello Anthony.'

'Hey Lucy, how's it going?'

'I hope I'm not disturbing you. I was looking for Amanda. She said she was coming up here today.'

'Amanda?'

'McCarthy. My friend. You know Amanda.'

'Oh right.' Anthony furrowed his brow. 'Why would she be here?'

'Oh, didn't Emma tell you? She's buying the grey.'

'She's buying...' He scrambled for the horse's name, "Zebbie?"'

Lucy smiled. Her teeth were unbelievably white, movie star white. Anthony noticed she was wearing lip-gloss. 'Yep, she reckons she's fallen head over heels in love with him.'

'Well, he's a fine animal.'

'She thought I might like to see him before the deal is concluded,' she laughed, 'and get my *hugely* valuable opinion on all things equine.'

'Oh, did you want to see him now?'

'I can call back later if you're busy.'

'It's no trouble,' he said. 'Sure I'm finished here anyway.'

He walked Lucy to the meadow and found himself blathering about Zebbie and his development, neglecting to mention how little input he had into the horse's training. Zebbie being, as Emma often said, a useful sort of animal, wandered up to the fence to greet them and laid claim to the polo mints Lucy produced from her pockets.

'Oh he's so beautiful,' Lucy scratched Zebbie under his chin like he was some type of dog. 'You know her dad wasn't sure about him at all, because he's so young and everything, but Amanda says he's got such a great temperament.' Lucy looked at him from under her long lashes. 'You can just tell, you know. If somebody is right for you or not.'

Anthony blinked. Was she flirting with him?

'Oh you're right. No point in having a flighty horse.'

'That's what she says.' Lucy leaned over the fence and rubbed the big grey's neck. 'How's the pub work? I called in the other evening, but you were on a day off.'

Anthony shrugged.

'Oh, you know.'

'You're not enjoying it?'

'It's fine; I mean it's a job.'

'I'm in Carlow now, at college.'

'You mentioned that before.'

'Did I? I'm still not a hundred percent sure what I want to do. Do you ever get like that?'

'All the time.'

'So tell me, what are your plans, Anthony?'

Anthony snatched up a blade of grass and chewed it for a moment before spitting it out again.

'Why does everyone have to have plans? Dad wants me to work here with him, but I don't really see myself spending my days running the farm.'

'What do you see yourself doing?'

'I'm thinking of going to Australia.' He wondered why he was telling her this. 'I haven't told anyone else yet.'

'Then I'm privileged.'

When she leaned forward to pat Zebbie, Anthony spotted the trim of a lacy bra under her v-neck jumper. He gazed at it for a moment, and then looked away. 'Is Martin happy about you being away in Carlow?'

'I wouldn't know,' she said. 'We broke up.'

'Oh. Sorry.'

'Why would you be sorry? I'm not.'

Anthony couldn't think of a rejoinder, so he concentrated instead on looking inscrutable.

'I think I'd better get going,' Lucy said, stepping back from him. 'Can you tell Amanda if you see her that I was here? And that I'll stop by her place tomorrow?'

'Sure.'

He walked her back to her car and waved her off. Evelyn was back from wherever she had gone. He spotted Emma sitting on the rockery wall struggling to pull on a pair of boots. He sat down beside her.

'I fed the horses and put them out.'

'Yes, thank you. Who was in the car?'

'Lucy Green, she was looking for her friend Amanda.'

Emma frowned. 'Here?'

'Apparently, Amanda is buying Zebbie.'

'Oh,' Emma snorted. 'Too much horse for her.'

'She likes his personality according to Lucy. How are you feeling? Still sick?'

'I am not sick.'

'Where did you and Mam go?'

Emma jammed her foot into her boot and stamped to make sure it fit right. 'I am not supposed to say.'

'You can tell me. What's the big secret?'

'I had to go and urinate on a stick.'

Anthony felt that weird scalp prickle again. 'What did you say?'

'I had to urinate on a stick.'

'Emma…are you…are you…pregnant?'

'Yes.' She put her hand on her stomach. 'Yes I am.'

Nobody could stop him – not Evelyn, not Anthony, not even Margaret, who, despite her frailty, grappled with him as he ripped the car keys from the wall hook so hard that the hook fell off the wall and pinged across the floor to the other side of the kitchen. But Jack was not to be reasoned with. His fury was so absolute God himself would have been hard pressed to hold him back.

He drove through the village like a madman. Everyone who saw him that day said they remembered his face, white and savage behind the wheel of the Ford Escort, the sound of the engine screaming as he hopped it over the hump-backed bridge with his foot to the floor. Nothing would stop him, not even the elaborate wrought iron gates of Sliabh Rua Stud, which buckled and fell from the force of being rammed by a car travelling at almost sixty miles an hour.

The gates killed the car too, so Jack climbed out and ran the rest of the lane, each step taking him closer to his target, Dody Molloy.

He found Dody standing in the narrow passage that linked the yard to the indoor arena, talking to his farmhand. Unaware that he was the cause of Jack's insane behaviour, he looked up with a faint, puzzled smile when he saw him bearing down.

'Jack? What are you–?'

Jack's first swing was a vicious haymaker that mashed Dody's nose into his face, splintering it bloody. Dody staggered backwards and went down. The farmhand, rooted to the spot with shock, did nothing as Jack's second blow dislocated Dody's jaw and loosened a number of his teeth.

'Stop. You'll kill him!'

Jack heard nothing: only white-hot rage filled his ears. Dody clutched his ruined face and curled up into an agonised ball as Jack kicked any section of his body that his hobnailed boot could reach.

'Stop!'

People were running towards them, shouting. Someone jumped on Jack's back. Still Jack kicked. He heard howling and realised that it was he who was making the sound. A hand grabbed his arm; more arms tackled him about the waist. He collapsed under the combined weight, baring his teeth, fighting against them in an effort to finish his task.

'Hold him down. Sit on him if you have to.'

'What's going on?'

'Isn't that Emma's father?'

'Hold him!'

'For fuck's sake. Is Dody dead?'

A yellow-haired woman ran past them to where Dody lay without moving on the ground.

'What happened?'

'This fucking lunatic attacked Dody, he came out of fucking nowhere and just beat the shit out of him.'

'Call an ambulance. Oh Jesus, are those teeth?'

Jack struggled, veins stood out like cable strands in his neck. *'Get off me!'*

'Call the guards.'

'Here, Jerry,' the woman said, 'help me get him into the house. Oh my God, hold on Dody, hold on, you're all right now.'

Another set of hands, massive and scarred, grabbed Jack and dragged him out of the passage and half lifted, half flung into a stable. He fell onto dirty straw, got up and charged the door. But, it was too late. It slammed shut and was bolted from the outside.

'Open this fucking door and let me out!'

'Ara shut the fuck up.'

Jack hammered the wood with his fists. 'He deserved it, the bastard. He deserved what he got.'

'And you'll be getting yours and all.'

The voices drifted away until the only thing Jack could hear was the sound of his own breathing. He kicked the door and squatted down against the wall to wait. It wasn't long before he could hear the sound of sirens wailing in the distance.

CHAPTER 44

Jack was arrested and brought to the local garda station where he was questioned, formally charged and remanded in custody for twenty-four hours. When Evelyn came to collect him, she was shocked by the sight that greeted her. He exited the doors of the station looking like a broken man. His right hand had swollen to twice its normal size; she wanted to bring him to hospital, but he refused, asking only that they go home.

In strained tones, Evelyn and Jack discussed their options around the kitchen table, while Anthony made Emma some toast and a cup of tea. He carried them up stairs, tapped on her door and opened the door with his elbow.

'Are you awake?'

'Yes. What time is it?'

'Almost seven. I brought you something to eat.'

'I am not hungry.'

'Don't be stupid. You didn't have anything to eat yesterday.'

She sat up in the bed.

'Dad's back.'

'Yes, I heard the car.'

'Do you know what he did?'

She shook her head.

'He went over to the stud farm and beat the shit out of Dody Molloy. Everybody's talking about it.'

'Why did he do that?'

'Because he thinks it was Dody who made you pregnant.'

'But he did not.'

'Then who was it?' He put the tray on the locker beside her bed, sat on the floor, and rested his arms on his knees. 'Talk to me.'

'Dad is very angry with me.' It was not a question, but a statement.

'He's not angry with you.'

She picked up a piece of toast and tore at it with her long, slender fingers.

'Emma, look. This is fucking weird, okay? But we need to talk about it. If Dody and you didn't have sex, then who did you have…sex with?'

'Nobody.'

Anthony shook his head and laughed. 'Oh so it was the Immaculate Conception. Is that it? Em, did the Holy Ghost get to you?'

'I do not want to talk about it.'

'Dad's in trouble for what he did. He was fucking arrested and formally charged. The whole village is talking about what happened.'

'Oh.'

'You need to tell me what's going on.'

Emma blinked.

'Was it Pete?'

'Pete is my friend. We do not have sex.'

'Well you had sex with somebody,' Anthony snapped, feeling himself lose some of his patience. 'I thought you trusted me.'

'I do.'

'Then why won't you tell me who you were with?'

'I can't…I don't know.' She closed her eyes and lifted one hand up to her head, shielding her eyes.

'Wow, are you having that much of it you can't remember who with? Fuck, I must be doing something wrong so.'

'Please stop.'

'*I'll stop* when you tell me.'

'It is like looking through fog. There are pictures, but they are all jumbled up.'

'*Think*, will you. This is important.'

'I… rode through the trees, and Red…she was fine, but then we heard shooting and I knew Red was afraid.'

'Jesus, not this again. Stop changing the subject; we're not talking about the fucking accident okay? I'm asking you about something else.'

'I heard shooting, wood splintering. Red was scared and wanted to leave. She was shaking, so I turned her towards the path that leads around the hill. I wanted to get her away from the shooting.'

'Why are you telling me about this?' Anthony balled his hands into fists. Emma's own hands whirled and twisted on the bedclothes.

'Then there was another loud bang, closer. I heard…'

Anthony leaned forward.

'What? What did you hear?'

'Dogs…dogs barking, coming closer to us, and I knew it was a shortcut back to the road if we took the path.' She shook her head, and took a long, ragged breath.

'You never said anything about dogs before.'

'They were barking. Red heard them, and she ran into the trees… I think I tried to stop her, but she…she would not stop.' Emma's face contorted with grief. 'She knew, she knew we were in danger. She wanted to take us home.'

'What do you mean, danger? How were you in danger?'

'I do not want to remember.' She buried her face in her hands and began to rock back and forth.

'You have to. *Tell me.*'

'Rain. I remember smelling rain. Rain, and my hands stung. I could taste blood. When I woke up, I was lying on the ground. I hurt a lot, very painful. There was a dog–'

'What dog?'

'The dog that licked my face.'

Something in Anthony's brain clicked, a glimmer of under-standing emerged. He stared at her, wondering how much further he could push her.

'Emma…when Red fell, what do you remember? Do you remember anything else?'

'*Screaming.*' Her voice cracked with anguish. Anthony shuffled closer to her.

'What type of dog licked you?'

'I do not know.'

'Bullshit, you know every breed of dog there is.'

She groaned. 'Anthony, I cannot talk anymore. I cannot remember anymore. I have a headache.'

'What breed was it?'

'I do not know. It was brown… maybe…' She closed her eyes and mumbled something.'

'What?'

'No…not, brown. It had a green collar, a green collar with a rusted lock. I heard…' Anthony held his breath, 'voices.' She started to shake uncontrollably. 'My head hurt and I could not see, but I heard voices, I heard voices, and someone laughed…and… then I don't remember, but Red was gone and there was blood everywhere. On my legs, on my hands… and I was hurt, but I had to find Red. She was screaming and…she trusted me and…'

Anthony stared at her, horrified. Suddenly everything made sense, her weird behaviour, her trauma, everything.

Emma wasn't being evasive… she had been raped.

CHAPTER 45

Evelyn had showered in the time Anthony had been speaking to Emma and was now standing by the kitchen sink in her towelling dressing gown. Her hair was loose and hung down her back in waves.

'How is she?'

Anthony had no idea how to begin what he had to say, so he blurted 'He didn't do it.'

'Who didn't do what?'

'Dody Molloy.' He glanced at Jack as he spoke. Jack stared at him, his hand resting in a bowl of ice. 'He didn't do what you think he did.'

'What the hell are you talking about?'

'I think she was raped. I think she was raped in the woods the same day someone shot at her.'

'Oh God...' Evelyn looked like she was going to be sick. 'Jack–'

'No,' Jack said, 'I got him, I got the bastard who did it.'

'She says he never touched her. Mam, listen to me; it makes sense if you think about it. Six weeks.'

Evelyn put her hand to her mouth, her eyes huge. 'Oh God. Oh God that poor man.'

'He did it, he raped her.' Jack jumped to his feet, knocking over the bowl and sending ice cubes slithering all over the floor.

'You were wrong.' Anthony shouted 'You were wrong.'

'Then who was it?'

'She's not sure. Okay? Her memories are jumbled up. Mam, listen to me, we need to report this, we need to ring the guards and tell them–'

Even as he was speaking, Evelyn was shaking her head.

'Why are you shaking your head like that?'

'If we get the guards involved they're going to want to question her. You know that.'

'Dad…he beat Dody Molloy to a pulp. He put him in hospital. We *have* to report it.'

'What good would that do now?' Evelyn said bitterly. 'What's done is done. It cannot be undone. You said yourself Emma doesn't really know anything–'

'But–'

'What would you have me do? She's confused and frightened enough already. Being questioned will only make things worse.'

'But the people who did this are still out there.'

'What's done is done.'

'God damn you,' Anthony said savagely. His eyes blazed. 'God damn you, you're as gutless as he is.'

Evelyn was stunned. 'You watch how you speak to me.'

'You don't give a shit about her, about Emma. You want to keep people from talking. You're happy enough to let people to think it was Dody Molloy because you're a fucking coward, you and–'

Evelyn slapped him. 'Don't you dare you accuse me of that.'

'Go to hell and take him with you.'

'Anthony–'

'No.' He held up his hand and backed away. 'Just fuck off and leave me alone.' He left.

The pub was busy that night, and Anthony was aware many a curious eye rested on his throughout the evening. But no one mentioned a thing about his father to him, not even Flicky.

Anthony waited until after closing time, and brought it up himself. 'I suppose you've heard what's going on?'

'A bit, here and there.' Flicky shrugged and flipped a tea towel over his shoulder. 'I suppose you could say there's a certain amount of curiosity regarding your father's actions.'

Anthony sat on one of the bar stools and raked his fingers through his hair. It wasn't that he didn't trust Flicky. He did and more, but where to begin? Flicky put two whiskey glasses up on the counter, filled them both liberally with Jameson and pushed one under Anthony's nose.

'To your health.'

Anthony picked up the glass and tipped it against Flicky's. He took a sip, savouring the burn as it tickled the back of his throat.

'We don't have to talk about it, if you don't want to.'

'Emma's pregnant.'

'Ah.'

Anthony's skin burned white hot. He tasted grass and blood; could almost feel the sensation of fingers on his balls.

'But Dody didn't do it, Dad's wrong.'

'You know who did?'

'Same person who shot at her in the woods.'

'You know or you *think* you know?'

'I know.'

'Listen to me now.' Flicky rested his hand on Anthony's shoulder. 'You need to be fierce sure of your facts son, before you accuse anybody of anything in this life. Talk like that can ruin a person.'

'Ruin? Ruin?' Anthony tried to smile, but he couldn't hold it in place. 'Oh I know all about ruin, Flicky.'

'You're a young man, with the whole world at your feet. Didn't you tell me you were thinking of travelling? Maybe that's what you should do. Go…get out of here. See the world, have an adventure.'

'I can't leave here now, not now, maybe not ever.'

'Anthony–'

The kindness in Flicky's voice was too much. Overcome, Anthony started to cry.

Flicky's comforting words died in his throat. He reached for the bottle and refilled their glasses almost to the brim.

'Quod non interficit nos fortiores facit.'

Anthony wiped his tears with his sleeve and looked at him. 'What does that mean?'

'That which does not kill us makes us stronger. Nietzsche.'

'Oh yeah? Well I hope that fella knew what he was talking about.'

Anthony returned to the farm the next morning, still slightly drunk. He and Flicky had stayed up late into the night talking and drinking. The barn door was open and inside he found Emma lying on a stack of square bales of straw with her legs dangling over the side. As he got closer, he could see she had a tiny black and white kitten sitting on her chest. He took off his coat and climbed onto the bale next to her.

'Hey.'

She glanced at him.

'Your eyes are very red.'

'Yeah.'

'You smell bad.'

Anthony sniffed his clothes; she was right about that too.

'Where did you get the kitten?'

'One of the feral cats had them a few weeks ago. This is the last one. The other two have been killed by a tom.'

'Poor things.'

They kill the offspring of rivals. That way, the females go back into heat and the males get breeding rights.'

'I know that, but I still think it's cruel.'

'It is the natural order of things.'

'How are you feeling?'

'Unusual.'

'Still sick?'

'No, but I do not feel like myself. I mean I am myself, clearly, but I do not feel as I felt yesterday.'

He leaned back on his elbows. He felt exhausted and slightly unwell in the sweet cloying air of the barn.

'Mam and Dad are worried about us.'

'Us?' Anthony said, barely mustering up enough energy for a sneer. 'You mean they are worried about *you*.'

'Yes, but you as well. I hear them talking. Whenever I come into the room they stop, but they are wearing their worried faces.'

'Big of them to give us their consideration.'

Emma rubbed the kitten's head with her thumb. 'They worry because of my condition.'

'It's a big deal.'

'I have managed my other condition.' She moved the tiny kitten over her clavicle and it snuggled under her chin. 'I have managed to be normal.'

'Who's to say what's normal these days?'

'I had a job, I interact with people regularly.'

'You've been pretty weird recently.'

'Yes, I thought I did not want to be with people anymore.'

'I feel like that sometimes.'

'Yes. I know you do.'

Anthony sat up and stared at her profile. 'Is that why you stopped talking to everyone?'

'It is hard to explain. I do not like metaphors, but sometimes I think people are a poison. Like alcohol is a poison, yet people drink it. It is bad for you, but in small doses it will not kill you. It is when people drink too much they become stupid and poisoned. I felt poisoned.'

'By people.'

'Yes. That was how I felt.'

'And now?'

'Now, I am not feeling as sick of people.'

'I suppose that's something.'

'I think it is.'

Anthony rested his chin on his arm and looked out across the straw to the yard beyond, washed golden by the early morning sun. He wished he could freeze-frame this moment, here in the barn, with the sleeping kitten and the dust motes dancing in the hazy sunlight.

'Anthony?'

'What?'

'You are angry.'

'I'm hung-over.'

'You are angry, I know your face.'

'Not with you, Emma.'

She hooked one hand behind her head and closed her eyes. He watched her, waiting for her to say something else, but she did not and, after a while, he slipped off the bales and went into the house to get some sleep.

CHAPTER 47

Though the family discussed Emma's condition with nobody, not even Pete, it did not take long for word to get round the area that Emma Byrne was pregnant, and immediately people began to speculate on who the father was, with Dody Molloy as prime suspect. Margaret was incensed by all the gossip, especially when one morning Eddie Yates stopped her at the post office and told her he was 'sorry for her troubles'. Margaret had sent him off with a flea in his ear.

'In my day, people didn't talk about such things,' she complained to Evelyn over a cup of near-scalding tea. 'Mind you, girls didn't go around flaunting their condition in my day either.'

Jack excused himself and left the kitchen.

'You know,' Evelyn looked Margaret straight in the eye. 'There was a lot done wrong back in your day. Thank God we now live in more enlightened times.'

'Well, what am I supposed to say to people when they ask me about her?'

'Say *nothing*. Say your granddaughter is doing well and leave it at that.'

'Oh now, if only it was that easy.'

'It's as easy or as hard as you want it to be, Margaret,' Evelyn said, 'Anyway, they've little to be worrying about if Emma's the main concern they have.'

Margaret sucked her dentures. 'We should never have let her get involved with that, that…Dody fellow in the first place. God knows what sort of carry-on he got up to when he was over there foreign.'

'I don't want to talk about him.'

'And he's brazen, strutting around Killbragh as though he's done nothing wrong. In my day, that yoke would have been made do the decent thing.'

'Margaret! Stop going on about it. At least he said he wasn't going to press charges against Jack.'

Evelyn was careful not to mention what Jack and Dody had spoken about. She would be grateful for the rest of her life that Dody Molloy really *was* a decent man and that he had promised to keep their secret, out of affection for Emma.

'Well, why should he press charges? What father wouldn't have done the same as Jack? Going around the place the way he does, after taking advantage of a girl like Emma. What way is that for any man to conduct himself?'

The only person who seemed unaffected by the pregnancy was Emma who, once she'd got over the morning sickness, had acquired what could only be described as a contented glow. She still refused to leave the farm itself, but she no longer stayed for hours in her room, and she no longer looked sickened whenever anyone spoke to her. She had also started speaking to Pete again – a good indication that whatever trauma she had endured, she was at least beginning to show some signs of fighting it.

Emma's pregnancy hit Pete hard. Not only because he cared deeply for her, but also because he discovered the wags had wasted no time in speculating that he might have his hat in the ring for paternity.

'Bastards,' he said to Anthony as Anthony helped him unload two jittery two year olds for Emma to 'educate' now that the drafts were gone.

'It makes me sick to think what that poor kid is going through, and those fuckers have nothing to do but talk flamin' rubbish,' he spat to the side. 'I see the way they look at me, like I'm some sort of pervert. People who've known me for near enough thirty years, questioning my decency like that.'

'Nobody thinks you're a pervert,' Anthony said, trying to squeeze his way past one of the horses to untie her. She swung her rump and pinned him against the trailer wall.

'I'd like to say that were true Anthony, but two fathers took their daughters' ponies out of the yard last week. Why would they do that if they weren't worried about me around their kids?'

'Who?'

'It doesn't matter who they were. Only that they did it.'

Anthony shook his head, shoved the mare over and clipped the lead rope onto the head collar.

'Let the fuckers talk all they want. You know it's not true and I know it's not true. My family knows it's not true.'

Pete huffed, and said no more about it.

The following Saturday was market day in the village, and Lakelands was hopping when Martin Harte and two pals landed into the bar.

'What can I get you lads?' Flicky asked, sweating up a storm as took orders.

'Three pints of the black,' Martin said, opening a wallet and extracting a note from the many in it. Flicky pulled up three pint glasses and began to fill each of them.

'Don't often see you in here, Martin. How's your father?'

Martin smiled and put his money on the counter. 'Busy. I'll tell him you were asking for him.'

'Do that.' Flicky took the note, gave him his change and moved down the bar counter to serve another customer while the three pints were settling. That's where he was standing when Anthony emerged from the cellar, having changed a keg.

'Oh now,' Martin said, loudly, 'is it yourself Byrne? I'd forgotten you worked here.'

Anthony shut the cellar door and ignored him.

'By God, that's some number your oul fella did on Dody Molloy. Have you seen him lately? Had to get his jaw wired shut, lost half his body weight. Don't think he'll ever be right again.'

'Shut up about it,' Anthony said through clenched teeth.

'Still though, I don't blame him. I'd be put out if I learned someone was sticking it to Grace on a regular basis. Not that anyone would, but the sentiment stands.'

'I said shut up.'

'Always thought your sister was a stuck-up sort. Just goes to show, it's always the quiet ones who–'

Putting one hand on the bar, Anthony vaulted it easily and, as his feet hit the floor, he loafed Martin Harte straight in the face. Martin fell back, crashing over a crowded table, sending drinks and ashtrays flying. By the time he managed to get to his feet, Anthony was on him, swinging mightily, landing a flurry of punches until Sam Delaney hooked his hand and hauled him back towards the bar.

'Hold on, hold on there now a minute!'

Martin scrambled to his feet. The bridge of his nose was gushing blood and his clothes were stained and soaked from beer. His friends stood there, gaping at Anthony, making no move to get involved.

'You're a fucking dead man Byrne.'

'Lads, I won't have any trouble here,' Flicky said, coming up the bar carrying the hurley he kept under the counter in case of trouble. 'Go on about your business.'

'Your barman head-butted me,' Martin said, smearing blood across his face with his hand. 'That's fucking assault. I could sue you. Have this place shut down.'

'Is that right?'

'I am the *victim* of assault,' Martin yelled theatrically, making sure the entire Saturday crowd heard his every word. 'You all saw it!'

'I didn't,' Old Charlie Barr, sitting in the corner, said. He was staring at Martin with his arms folded across his chest.

'I saw nothing either,' another man said from a nearby table. 'And the only thing I heard was some gobshite looking for trouble.'

'I didn't see any assault,' Sam said, staring at Martin's friends with such intensity that they both looked away. 'I'd say you fell and hurt yourself and now you're looking for a pay out.'

'Some kind of insurance scam,' another voice said. 'You hear about that kind of thing, don't you?'

'You do,' Flicky said, bouncing the hurley against the palm of his hand. 'Seems to me like this has been an unfortunate accident, and since we don't want another one, you boys had better head on with yourselves.'

'He fucking assaulted me!'

'I'll fucking assault you with a foot up your arse if you don't get out of here,' Sam said, releasing Anthony and taking a step towards Martin, who blanched a little. Sam was not a small man.

'Those are my pints,' Martin said, pointing at the bar. But his bravado was fast failing and the tremor in his voice didn't help matters.

'Marty, let's go,' one of his friends said.

'This isn't over,' Martin said to Anthony. 'This is far from over.'

They left.

'Three pints going a begging lads!' Flicky roared. 'Three of the sweetest-tasting pints you'll ever have.'

CHAPTER 48

Anthony began to spend even less time at the farm. He asked for and was given more shifts at Lakelands, and stayed over most nights, staying up late to drink or play cards with Flicky. Evelyn worried about him, but whenever she broached the subject with him, he brushed it off.

'Makes sense to stay over if I'm working the next day. No point trying to get home alone on the roads at one in the morning.'

He took to cycling the surrounding area in his free time, carrying a notebook and pen in his pocket. People saw him hither and yon, and if a curious person asked what he was up to, he said he had taken up an interest in ornithology.

'Seen any decent-looking birds on your travels, Anthony?' the wags in the Lakelands bar would ask, wiggling their eyebrows. 'Are you sure it's the feathered kind you're looking out for?'

Anthony would smile and go back to reading the newspaper or watching the horseracing.

Jack kept his own counsel; he was sorry that Anthony had all but moved out, but he was too caught up in his own inner turmoil to address the issue.

'Please talk to him Jack,' Evelyn pleaded. 'There's a pair of you in it.'

'Ara stop, would you,' Jack replied. 'Let him do what he wants. He'll do what he wants anyway, that fella.'

Emma's work continued without mishap, which was just as well, as she steadfastly refused to make any variation in her daily routine with the horses.

'I don't think you're being practical,' Evelyn said. 'It's not safe for you to be riding when you're pregnant.'

'Riding is fine,' Emma stated with conviction. 'Statistically speaking, it is unlikely that I will fall off or be hurt.'

'You must have some fears,' Evelyn said, exasperated by her nonchalance.

'I have *many* fears. I fear enclosed spaces, I fear the supermarket, I fear–'

'Not those kinds of fears. That's not what I'm talking about and I think you know that. I mean fears for your safety and if not for you, then for the baby's safety.'

'I do not feel safe in the hairdressers. That is why I do not go there.'

'Oh for God's sake. You'll get hurt,' Evelyn said. 'Jack, tell her will you?'

But Jack had nothing to say on the matter and so he remained silent. In his heart, he wanted to accept the pregnancy, but no matter how hard he tried, he found he could not. Every time he looked at Emma, he was reminded of the day he found her in the woods, bloodied and disorientated. He thought about what happened to her and he hated himself and felt less of a man than ever before. The anger never abated: it bubbled under his skin, ready to surface at the slightest provocation. Even Pat could get no good from him, and stopped calling in or asking him to come out for a pint.

Despite Evelyn's warnings, Emma worked as hard as she had always done, but as the weeks progressed the strain began to show. Aside from her growing bump, she was skin and bone and exhausted a lot of the time. She now had six horses in the stables, and worked them daily, with little or no help from anyone else.

She dropped off to sleep in the sitting room one evening with the television on, something that no one could ever recall happening before. The following day she was returning one of horses to the stables when she tripped over the loose coils of the lunge rein and fell, scraping her elbows and her knees.

Evelyn phoned Pete on the quiet and pleaded with him to take some of the horses, but the hunting season was in full swing and Pete's livery yard was filled to capacity. He promised Evelyn he would talk to Jack, and failing that, he would talk to Anthony. Evelyn hung up and realised that she had to do something to prevent the implosion of her family.

'Jack,' she said that night, lying in the darkness. 'I don't want a fight, but I need you to listen to me.'

'What?'

' I love you; I think you know that, but you can't go on the way you've been carrying on. I need you to talk to me, I need…I need my husband and Emma needs her father. Jack we need you.'

'I don't know what you want from me, Evie.'

'I don't want anything *from* you except your support.'

'No, what you want is for me to pretend like you are doing. Well I can't. I won't do it. I can't act like this pregnancy is some sort of weird blessing, that everything's okay. Because it's not okay, Evie, it's not. You asked me not to go to the guards and I did what you asked. But by God don't ask any more of me.'

Jack rolled over onto his other side and gave her his back. He thought of his daughter, lying in the mud with blood seeping from her head and a dark shadow bent over her. He squeezed his eyes shut and lay rigid until his heart slowed and he could breathe normally again.

CHAPTER 49

A few days before his eighteenth birthday, Anthony was standing outside a chipper on Main Street in Arklow, eating a battered cod and chips, when he saw Lucy Green walking up the street.

She was wearing black velvet trousers and a black jacket with a furry hood, pulled up against the cold evening air.

'Hello stranger,' she said, smiling when she recognised him.

'Aren't you a sight for sore eyes?' Anthony offered her a chip and she took one.

She put it in her mouth and began to splutter almost immediately.

'Hot', she said, waving her hand in front of her mouth, laughing. 'And vinegary! Wow, how much of that stuff does one person need?'

Anthony shrugged and shifted over a little on the window ledge, so that she could sit down beside him.

'So, how are you?' she said.

'I'm okay. How's college?'

'Oh, you know…a lot of work. More than I realised there would be frankly. How's the pub?'

'Same as always.'

'How come you never got away to Australia?"

'Things came up.'

'I heard about Emma.' She turned her head to look directly at him. Anthony was surprised: hardly anyone ever brought up the subject of Emma with him these days. 'How is she doing?'

'She's okay.'

'Is it true about Dody Molloy? I always thought he was such a nice person when I used to meet him.'

'Who says he's not nice?'

'Oh, well I just…'

Anthony looked across the street. A group of lads were coming out of a bar. He recognised a few of them, and then spotted Gully Donovan and Martin Harte bringing up the rear. Lucy followed his gaze, saw what he saw: her mouth tightened into a thin line.

'You want to go for a walk, Anthony?'

'Sure.'

They got up and walked down the street, turning left into the lane past the bandstand, and then on towards the riverbank. A flock of speckled geese sat dotted about on grass, some with their heads tucked under their wings.

'So what's Carlow like?'

'Oh, it's a real student town, lots of bars and stuff. I'm sharing a flat with a girl from Mallow. You should see it. It's like a shed with a toilet, and the landlord is always hovering about,' she laughed. 'He claims he likes to keep a close eye on us *wee girtles*.'

'Girtles?'

'That's what he calls us, his wee girtles. He's a total creep. But the flat is dead handy for college, so we sort of ignore him. I reckon he's harmless really.'

'Be careful with him anyway,' Anthony said. 'You never know.'

Lucy nodded, not smiling now. 'I will.'

They walked on.

'I met Mark Bradshaw the other day. He's training to become a guard. Can you imagine?'

Anthony rolled up the chip bag and tossed it in a bin. He rubbed his hands together to remove the grease. 'I know. I was with him when he applied. He filled out the form sitting in the snug in Lakelands. Then he had a few pints and drove home. Getting the practice in early I suppose.'

'What practice?'

'Saying one thing, doing another.'

'I thought you and he were friends?'

'We are. But that doesn't mean I can't call a spade a spade.'

'When did you get so cynical?'

Anthony shrugged. 'There's nothing cynical about knowing the way the world works.'

They reached the end of the walk and climbed the steps onto the bridge.

'Hey, what are your plans for this evening?' Lucy asked.

'Dunno, head back out to the village I suppose. I have Flicky's car with me.'

She stuck her hands into her pockets and rocked back on her heels. 'Fancy going for a drink first?'

'With you?'

'Yes Anthony, with me.' She laughed and linked his arm. 'I promise I won't bite.'

He glanced out across the pewter-coloured water. 'I don't know.'

'Wow, it's a drink. Are you always this serious?'

'I don't know, I hadn't noticed.'

'Come on, one drink won't hurt.'

They found a quiet seat in a bar called The Old Ship. Anthony bought them two drinks. Initially, he hadn't got much to say. In truth, he felt shy and a little awkward around Lucy; but it didn't matter, Lucy was happy enough to do the talking for both of them and, after a while, he found he could relax in her company. Before he knew it, an hour had passed.

'See?' Lucy said, when he mentioned it. 'Time flies when you're having fun.'

'Are you having fun?'

'I am actually,' she said, her blue eyes twinkling with mischief. 'Are you?'

Anthony smiled. 'I suppose so.'

'Oh you *suppose*,' she punched him playfully on the arm. 'You're a hard one to impress Mr Byrne. A real cool cat.'

'You don't need to impress me. Still, I'd better get this car back to Flicky. He'll think I've run it into a ditch or something. Do you need a lift anywhere?'

Lucy shook her head. She stood up and put on her jacket. 'I'm going to head over to a friend of mine. Thanks all the same.'

They left the bar. Outside, the temperature had dropped another few degrees. Anthony could see his breath in the freezing air.

'I had a good time,' Lucy said.

'Yeah, me too.'

'You should try doing that more often.'

'What?'

'Smiling.' She leaned in and kissed him square on the mouth. Before Anthony could even think of saying or doing anything, she pulled back, winked and walked away.

Anthony watched her go. He could taste her lipstick on his lips, her perfume in his nose. When she disappeared from view, he turned and walked back down the street to where he had earlier parked the car.

'Hey Byrne.'

He turned around. That was his first mistake. Gully's big punch was slow, but not slow enough to duck, and what it lacked in speed it more than made up for in force. Anthony tried to stay on his feet, but it was hard when he couldn't see straight because his eyes were watering.

'Hit him again,' Martin Harte's voice in his ear was high with excitement. 'Make the fucker drop.'

Anthony aimed his fist towards the sound, clipped flesh and heard a yelp, but not a cry of real pain. Then something, a truck or a sledgehammer hit him in the stomach and he collapsed. The second he hit the ground they were on him, kicking him all over.

'Hey!' somebody shouted, 'get off him.'

Gully leaned into his ear, his breath reeking of cigarettes and beer. 'You think you can decide to stop paying, Byrne? You're mine. I told you, you're mine.'

Anthony's head was swimming. He tried to get up, but he could not get his feet under him.

'Jesus, it's that young lad from the bar earlier?'

'Aw fuck, look at his face.'

'Call an ambulance.'

'No.' Anthony waved a feeble hand. 'Help me up.'

He felt arms under him and he was hoisted to his feet. He blinked and wiped the blood from his eyes.

'Here young lad, you're bleeding all over the place so you are.' Two old men stood before him. He tried to get a lock on them but their faces blurred and swam. 'Were you robbed, son?'

He shook his head, leaned forward and spat; blood splattered against the pavement. 'I'm all right.'

'You are in your bollix. Look at the cut of you. Sure you're half dead.'

'I'm all right' he repeated.

The men exchanged glances. There was no point trying to help those who didn't want to be helped, and anyway it was too cold to be standing around.

'Well, if you're sure…'

'I'm grand. Thanks for your help.'

Anthony staggered back to the car. He managed to lower himself into the driver's seat but had to wait for a few minutes until his head stopped spinning before he could start the engine. As he drove across the bridge he was shivering with cold and shock and his eyes were swelling to slits.

By the time he reached Flicky's the pain in his lower back was so bad he could barely walk from the car to the pub. Somehow he made it inside, but collapsed in a dead faint among the barrels in the hall, where Flicky found him half an hour later.

CHAPTER 50

'Where's Anthony?' Jack asked Emma as he met her making her way across the yard, leading Lily, a beautiful but skittish animal. Lily refused to walk in a straight line and tripped over the cobbles crabwise instead, snickering and throwing her head about until Emma gave her a correction.

'I do not know.'

Jack looked at his watch. 'He's not working in the pub today. I thought he was supposed to be giving you a hand this morning?'

'He said that he would.'

'What's wrong with that horse?'

Emma passed him. 'She is the giddy sort.'

Emma led Lily to the paddock and turned her loose. Earlier that morning she had set up a number of jumps ranging in height from two feet to four and a half feet. She wanted the mare to have a good look at them before she sent her over them later that day.

She thought – as did the owner – that Lily would make a spectacular jumper someday, but she was fiery and prone to exaggerated flightiness. If you pushed her she pushed back. Instead, Emma let the mare think that she was the one calling the shots, even though she was doing nothing of the sort. That meant working her offline and giving her as much freedom as possible in a safe environment.

She left Lily and walked back to the barn, hoping to do something about the state of the makeshift tack room. These days, she felt more tired than usual and things were sliding a little.

She was brushing dried mud from the rugs when Jack entered the barn.

'Need a hand?'

Emma glanced at him for a second and turned her back on him.

'If you want.'

Jack picked up a stack of numnahs and hung them so they might dry better.

'I'm sorry I shouted the other evening.' Jack said, as he worked. 'I'm sorry for how I've been acting this past while. You know I am not angry with you, right?'

'Anthony told me you were not.'

'I'm…it's whoever hurt you, Emma. I'm angry with them. They deserve to be locked up.'

'I understand. You feel protective.'

'I do,' Jack tried to think of something appropriate to say. He glanced at her, but her focus was on a tangle of reins. Why was it always so hard to say what he wanted to say? 'I feel like I've let you down.'

'You have not. But you should tell Anthony you are not angry at him.'

'He knows I'm not angry with him either.'

'You wear your angry face all the time now. If you wear your angry face, how are people supposed to know that you are not angry?'

'I don't know.' Jack straightened a saddle. 'I hadn't thought about it.'

'I do not know either.'

Later, he couldn't get the conversation out of his head. Everything she said was true; he had made the pain all about him and, in doing so, he had let his entire family down. It was time to try and make amends. He finished hosing down the byre and went into the house to shower and change.

'Where are you going?' Evelyn asked, surprised by his unexpected appearance in good clothes.

'I'm going down to Lakelands to talk to Anthony.'

She looked at him, anxious, even slightly fearful. Good God he thought, had it come to this? 'Evie, I want to talk to the lad. It's only a few days from his birthday and I want to tell him I'm sorry. That none of this is his fault.'

Evelyn looked at him coolly. 'Good, I think it's high time.'

Jack drove down to the village and parked outside the pub. The main bar was locked up, but the cellar door was open and he could see a number of kegs resting between sacks of sand on the footpath outside. As Jack approached, Flicky popped up though the opening and grabbed the nearest keg.

'Need a hand there?' Jack asked.

'Ah how are you Jack? No, I'm grand thanks. It won't take too long getting this lot in.'

'Is Anthony not giving you a hand?'

Flicky hesitated before answering. 'I thought I'd give him the morning off.'

'Is he about? I wanted to have a quick word with him.'

'He's upstairs. Look Jack, I think we'd better have a chat about something first.'

'Oh aye?'

'I don't want you seeing him the way he is without warning you first.'

'What do you mean the *way* he is?'

Flicky climbed up the cellar steps and stepped out onto the street. 'He took a bit of a pasting last night. No real harm done as far as I can see. Looks worse that it is, but in saying that, it does look bad.'

'He was fighting?'

'He says he wasn't. He was in Arklow grabbing a bite to eat. He says he caught some lads trying to break into my car and they gave him a going over.'

'Jesus. Did he call the guards?'

'He didn't and he wouldn't let me do it either.'

'Why not?'

Flicky pulled a set of keys from his pocket and used the largest one to unlock the door of the pub. 'When you find out, maybe you could tell me. He's upstairs, second door on the right.'

Jack stepped past him into the hall.

'And Jack?'

He stopped.

'Don't be too hard on him, he's a good lad.'

'I don't need you to tell me that,' Jack said, and walked up the stairs.

CHAPTER 51

Jack pushed open the second door and paused in the doorway to allow his eyes become accustomed to the dim light. It was an untidy sitting room, crammed with old-fashioned furniture, rugs and bookcases. A small portable television was playing an *I love Lucy* re-run. Jack could see feet jutting out from the side of a tattered sofa.

'Anthony?"

'Dad?'

A hand crept over the top of the sofa. 'What…what are you doing here?'

Jack stepped into the room and closed the door behind him. He walked around to the front of the sofa and caught his breath.

'Jesus Christ son.'

'It looks a lot worse than it is.'

Both of Anthony's eyes were swollen shut and the skin across his nose was split and shiny. He had cuts and bruises on his cheeks and dried blood in his hair.

'What in the Sacred Heart of Jesus did they do to you?'

'I was jumped. It's all right.'

'All right? Son, have you looked at yourself?'

'I've looked.'

'Who did this? Did you know them?'

'No.'

'Well, what did they look like? Were they young or old, local or–'

'I didn't see Dad. It was dark.'

'I don't understand. Did they take your money or what were they after?'

'They were at Flicky's car and I surprised them.'

'Where was it parked?'

'The car park off Main Street.'

Jack thought about it. 'There's plenty of streetlight there.'

'I didn't see who it was. I came around the corner and I saw them at the car.'

'How many?'

'Two, I think.' Anthony pressed his fingers to his temple. 'I don't know, it might have been two. I can't be sure.'

'They gave you a right good going-over.'

'Aye.'

'Not like car thieves to hang around and do that.'

'Well, they did.'

Jack lowered himself onto a battered leather armchair. He reached out and tilted Anthony's head towards the faint light coming through a chink in the drawn curtains.

'Your mother's going to lose her reason when she sees this.'

Anthony jerked his head. 'I'm not going to let her see it.'

'Humph. And how are you going to avoid that? You're going to lie low in this place until after your birthday? Is that it?' Jack said.

'What do you care about my birthday?'

Jack rested his hands on his knees. There was a challenge in his son's voice.

'I care for you, son.'

Anthony laughed, or tried to, but the slightest movement made him wince with pain.

'I should bring you to a doctor.'

'I don't need one. I want to be left alone.'

'Look lad, I'm sorry about the last while. I was out of line.'

Anthony closed his eyes.

'I was angry Anthony. I know I've handled everything all wrong. I shouldn't have said the things I said. I didn't mean them.

Anthony, I didn't mean what I said to you. Why don't you come on home son?'

'I don't want them see me like this.'

'We'll look after you.'

'I don't need looking after. Don't tell Mam about this.'

'If I don't, she'll hear it from someone else anyway.'

'I'll be over in an few days.'

'What about your birthday?'

'What about it?' Anthony grimaced. 'Close the door on your way out.'

Flicky was behind the bar washing ashtrays, with the television on low in the background and turned to horse racing. He looked up when Jack entered and shrugged a shoulder.

'Well?'

'He's lying about the fight.'

'Aye, I thought that too.'

'Why would someone beat him like that?'

'Some people are bastards.'

'Did he tell you who did it?'

'No, he didn't.'

'He must know, why won't he tell me?'

'I'm sure he has his reasons.'

'Reasons? What the hell kind of bloody answer is that?'

Flicky looked at him, coldly. 'The only one I have at the moment, Jack.'

'He says he won't come home. He says he doesn't want his mother or sister seeing him like that.'

'Are you going to tell them?'

Jack shrugged. 'I may. I can't have them hear it somewhere else.'

Flicky stacked the last ashtray on a rack and dried his hands on a tea towel. 'I can tell him he can't stay here if you want him home.'

'I want him home of his own accord, not because he's been backed into a corner.'

'Suit yourself.'

Jack drove back to the farm with his mind in turmoil. Everything was spinning out of control, first Emma and now Anthony. If he was a superstitious man, he might have wondered if they were cursed. He didn't buy Anthony's story at all. The lad had been assaulted, and badly at that, but such a response from would-be car thieves was highly unlikely. He was hiding something. Of that Jack was certain, but what the hell could it be?

He turned into the yard and parked under the chestnut tree. He caught a brief glimpse of Evelyn standing at the window and then she was gone. What was he going to tell her? There was no point in lying, at least not to her; the woman could read him like a book.

'Did you see him?' she asked the moment he put his foot in the kitchen door. She had been baking; there was flour on her hands and on her cheeks. The kitchen smelled of cinnamon.

'He's not coming home.'

'What do you mean he's not coming home? It's Christmas.'

'That's what he said.'

Did you have another row??'

'No, I didn't.'

Evelyn searched his face. 'Then what is it?'

'He was in a fight last night. He says he caught someone trying to break into Flicky's car in Arklow and they gave him a few digs.'

'A fight? Is he hurt?'

'Black eyes, few cuts and bruises.'

'Then what's he doing down there? He should be back here, in his *home!*'

'He doesn't want you or Emma to see him all banged up.'

'That's ridiculous.' She wiped her hands on her apron and untied it. 'Give me the car keys. I'm going down there to get him.'

'Evelyn, he's almost eighteen. You'll only embarrass him by trying to drag him home.'

'I don't want to ask you again,' Evelyn said, her face darkening. 'Give me the car keys.'

Jack sighed. He handed them over and she left.

He went upstairs and changed into his work clothes. He was splitting logs for the woodpile when Evelyn arrived home. Anthony was in the passenger seat. Jack shook his head and swung the axe; he should never have underestimated her.

CHAPTER 52

'You are injured,' Emma said, looking at Anthony's face. She was hosing down Garryowen, the last animal to be exercised that morning. The second the cold water hit him, the bay lifted his feet and tossed his head irritably. 'What happened to your face?'

'I caught someone tampering with Flicky's car, but instead of running away, they gave me a thumping.'

Emma turned off the hose and retrieved a sweat scraper from her tack box. She began to squeeze the excess water from Garryowen's hide.

'Do you know who hurt you?'

'No, it was dark, I didn't see their faces.'

'That is a lie. I can see that you are lying.'

'Here, give me that.' Anthony pried the scraper from her hand and took over.

'Why do you lie to me?'

'I'm not.'

'Anthony, I know that you are.'

'Look, it doesn't matter. That's my story and that's it.'

Emma sat down on the wall. She rested her hand on her bump and watched her brother work.

''You okay?'

'I think I can feel this baby moving.'

Anthony did not reply. What was there to say? How could he explain that he felt sick to the pit of his stomach, that he could hardly bring himself to look at her, that he was now convinced more than ever that Emma was carrying a Donovan spawn? That it was he who had failed her; that he had tried but it hadn't been good enough? How would he explain any of that to Emma? It was impossible, she would never understand.

The night before, he had lain in Flicky's spare room, watching the shadows on the ceiling, trying to think, trying to piece together some plan of action. It's all boiled down to two things: Emma had to be protected and the baby had to be protected. There was no telling what Gully might do, what he was capable of. Minutes had stretched to hours. He had taken more painkillers and drank room-temperature water. Close to dawn, his thoughts took a darker turn. It was simple really: so simple it scared him. Emma would never be safe, and neither would her baby, with Gully Donovan around. He had to be eliminated.

'Anthony?'

'What?'

'I said he is finished. Please throw the sweat blanket over him and I will walk him dry.'

'Want me to do it?'

'No. You are making him nervous.'

Anthony did as she asked. Emma walked the bay up and down the lane until he was dry, rugged him and put him in his stable.

'You look tired,' Anthony said as she closed the barn door and leaned against it.

'Anthony,' she said, her brown eyes travelling over him, 'I will not pretend to understand what is going on in your life, or why you lie to me. But I do not like to see you hurt.'

'I know that.'

'I think you should take better care of yourself.'

Anthony erupted with laughter. 'Oh, that's the pot calling the kettle black right there.'

'What?' Emma asked, a little confused. 'Did I say something funny?'

'Not really.'

'Then why are you laughing?'

'I don't know,' Anthony replied, 'I honestly don't.'

The day after their birthday, Anthony cycled up to Ballycreen. He stashed the bike under some holly bushes and hiked along a steep hillside for a couple of miles, a small rucksack on his back containing his notebook and some water, a pen and a set of ancient binoculars once owned by Margaret's husband.

At the upper ridge of the hill he turned west and walked a mile until it descended into a shallow gully made up of shale and rock. He slithered down the loose face until he came to rest on a small shelf overlooking the valley, and more importantly, overlooking the Donovan farm, a scant few hundred yards below him.

From there, he was able to see into the side yard and the rear of the farmhouse. He raised his binoculars and scanned the area. Donovan's battered Volvo truck was nowhere to be seen and the place looked empty. Behind the house, in a scrubby-looking field surrounded by rusty barbed wire, two shaggy-haired horses stood fetlock deep in mud, nose to tail, standing next to a round bale of rotted hay.

At two-thirty, Sean Donovan cycled into the yard, wearing dirty jodhpurs and a green waxed jacket. Anthony knew he worked part time as a trainee jockey in Ballymoney Stud. Dogs barked and went to greet him. Anthony wrote the time in his notebook. He also took note of the dogs, two mutts and a large German shepherd with bad hips.

The Volvo appeared shortly after noon with Donovan Senior driving and Gully riding up front in the cab.

Anthony touched his bruised jaw involuntarily as he watched Gully climb down from the cab while cracking a joke with his father. Sean came out to the yard to join them and together the three men unloaded heaps of scrap metal into a dilapidated shed made of corrugated iron.

At one, Gully tacked up a good-looking chestnut mare and rode out from the farm, heading along a rutted track that ran along the foot of the hill below where Anthony was hidden.

Anthony waited until he was gone past, then tracked him with the binoculars until he disappeared from sight into a small copse.

Anthony settled back to wait. Gully returned in under the hour, un-tacked the mare and turned her out into the field with the other horses. After that Gully went into the house without removing his boots and shut the door. Through the binoculars Anthony was able to make him out, moving around in what he surmised was the kitchen.

Aching from cold and immobility, Anthony packed up his things and climbed back out of the gully. Despite the hour, light was already fading and he had no choice but to move carefully and deliberately. Breaking an ankle here was not an option.

CHAPTER 53

'Hi Anthony. Beautiful day.'

Anthony put the bags of groceries into the back of the Ford and closed the boot. Amanda McCarthy, Lucy's friend, was standing smiling at him.

'Oh howya'

'Oh my God, your poor face. I heard you were attacked in a robbery?'

'Attempted,' Anthony smiled and pointed to his face. 'Fortunately, my face was too strong for their fists, so they ran away.'

She laughed, a light tinkle that sounded as fake as her blonde hair looked. Well I'm glad you're okay. Scary really. I mean, it goes to show you're not safe anywhere these days.'

Anthony nodded. She stood there, the same dumb smile on her face. Was she waiting for him to say something?

'Em, so the horse, Zebbie, how's he working out for you?"

'Oh he's great.'

'Done any hunting this season?'

'Well, no. I mean, he's still pretty green, but it's actually me who needs the help.' She smiled coyly, as though she was telling him some massively important secret. 'It's nothing to do with how Emma trained him or anything.'

'I didn't think it was.'

'Although he can be a bit of a brat when I'm mounting him. He walks off the minute my foot is in the stirrup.'

'Horses do that sometimes,' Anthony said, thinking he had

seen Emma get on Zebbie countless times without ever noticing him do that.

She leaned in closer. 'She's so brave you know. It can't be easy working and being pregnant, alone.'

Anthony smiled stiffly. 'Yeah.'

'I mean, my brother is friends with Dody, and he just can't believe it, you know? You think you know a person.'

'Yeah, well, I've got to get back to—'

'I heard you had a drink with Lucy the other week.'

'You heard?'

'Well, okay… Lucy told me.' She did the smile again. Anthony was starting to get sick of her.

'Do you like her?'

'She's a nice girl.'

'No…I mean…look you should give her a ring sometime.'

Anthony searched in his pockets, making a big deal out of trying to find his car keys. 'She's in college in a different county. I don't think there's much point.'

'Well, if you change your mind, I think she'd be glad to hear from you. Give my regards to Emma, won't you?'

As if she'd even know who you are, he thought, getting into the car and driving away.

Lakelands was crowded that evening, it being the last Saturday before Christmas. The atmosphere was festive, bar and lounge humming with regulars and not-so regulars. A loud and fractious contingent from Rathdrum arrived in a minibus, lending an air of unpredictability to the crowd. Not that Flicky noticed; he was three sheets to the wind by eight o'clock.

Anthony didn't drink anything at all that night, no matter who offered to buy him a pint. A few people commented on his face but, by and large, he was rushed off his feet and happy to let the work occupy his mind. He was so busy serving pints and shorts to the three-deep bar crowd that he almost missed Arthur,

Gully, Sean and Sylvester Donovan, Arthurs's older brother, the one who had been in jail somewhere in England, sitting around a table.

'What are they doing here?' he asked Flicky.

'Who?' Flicky said, weaving slightly on his feet, exhaling enough whiskey fumes to fell an elephant

'The Donovans. They don't normally come in here.'

'Christmas Ant'ney. Arthur always comes for a drink at Christmas. Doesn't normally bring the sons though.' Flicky burped into the back of his hand. 'S'cuse me.'

Anthony tried not to think about them, sitting there like malignant vultures. He worked on, smiling, wishing good cheer and so on to everyone who offered him season's greetings.

He held it together pretty well until Gully appeared at the bar. He was drunk, belligerent, reeking of entitlement.

'Hey chief, four pints when you're ready there.'

Anthony looked across to where the rest of the family were deep in conversation.

'I can serve you three, but not one for Sean. He's under age.'

Gully shrugged. 'Not your business, head. Get 'em up there.'

'If Flicky wants to serve you, that's up to him, but I won't.'

A number of people seated nearby were starting to pay attention to the exchange. Gully rested two hands the size of shovels on the bar and glowered at Anthony. 'I'm not fucking asking ye. This is a public bar.'

'What's going on?' Flicky wobbled up, wearing a party hat from a cracker.

'This gobshite won't serve me,' Gully said.

'Anthony?'

'His brother is over there. I said I can't serve him alcohol. Gully here seems to have a problem with people who say no to him.'

Flicky squinted across the crowd. 'What age is your brother there?'

'He's near enough eighteen so—'

'He's fifteen,' Anthony said.

'Ah here,' Flicky said. 'That's taking the piss. Do you want me to lose my licence or what?'

Gully's eyes never strayed from Anthony's face. 'This how it's going to be?'

'Go fuck yourself,' Anthony said, and suddenly the bar grew very quiet.

Gully grinned. 'Give me three pints and a Coke.'

Flicky slipped under the hatch and set about pulling the pints himself. 'Anthony, why don't you go keep an eye on the snug for me? Old Andy's half-cut down there and threatening to stab anyone who sings a Christmas carol.'

Anthony stalked off. Flicky finished pulling the pints and got a Coke and a glass with ice. He put the whole lot down on the bar.

'There you go.'

'How much do I owe you?'

'Nothing. On the house.'

Gully raised an eyebrow. 'Oh yeah?'

'Aye,' Flicky said, with a smile that did not reach his eyes. 'Now, make sure you drink them up and get the fuck out of my bar.'

Gully stared at him.

'Happy Christmas,' Flicky said. 'Safe home now.'

CHAPTER 54

Christmas week the weather took a turn for the worst. Every day became progressively more miserable. The rain turned to sleet and, finally, towards the weekend, the village awoke to a couple of inches of snow on the ground.

Anthony rose, dressed and made his way downstairs to the kitchen. He was not surprised to see that Emma was up before him.

'Don't you ever sleep?'

She glanced at him fleetingly, unwilling to move away from the Aga. 'I sleep.'

Anthony wiped the condensation from the window over the sink with his sleeve and peered out.

'Snow.'

'Yes.'

'Need a hand feeding the horses?'

'No. Thank you.'

Anthony watched her shrug on her coat over her clothes. Even with all the extra layers she was wearing, he could see she was just skin and bone. Her wrists, shoulder blades, cheekbones jutted out. Everything looked sharp.

She paused at the door, pulling on a blue woolly hat. 'Can you ride today? Garryowen will need to be ridden. He is starting to get very stable bound.'

'Not a problem,' Anthony said.

'Thank you.'

He had a slice of toast and a cup of tea. By the time he was finished eating, Jack was up too.

'Morning.'

'Morning.' Jack looked out the window and sighed 'I see it snowed during the night.'

'Can I borrow the car later on? I want to pick up a few bits and pieces for Christmas.'

'Check with your mother. I think she mentioned something about going into town.'

'Will do. I'll go get the cows and bring them down.'

Jack looked at him in surprise.

'I might as well,' Anthony said. 'Sure I'm up aren't I?'

He left quickly before Jack ruined it. He whistled to the dogs and they came running from their kennels. The wind was bitingly cold and some of the overnight snow had drifted against the garden walls. He wrapped his scarf around his mouth and tramped up the lane. Too cold to be outside for long, he thought. Luckily, the cows had much the same view as him and they were milling around the ditch waiting for him. No sooner had he opened the gate than they hurtled down the lane towards the byre.

After lunch, he arranged to take a lift into town with Evelyn. She was excited about an invitation to the hunt ball, something she and Jack almost never attended. She wanted to buy a new dress.

'I don't know why he agreed to go this year. It's most unlike him, maybe he's getting sociable in his old age.'

Anthony turned the car heater up as far as it would go. He thought he knew the reason why his father had agreed to go to the hunt ball. Jack was squaring his shoulders to the world, as only Jack knew how. At the most prestigious event on the local calendar, Jack would represent his daughter and his family, and let the chips fall where they may. About fucking time, Anthony thought. There was hope for his father yet.

In town, Anthony and Evelyn went in separate directions. He wanted to buy presents, he told her, and didn't want her to see what he was getting. But that was not the reason he was in town.

First, he called to Lucy Green's house. Lucy's aunt opened the door. Clodagh Green was an attractive woman with sad blue eyes and a gentle smile. Anthony thought of all the times she had come in to the bar to collect her husband Larry, and he felt a little sorry for her.

'Hello there, Anthony, I almost didn't recognise you for a minute.'

'Hello Mrs Green.'

'How are you?'

'I'm fine thank you. I was wondering if Lucy might be home.'

She tilted her head slightly. 'She is. Come in for a moment out of the cold. How are the family?'

'Great thank you.'

'Well, glad to hear it.'

She showed him into a large, comfortable living room, over furnished and overheated. The Christmas tree taking up most of the available space in the bay window was garishly decorated with multi-coloured ribbons, tinsel and flashing lights.

'Have a seat Anthony. Can I get you a cup of tea or anything to drink?'

'I'm fine, thank you Mrs Green.'

She nodded and left. A few minutes later Lucy came bounding into the room.

'Oh!' she said, when she saw him. 'I thought she was joking.'

'Hello Lucy.'

'Hello yourself.'

She gazed at him as though he was something exotic. He shuffled his feet, feeling awkward and out of place.

'I…I was wondering if you'd like to go for a drink with me again, sometime. Or if you're you know, busy and stuff, I–'

'I'd love to.'

He blinked, a little surprised at how easy that was. 'I'm working Friday and Saturday. How about Sunday?'

'Sure. Where had you in mind?'

'I can pick you up and maybe we can go to Wicklow or somewhere different.'

'Okay.'

He stood. 'Okay, I'll come by about seven.'

'I'll see you then.'

She walked him out to the front door. Over her shoulder, he could see Clodagh and Mrs Green, Lucy's mother, laughing and sipping red wine from over-sized glasses.

'Goodbye,' Anthony called out.

'Oh good luck, Anthony. Happy Christmas and give my regards to the family.'

He waved.

Lucy winked at him. 'I didn't think you had it in you.'

Anthony's mouth twitched. 'You don't know what I have in me.'

'I can't wait to find out.'

Anthony's blush was genuine and it went straight to the top of his ears.

On the way home, he asked if he could borrow the car for his upcoming date, and then he had to endure almost eight miles of questions and gentle ribbing from a highly amused Evelyn about his sudden foray into romance.

Back at the farm he went up to his room and closed the door. He carefully extracted his purchases from the inside pocket of his jacket and added them to the rucksack he used on his so-called bird watching expeditions.

Sunday could not come soon enough.

He lay down on the bed, his hands hooked behind his head. If Evelyn had glanced in at that moment and saw the smile he wore, she would have guessed – wrongly – that he was thinking of Lucy Green.

CHAPTER 55

The day of his date Anthony got up early and mucked out the stables himself without being asked. At seven, Emma joined him, wearing so many layers of clothes she looked like a zeppelin.

'You are up early.'

'I couldn't sleep so I thought I might as well get on with it.'

Garryowen stuck his head over his stable door when he heard Emma's voice. She stroked his muzzle absentmindedly. 'Why could you not sleep?'

'Dunno.'

Emma watched him load the wheelbarrow with soiled straw. 'You are worried about something.'

Anthony didn't see any point in pretending otherwise.

'Is it on my face?'

'Yes.'

She watched him for a while. 'I miss Pete.'

'Yeah, well I know he misses you too. Why don't you go back to work for him?'

'I do not think that is the best thing to do.'

'Emma.' He leaned the fork against the stable wall and grabbed some fresh straw from a bale by the door and began to shake it all over the floor. 'You've got to get back in the saddle, metaphorically speaking.'

'There is no need to speak in metaphors.'

'Okay, what I'm saying is you need to start dealing with the real world again. You know, the world beyond the farm.'

'Why?'

'Well, for one thing, you're about to have a baby. So, you're going to have to do things with your child, go places, talk to people, doctors, schools, that sort of thing.'

She said nothing, but he knew she was thinking, taking in everything he said.

'You can't just stay hiding out here forever.'

'I do not feel safe,' she said softly. 'I do not feel safe when I am with people I do not know. I can confide in you, because I know you understand. I am safe by myself.'

Anthony finished the stable, untied the mare and walked her back inside. 'I'm not going to patronise you. But I'm not going to mollycoddle you either. It's not going to be about *you* in the future. It's going to be about you plus one.'

'I know that.'

'And that one is going to need you, he or she is going to need you to go places, talk to people, you can't just hide out here and expect Mam and Dad to do it all.'

'I understand that.'

'You know you can do it Emma. You're as tough as old boots when push comes to shove.'

'Yes.' She looked at the floor. 'Sometimes it is hard to not be afraid.'

'I know that too.' He glanced at her. ' I really do.'

Later that morning, Anthony tacked up Garryowen and rode him out of the yard. He hacked across the woods and came out through the woodland opposite Sam Delaney's farm. He rode along the road for a while, then turned into the forest and trotted the bay up through the woods and out onto the hillside, three miles north of Donovan's farm. There he left the trees and rode the horse over snow covered scrubland. Garryowen was a little spooked by this new route. He shied and snorted at the scents of fox and mink, but when Anthony pressed him on he did as he was asked.

When they reached a small stream, Anthony dismounted and looped Garryowen's reins around the branches of a holly bush. He patted the horse and walked away. Garryowen whinnied, but Anthony did not look back and he hoped the bay would settle down and not make too much of a fuss. He climbed over the rocks and emerged on a sharp bend on another track where the hedges either side were overgrown and covered with briars. He checked his bearings. He was correct; this was the road Gully Donovan rode every day.

The snow here was thicker, and harder to walk though. By the time reached where he wanted to go and scrambled up onto the rocks to attach the first wire, he was sweating a little despite the cold.

He found the tree he had selected earlier in the week, slipped his backpack off his shoulder and opened it. Reaching inside, he removed a roll of wire and a pair of pliers. He wound wire around of the thicker branches of the tree, climbed back down and unravelled the spool behind him. On the opposite side of the track, he jumped the briars and the drainage ditch and scaled a small fir tree. He attached the end of the wire to the trunk, hoping he had judged the height correctly, and used the pliars to twist it until it was taut.

Back out on the track he tested the wire, thrumming it his forefinger; there was not a lot of give and for the first time he began to have doubts. He hoped it would not snap under the pressure.

He did not have to wait long. Shortly after noon he heard the unmistakable sound of a horse approaching. He climbed the bank and hid behind a boulder, beneath the first tree he had wired.

Closer and closer came the sound of hooves. Anthony pressed against the boulder, holding his breath. The horse passed beneath where he hid without pausing; he heard the wire twang and snap as snow tumbled from the branches above him and landed on his head and shoulders.

Slowly Anthony stood and looked down.

Gully lay on his back, with one leg bent at an odd angle almost beneath him. He held his right hand to his throat, the left raised above him, his fingers clenching and unclenching, gripping nothing but air. He was making some kind of unintelligible sound and even as Anthony jumped down and approached him, it seemed as though he might get up any second, dust himself off and kick Anthony's arse.

Then Anthony saw the blood, bubbling through Gully's fingers. He pulled off his gloves and squatted down beside him. Gully's eyes widened when he saw him. He opened his mouth to speak, but more blood filled it and spilled down his cheeks into the snow beneath his head. With each blink, Gully's eyes lost a little focus.

'Gully,' Anthony leaned over him. 'Look at me.'

Gully did so.

'I did this.'

Gully grabbed the front of Anthony's coat with his left hand. His fingers twisted, but there was no strength in them. He tried to speak, more blood, crimson and flowing freely dribbled through the savage wound to his throat. Anthony grabbed his wrist and shoved it away.

'I did this for Emma.'

Gully's hand grew weaker, his eyes lost a little focus.'

'I did it for me too.'

Gully stopped moving. He blinked: Anthony watched the light fade from his eyes and then he was dead.

There was no time to waste. Anthony shoved Gully to the lip of the bank and rolled him down the bank into the ditch into the rotten bracken. He snapped off a few fir branches and flung them on top of the body, and kicked the bloodied snow until it dissolved into a mucky paste.

Removing the wire proved to be the most difficult part of the operation. The force of Gully's collision and dug the ties into the trees and for one horrible moment Anthony feared he might have to leave it behind. But he finally managed to undo the knots, bundle everything into the backpack and hike back through the woods, where he hoped Garryowen was waiting for him.

The bay had managed to loosen his reins, but, luckily, he had not wandered far. Anthony threw himself up into the saddle and rode back towards the road. He paused at a stream, flung the wire into it watched it sink without a trace, then turned the bay for home.

Later that afternoon, driving his parent's car, he collected Lucy Green from her home and drove slowly and carefully along the near-deserted roads to Wicklow town. They enjoyed a pint in the Grand Hotel and then stopped in Jack White's for a second. When Anthony dropped Lucy back home, they sat outside her house and talked for a while with the radio playing softly in the background. They kissed and Anthony promised he'd call her the next evening he had off from the pub. When they kissed for the last time, Anthony realised he felt nothing: no anger, no passion, no relief and no guilt.

He tasted Lucy's berry lipstick and thought about Gully Donovan lying in the ditch, his blood congealed beneath him and he felt... nothing.

CHAPTER 56

December 23rd

The day before Christmas Eve, Anthony woke from deep sleep with a sore head and no memory of coming home the night before. The last thing he could recall was losing a game of cards in Lakelands and vomiting on stones somewhere.

He sat up gingerly and pulled on a pair of black jeans covered in…something, and a Metallica T-shirt. He couldn't find his runners anywhere, so he had to go downstairs in his bare feet.

Pat Kinsella and his father were sitting at the kitchen table, drinking tea and eating hearty slices of Christmas cake. The smell of food made Anthony's stomach threaten a rematch of the night before.

'Ah look; there's the boyo now. Happy Christmas to you,' Pat said.

'And many happy returns' Anthony said automatically.

'Is it women or song that has you looking so fragile?'

Pat said this slapping his hand on his thigh. But it was a curiously forced joviality and Anthony wondered what had the two men looking so serious at this hour.

'A little of both maybe.' Jack winked at him over the top of his cup, and Anthony knew Evelyn had been filling his head with talk about Lucy Green. 'Must have been a hell of a night.'

'Aye,' Anthony said filling a cup from the pot and dropping heavily into Margaret's seat by the Aga.

'Where were you?'

'Lakelands.'

'That place must never close. I suppose you've heard what's happened?'

'What's happened about what?'

'Young Donovan's missing. Gully.'

'No one said anything to me about it last night down in the pub,' Anthony said. His voice was steady.

'Seems he went out riding yesterday afternoon and hasn't been seen since.'

'Oh?'

'His horse arrived back in the yard alone.'

Anthony took a sip of his tea. It scalded the roof of his mouth.

'Could have had an accident anywhere,' Pat said. 'Of course that young lad rides like a madman.'

'He does that.'

'Remember that time he jumped the school wall on that grey yoke of his father's?'

'Bloody fool. Could have killed the kids playing in the yard.'

'Some jump all the same.'

'Aye.'

'Well, I hope he's all right. He's not the worst of them.'

Anthony suppressed a comment.

Jack's gaze drifted towards the window. 'It was fierce cold last night. A lot of snow fell. If he's fallen or hurt himself up in those hills, he'd be in a lot of trouble out in that weather.'

'He might have found a bit of shelter, though. Sure them Donovans are used to a bit of hardship. I don't even think there's running water in that cottage of theirs,' Pat Kinsella said.

'Even so,' Jack said. 'He wouldn't be the first to come a cropper up there.'

'No, no and indeed he wouldn't.'

They finished their tea in silence. Anthony tossed the last of his own tea down the sink and left them too it. He showered, dressed and went across the yard to look for Emma. She was not in the barn and he found her lunging Lily in the paddock. The ground was completely covered in snow, except for a track the mare had made and the spot where Emma stood.

'Morning.'

'Hello.'

'How's she getting on?'

'Okay. She bucked once but that was all. Were you out late last night? I did not hear you come in.'

'I was playing cards.'

'Gully Donovan is missing.'

'Dad told me.'

'He has not been seen since yesterday.'

'So I'm told.'

Emma raised the whip and Lily moved from a trot to a canter smoothly. 'It is very cold. If a person was exposed to last night's elements, it is likely he is dead.'

Anthony thought of Gully's eyes, the way his fingers clenched and unclenched as the blood seeped from his body.

'Well, we'll have to wait and see.'

'Yes. We will.'

That afternoon a bitter wind rose and drove heavy, dark clouds, leaden with snow, across the mountains. At three o'clock, a blizzard struck and visibility became so bad Anthony could hardly see from one end of the yard to the other. He called Flicky at four o'clock to see if he was needed for work.

'No, that's okay. Sure there's not much stirring. So much for it being the busiest time of the year, I reckon I'll probably close up early at this rate.'

'Did you hear anything about Gully Donovan?'

'That's a right quare one. Arthur was in here earlier asking if anyone had seen hide or hair of him.'

Anthony looked out the window at the swirling snow.

'Anthony?'

'Yeah?"

'He was asking about you.'

'Me?' Anthony replied, watching Jack struggle across the yard, holding his coat shut. 'Why was he asking about me?'

'He wanted to know what happened the other night between you and Gully.'

'Nothing happened. I didn't want to serve Sean. That's all there was to it.'

'That's what I told him.'

Anthony's scalp prickled. He turned his head and noticed Emma watching him from the stairs.

'I've got to go Flicky. See you tomorrow.'

'If the Gods allow.'

Anthony hung up.

'Stop spying on me.'

He went into the sitting room and turned on the television. At five o'clock the electricity went.

'Well doesn't that beat the band,' he heard Jack say from the kitchen. Moments later Evelyn popped her head around the door, carrying candles.

'Anthony, will do me a favour and run across to the barn and see if we've any oil for the paraffin lamps.'

Anthony pulled on his boots and a jacket, and grabbed a torch. He wrapped a scarf around his neck and pulled a hat down low on his head. He squeezed out the door and barely managed to get it closed. The wind was fierce and filled with ice, and was so cold it made breathing difficult. He had to bend almost double to fight against the howling wind, his journey made more difficult because his boots kept sinking into knee-high snowdrifts.

He made it to the other side of the yard and noticed the barn door leading to the horses' stalls was slightly ajar. He frowned.

Emma would not have left it like that. He entered the barn and switched on his torch to check on the animals. Garryowen's blanket had become twisted somehow, so he rested the torch on the ledge outside his stall and went in to fix it, tugging it higher up his withers and adjusting the straps. He checked that the horse had enough water, and as he turned to leave, his gaze met a snow-encrusted face staring at him from the shadows.

It was Arthur Donovan.

'What are you doing in here?'

'I've been up and down those hills all night and all day,' Donovan said. 'I can't find my boy.'

'Jesus you put the heart crossways in me.'

Donovan stepped closer. His scarred face looked more gaunt and haggard that it had ever been; small particles of ice hung from his eyebrows.

'Andy Delahunt says you've been riding up around our way a lot lately.'

'I ride out near enough every day at the moment. I'm helping my sister. You might have noticed she's not really her normal shape.'

'You and my boy had words in the pub the other night.'

'Aye, me and Gully have a few problems between us.'

'What kind of problems?'

'A clash of personalities.'

Arthur's arms snaked out and, before Anthony had a chance to react, he was dragged out of the stall and slammed against a wooden joist with enough force to rattle his teeth.

'If you're lying about something boy, so help me I'll cut the fucking truth out of you if I have to.'

'Get off me, I don't know anything. Maybe he decided to leave Killbragh.'

'You're lying.'

'I'm telling you I don't–'

'Get your hands off him,' Jack's voice boomed.

Arthur let him go, but his eyes never left his face.

'What the hell do you think you're playing at?' Jack appeared, shining a torch into Arthur's face. 'What are you doing here Arthur? What's going on?'

'This boy of yours knows more than he's letting on.'

'What are you saying? Are you accusing Anthony of something?'

'Gully,' Arthur pointed to the snow swirling beyond the barn door, 'is out there somewhere and God alone knows what's happened to him. I need to know where he is. I need to bring him home.'

'Jesus Christ, Arthur. Look, I know you're upset. I'll help you search for him when the weather breaks, but you can't go around accusing people of…whatever you think. Anthony doesn't have anything to do with him being missing.'

'They had words in the bar. Everyone heard it.'

'For God's sake, haven't we all had rows and fights in our time. That means nothing.'

Arthur pushed past Jack and made his way to the door. When he reached it, he turned to look back at Anthony, his face half hidden beneath his hood.

'You mark my words, if anything has happened to my son, you will be the first one I come calling for.'

The worst of the storm blew itself out sometime during the night. But the following morning, Christmas Eve, the resident of Killbragh awoke to find that most of the roads surrounding the village were impassable.

Unfortunately for Jack, Evelyn needed some last minute supplies for the Christmas dinner, so he was dispatched to the village on the tractor. Anthony cadged a lift with him as soon he heard where his father was going, unable to bear another day in the house cooped up and wondering about Gully.

They pulled into Larry Green's petrol station to stock up on gas cylinders and coal. Larry, his nose as red as the scabby-looking holly wreath hung from his door, came out to watch them load the coal onto the trailer without offering to help.

Anthony scanned the petrol station window, but there was no sign of Lucy.

'Cold day, by God.'

'It is that,' Jack replied. 'How did you get in from Arklow? I thought the roads were bad everywhere.'

'I didn't. I had to get Flicky to put me up for the night. I'll be keeping a close eye on it today.'

'Forecast has it coming in around four o'clock.'

Anthony flung the last sack of coal up onto the trailer and glanced at the sky. Judging by the clouds, it would be coming in sooner than that.

'Still no sign of Arthur's lad?' Jack was asking.

'No. Divil a sign. And if he was out in that last night, he's surely a goner.' Larry waved his hands toward the expanse of white beyond his yard. 'There's a meeting at the Community Centre at ten. We're going to try and organise a search party.'

'Is that so? I'll come down myself.'

'The more the merrier, Jack. My God isn't it an awful thing? Especially at this time of year.'

'Dad,' Anthony interrupted, 'I'm going to head over to the pub.'

'Go on ahead,' Jack said, before turning back to Larry.

Anthony stuck his hands into his pockets and hurried across the street to Lakelands.

Flicky was standing at the bar when he entered, eating a toasted ham and cheese sandwich, gloomily listening to the weather forecast on the radio. The fire was blazing in the hearth, making the room smell of turf. Two of the regulars sat at the end of the bar, their clothes gently steaming, half-finished pints of Guinness standing on the counter in front of them.

'Good morning Anthony.'

'What's good about it?'

Flicky glanced at him. 'You all right? You look terrible.'

'I didn't sleep too well.'

Flicky rolled his eyes. 'Oh aye, there's coffee on. Make sure you grab a cup while you have the chance. It's going to be a long day.'

Anthony slipped past him and hurried upstairs to hang up his coat. In the short time it took him to do that, Ivan Harte had arrived into the bar, with Martin trailing behind him.

'Bitter out there today,' Ivan said to Flicky, pulling out a stool and sitting on it.

'I'm dreaming of a White Christmas,' Flicky sang, as he reached under the counter for two pint glasses. 'Pint lads, or is it too early?'

'Never too early for a drop of the black.' Ivan rubbed his hands together. 'We won't be stopping long though. I need to drop the messages home first before we come back in for the search.'

'Arthur's lad?' Flicky grimaced, as he poured. 'A bad business all round that. I hope he's found.'

Anthony bent and unloaded the dishwasher. As he took the glasses out of the tray and placed them on a shelf, he became aware that Martin was watching him, following his every move.

'I believe the horse arrived back safe and sound without a scratch on him' Flicky said.

'It's a queer one. Arthur says he's scoured the route Gully usually rode, but there's no sign of him anywhere. It's like he vanished into thin air.'

'Something happened to him,' Martin said, his gaze on Anthony. 'Gully knows the hills up there like the back of his hand; there's no way he could have got lost.'

'He wouldn't be the first, not in this kind of weather,' Ivan said, taking a sip of his pint, then licking the creamy froth from his upper lip.

'We'll find him,' Martin said, 'and when we do, we'll know soon enough what happened.'

Anthony filled the detergent section of the machine and snapped the door shut.

CHAPTER 58

Throughout that morning, men drifted into the bar wearing warm clothes and dour expressions. They carried sticks and poles and a number of them had left their dogs tied to the railings outside the door while they were in the pub. Outside, the sky looked as though it hung mere inches above the trees; by ten o'clock, the temperature struggled to reach two below freezing.

Anthony stepped outside to grab some fresh air and have a smoke. He surveyed the scene. Jeeps and tractors lined the village street; inside the myriad vehicles, dogs barked with excitement. The bar continued to empty as quickly as it filled – an endless procession of searchers toing and froing between it and the small community centre nearby.

When he could bear the cold no longer, Anthony returned inside, where Flicky asked him to look after the bar while he joined some of the searchers in the community centre. Flicky was standing near a radiator in the centre, warming his hands when Jack and Pat walked in and joined him.

'How are we men?' Flicky said.

'Good enough,' Pat said, swivelling his eyes around the room. 'Big crowd.'

'Ah for a thing like this? Couldn't be any other way.'

Arthur Donovan stood to the left of the raised platform that often doubled as a stage, talking to Jim Breen, the heavy-set local detective sergeant from the neighbouring village. Two other guards from a different station stood by the door to the kitchenette sipping tea and nibbling on sandwiches provided by the wives of some of the searchers.

Arthur looked tired and gaunt. Pat muttered to Flicky that he had been up since early that morning, searching the hills until it got too dangerous to do so. As well as having to contend with thick snow, a dense freezing fog had descended, reducing visibility to almost nothing. It did not need to be said by anybody that as each hour passed, hopes of finding Gully alive reduced considerably.

Jim Breen walked to the front of the room and cleared his throat.

'Folks, it's good of everyone to have come out on a day like this. We're fighting against time and weather conditions. The forecast is not good and we've got confirmation that another blizzard is heading our way later this afternoon. As we know, the snow is likely to come down thick and fast, so the last thing we want is anyone getting stranded or lost. So, we're going to stick in groups of five or six. We'll take four by fours up as far as possible and comb our way across the west side of the hill. Bray Search and Rescue have sent us down a number of dogs that we will be using. I want those of you who brought your own animals to keep a tight rein on them; don't let them be more of a hindrance than a help. Okay, let's get moving while we can.'

Together with the other guards he divided the local men into groups, making sure each had a guard with a working walkie-talkie. By eleven o'clock, the groups were filing out of centre and heading for various transport vehicles.

Jack and Pat walked down the street towards Pat's jeep, with Flicky and Sam Delaney in tow.

'We'll hopefully find him today,' Pat said, eyeing the clouds.

'Aye, there's drifts nearly five feet high at my place,' Sam said. 'Imagine what it's like up on Creen's Face.'

Ivan Harte walked behind Pat's group with Martin, Robert, his brother-in-law and Andy Delahunt. Ivan raised his hand and waved at Pat, who returned the gesture.

Anthony watched them from the window of the pub. Ivan's group had a number of dogs with them: two shepherd crosses, a wire-haired German pointer, and on the end of a leash held by Martin, a chocolate brown Labrador. The Labrador wore a green collar and from it hung a rusted lock.

Anthony jerked back from the window and walked stiffly back behind the bar.

Charlie Barr, who was too old and infirm to join the search, glanced at him and narrowed his eyes. 'What's wrong with you lad? You look like you've seen a ghost.'

'Oh, it's nothing,' Anthony said, 'I'm grand.'

But he was not grand, and when Lucy Green popped her head into the bar to say hello, he dragged her into one of the snugs and shut the door.

'Whoa tiger,' Lucy said, extracting her arm from his grasp with a laugh 'Are you sure you want it to be so public?'

'I was…have you heard about Gully?'

'Of course I have. Sure wasn't it on the radio and everything this morning'

'Him and Martin, they were good friends, weren't they?'

'*Are* good friends, Anthony,' she said. 'You're talking like he's dead and buried.'

'Do they go out hunting together?'

'Anthony, what's going on, why are you acting like this? We broke up, okay? It's over between me and him.'

'Will you answer me?'

'Stop. You're scaring me.'

'I'm sorry…I'm just…things are a bit weird right now, okay? I'm…I'm not myself.'

'I think I'd better go.'

'Okay.'

She looked hurt. 'Okay? Is that it?'

'What did you want me to say?'

'Nothing, don't bother saying anything at all.'

She picked up her bag.

'And yes, they do go out hunting together. It's one of the many reasons we broke up. He never stopped bloody going on about shooting things.'

Up on Creen's Face, search and rescue groups fanned the hillside. But long before they had even reached the upper tree line, clouds descended and it began to snow again. By two-thirty, visibility was reduced to less than ten feet and Dessie Lynch, Larry's brother, had fallen and twisted his ankle. Shortly before three the garda walkie-talkies crackled and everyone was ordered to return to the village

Arthur Donovan remained on the old quarry road after the last person had left, his expression stony, his face blue from the cold. It was his son, Sean, who finally managed to persuade him to return to the truck, but when he walked, he walked like a broken man.

CHAPTER 59

On Christmas morning the Byrne family got up early to exchange gifts, as they had done ever since the children had been old enough to escape from their cots.

Anthony stood at the kitchen window, looking out. It was snowing heavier than ever, and no let-up was forecast for another day at least.

'It's so pretty isn't it?' Evelyn said, mistaking his silence for contemplation.

'Mmm.'

'I do not see what is pretty about snow. It will be difficult to ride in,' Emma said, stacking her new books in order, based on her assessment of their readability.

'Maybe you should let them horses have a day off,' Margaret said, smiling because the book that she had given Emma as a Christmas present was top of the reading pile.

'Why give them a day off?'

'Because it's Christmas.'

'They do not know that.'

'Emma, it's too cold to be out with the horses today,' Evelyn said, taking out the frying pan and wiping it with a piece of dripping.

Emma scowled. 'I do not like snow.'

'Remember the big snow in '82?' Jack asked. 'High as the ditches it was, and we had to buy in condensed milk.'

'We may have to do that this time around too, if we don't go easy on it,' Evelyn said, smiling at him.

'I'm not the one who has to have hot chocolate every night before she goes to bed.'

'Oh do you hear that?'

Anthony tuned out their chatter. He felt cold: no matter where he was in the house, he felt chilled. He had not slept well again the night before. Every time he closed his eyes he thought of Gully, and wondered if he had made a terrible mistake. He thought of the Labrador. He thought of Martin Harte's watchful expression. He thought of the body, lying up there in the ditch, frozen under the falling snow.

When the phone rang, he tensed, waiting for what he now felt was the inevitable.

'It's for you,' Jack said, stepping in from the hall with a smile. 'A girl.'

Anthony rose unsteadily, took the receiver from his father, stepped into the hall and closed the kitchen door. He took a breath before he spoke.

'Hello.'

'It's me, Lucy.'

He did not reply, so after a moment she began to speak again.

'Look, is everything all right? The other day… you were acting so strange and I–'

'Everything's fine.'

'Anthony, you know you can talk to me, right? About anything.'

'There's nothing to talk about. I told you, everything's fine.' He made a half turn, caught his reflection in the hall mirror and quickly looked away.

'When will I see you again?'

'I don't know. I've a lot going on at the moment.'

'Oh.'

'To be honest I think it's better if we, if we just leave things as they are…at the moment.'

'I see.' Her voice trembled. 'I suppose I've only myself to blame, sure I practically forced you to go out with me.'

'You didn't force me to do anything.'

'I really thought you liked me.'

Anthony leaned his forehead against the wall, and felt his shoulders sag under the weight of it all.

'I like you…but I can't do this right now.'

'Anthony–'

He hung up before she could say anything more, and waited. She did not call back. It was done.

He went back to the kitchen, ignoring the knowing looks his parents exchanged between them. Bless them, he thought, they haven't a clue.

'Emma,' he said. ' Look, it's stopped snowing.'

She looked up from her book. 'What?'

'The snow, it's stopped.'

'Oh.' She glanced out the window. 'Yes.'

'Want to take a soft ride? We can lead some of the horses out.'

'They will like that.'

'I don't want you riding today,' Evelyn said, glaring at Anthony for even suggesting such a thing. 'It's not safe.'

'We'll be walking the horses. It's hardly riding.'

'It's freezing outside.'

'Exercise keeps you warm,' Emma said, rising from her chair a little awkwardly.

'Jack, will you talk sense to the pair of them.'

'Dad, we're just going to walk the horses out and back. It means we'll exercise the lot of them in one go and have the rest of the day free.'

Jack sighed, as Anthony knew he would. Appeals to logic flummoxed his father. 'Well. If you're careful, I don't see–'

'Oh for God's sake,' Evelyn said and went back to stuffing the turkey using more force than was absolutely necessary.

Jack picked up his newspaper and retreated behind it.

'Go do what you want,' Evelyn said, 'but don't come running to me when you catch your death.'

'Why must people say that? People do not catch death,' Emma said, stamping across the snow to the stables. 'They catch sickness, and death is the outcome. For that matter, if we did *catch* death, we would certainly not be running anywhere.'

'Figure of speech,' Anthony said.

'Yes …well, I do not understand the expression at all.'

They tacked Lily and Garryowen and threw head collars on the other four, taking two horses each.

As they rode, Anthony was acutely aware that the countryside was absent of birdsong or other sounds, the silence punctuated by an occasional snort from one of the horses. It felt as though he and Emma were the last two people on earth. About a mile from the house Emma said.

'You talk in your sleep. Do you know that?'

Anthony was surprised. 'No, I didn't know that.'

'You call out and you cry.'

'I see.' He rode on for a moment.

'Last night I heard you crying. You were talking about Gully Donovan.'

'Oh?'

'Yes.'

'Well, he's…everyone's talking about him at the moment, it's probably my subconscious acting the maggot.'

Emma stopped Lily and the other horses fell into line beside her. 'I am not stupid Anthony. I have a condition, but I am not stupid.'

'Jesus, I know that. I know you're not stupid. Sometimes I think you might just be the smartest person I know.'

'I have been thinking about things. I have anxiety because I think you know what happened to Gully Donovan.'

Anthony stared at her. 'What the hell makes you think that?'

'Garryowen was very tired and you were gone for a long time. Longer than it would take you to ride the route you said you had taken. Garryowen had holly in his tail. I saw it when I groomed him. There is no holly by the river.'

'So what …so you think I did something to Gully Donovan over some fucking holly in a horse's tail? Holy shit Sherlock Holmes, your talents are wasted.'

'You wear a guilty face all the time when no one is looking.' Emma lifted her head and did something she rarely did. She looked at him square in the face. 'Did you kill Gully Donovan?'

'No, I did not.'

Her eyes never left his. 'You are lying.'

She wheeled Lily to the right and began to trot her back the way they had come.

Anthony turned his own horses and rode after her. 'Wait. Why do you even care what happened to that prick?'

'I do not, I care about what happens to you.'

'He hurt you.'

'He did not.'

'What, what are you saying? You remember what happened to you now?'

'Yes.'

Anthony felt sick to his stomach. Even though he knew, having it confirmed was like a punch to the gut. 'Then it wasn't Gully Donovan?'

'No,' Emma said, pressing Lily on a little faster, 'it was not.'

Two days after Christmas, the temperature rose slightly and it began to rain. All morning Anthony sat, listening to the rain beating on widows slumped on the sofa, watching television with Margaret. The rain changed everything: it would only be matter of time now before Gully's body was found.

'Lying up there all that time,' Ivan Harte said, ordering his second pint in Lakelands that night. 'Eddie Yates told me they had to stretcher him down the mountain because the ambulance couldn't make it up through the mud.'

'Any idea what happened?'

'Nah, but had to have been an accident of some kind.'

'Excuse me,' Anthony said. He headed to the men's toilets and sat in one of the two cubicles for a few minutes. As soon as he felt a little bit more composed, he opened the door and washed his hands, letting the water run over his wrists until he could bear the cold no longer.

The next day the entire village was talking about the discovery. Speculation was rampant: he'd been shot some said, attacked by Travellers, struck by lightning, thrown from the horse. Then news began to circulate about the injuries some members of the search team had reported seeing on the body, local talk of gunshot wounds, lightning strikes and the rest receded, and people began to openly speculate about the possibility of murder.

Anthony listened for whatever scraps of information he could glean. Squad cars drove through the village, heading for Creen's Face; endless photographs were taken and the State Pathologist was spotted. By the weekend everyone in the village had an opinion and everyone a suspect in mind.

Anthony was so on edge he barely ate or slept.

'Ever since he broke up with that girl, he's been in an awful state,' Evelyn said.

'Time will heal a broken heart,' Jack responded with a sigh.

'It's funny, I didn't even think they were that serious to begin with.'

Anthony tried to talk to Emma, but she shunned him at every turn. This caused even more curiosity in the Byrne household than did his hollow eyes and his pallor.

'What's going on with those two?' Evelyn would ask no one in particular after another silent lunch.

Anthony rose, worked, went to the bar, came home and slept fitfully, exhausted but terrified that he would talk in his sleep. His waking hours were spent listening to the endless rehashing of events and speculation. He lost weight and found it hard to concentrate on even simple tasks. Flicky noticed and tried some gentle prodding, but was met with a stone wall. What could Anthony tell him? That he had killed the wrong man? That he was guilty of cold-blooded murder?

'Had to be someone who knew the terrain up there fairly well,' the old fellas sitting at the bar in Lakelands said.

'Maybe he was carrying on with someone? Remember his mother?' the women in the shop whispered. 'The apple never falls far from the tree.'

The guards questioned everyone and anyone "of interest".

Anthony was not surprised to find he was on that list.

'I hear,' Jim Breen said, taking off his cap and laying it on the table before Anthony, 'there was no love lost between the pair of you.'

Anthony shrugged, decided to aim for the truth. 'He was a bully. I never liked him.'

Breen leaned back in his chair and studied him. Anthony stared back. He would not offer up any information that was not asked of him. Years of living with Emma had taught him how to play *that* game well enough, in fact, far better than most people.

'I'm told you wouldn't serve him in the bar before Christmas,' Breen said after almost three minutes of silence had elapsed.

'I had no problem serving *him*. It was his fifteen-year-old brother I wouldn't serve. Gully had a problem with me telling him that, but then my boss made the decision for all concerned.'

'Very conscientious of you.'

Anthony said nothing.

'I *hear* you had a run-in with someone yourself not too long before that evening. Had a few cuts and scrapes,' Breen said staring at him levelly.

'That's right.'

'Care to tell me what happened?'

'I was attacked in a car park in Arklow. Look Sergeant, what has that got to do with anything?'

'Did you report it?'

'No.'

'Why not?'

'What was I going to say? Sure I hardly got a look at them.'

'Them?'

'Aye, there were two of them, I think.'

Breen eased his considerable bulk back in the chair. He had a way of tilting his head to the side, as though he could hear a sound from far away: it made Anthony feel very uncomfortable.

'So you had a couple of run-ins with Gully then?'

'When we were growing up, but then I'd say so did everyone else. He was indiscriminate when it came to bullying people.'

'So he bullied you?'

'I told you he did – me and anyone smaller than him. If you don't believe me ask around.'

'You've got a reputation as a bit of a hothead yourself.'

'Me?' Anthony laughed. 'I don't think so. I'm the last person who wants to get into a brawl.'

'So you didn't head-butt Martin Harte in Lakelands, almost breaking his nose?'

'Did he say that?'

'He did.'

'Accident. Ask anyone in the bar.'

'How do you accidently head-butt someone?'

They played the waiting game for a few more minutes.

'The day of the twenty-second of December …you were out riding that morning I believe?'

'I ride out a bit at the moment, I'm helping out my sister.'

'Ah yes, your sister. I noticed her earlier, outside. Shy sort of a young one. Gifted lady I believe.'

Anthony did not reply.

'So where did you ride?'

'Down along the river, loping back to the farm.'

'People saw you?'

'They must have, I'm sure I passed plenty of people.'

'Do you remember any of them?'

'Not off the top of my head.'

'And then what did you do?'

'I came home, untacked my horse, hosed him down, gave my sister a hand feeding the other horses, had a shower, changed, borrowed Dad's car, picked up my girlfriend, went to the Grand Hotel in Wicklow, then Jack White's. Came home, dropped off the car, met up with my friend Mark and played some cards. Had a few drinks. Came home and went to bed.'

'That's very concise.'

Anthony shrugged. 'That's what I did.'

'Do you know of anyone who might want to hurt Gully Donovan?'

'Hurt him, sure, kill him, no.'

'Can anyone verify what time you arrived back home?'

'My parents were not at home, but my grandmother was.'

'What about your sister?'

'My sister's not great with time.'

'I'll want to talk to her.'

'I'd rather you didn't bother her.'

'You'd *rather?*'

'My sister finds it incredibly difficult to talk to strangers.'

'Even so,' said Breen, closing his notebook and standing up. 'I might want to talk to you again too, Anthony.'

'I'll either be here, Sergeant, or at Lakelands Bar.'

'You take care now.'

'Will do.'

Breen walked out of the kitchen and found Evelyn in the hall, pretending to dust a few ornaments, though it was pretty obvious she was waiting to have a private word with him. 'Was he able to help you at all?'

'No, not really.'

'It's so terrible. I feel so sorry for Arthur. It makes me sick to my stomach to think of the poor lad lying up there all that time, and especially over Christmas.'

'Anthony tells me your daughter does not relate well to people.'

Evelyn put down the duster. 'Some days she's more communicative than others.'

'I'd like to talk to her if that's all right?'

'You don't need my permission. But why would you need to speak to her?'

'I'm talking to everyone.'

'But Emma wouldn't have any notion about Gully Donovan's death. I doubt that she even knows who the lad is.'

'Didn't they go to school together?'

'That wouldn't make a blind bit of difference to Emma.'

Breen smiled. 'It's amazing what little things people know without even realising it.'

'Well, she's across the yard there. But, just so that you know, she might not speak to you at all.'

'Thank you.'

Breen left the house and entered the barn; a number of horses gazed at him curiously. A girl with strawberry blonde hair was cleaning out the hooves of a dark brown horse. He approached and stood a few feet away, waiting for her to acknowledge him. When she did not do so, he cleared his throat loudly.

'Emma Byrne?'

He waited for her to respond or acknowledge his presence in some way but she just put one hoof down on the ground and then lifted another.

'They've got very big feet,' he said after a moment.

'Not in relation to their size,' she replied. Her voice, he was surprised to discover, was deep and pleasant on the ear.

'I'm Detective Inspector Jim Breen. Do you know why I am here?'

Emma dropped the hoof and straightened up. She pressed her left hand against the small of her back and glanced at him, not quite making eye contact. Breen was surprised to see she was pregnant.

'You are here to ask about Gully Donovan.'

'That's right. Did you know him?"

'Yes.'

'Well?'

'Well?'

'No. I mean did you know him well?'

'He was in my primary school.'

'You know he was found dead, right? Possibly murdered.'

'Yes. My father told me.'

'How do you feel about that?'

She frowned. 'I don't know.'

Breen took off his hat and scratched his head. This was proving more difficult that he could have imagined.

'How about your brother…did he know him well?'

'I do not know.'

'He must have known him well enough. He said Gully used to bully him.'

'Yes.'

'You knew about that?'

'Yes. He hit Anthony in the stomach one day. He was angry, always angry.'

'What did your brother do when he was hit?'

'He fell down.'

'No…I mean what did he do afterwards?'

'He walked home.'

The horse sighed and nuzzled the back of Emma's neck.

'The day Gully went missing, your brother rode out of here didn't he?'

'Yes.'

'Do you know how long he was gone?'

'No. I do not. I am not good with time.'

Breen nodded. 'I hear you're something of a genius with horses. Must be tough going with all the manual work involved.'

'My father helps, Anthony too.'

'That's good. He's a good brother.'

'Yes.' She raised her eyes to his for a split second. 'He is.'

'Well, I'd better let you get back to it. It was nice to meet you Emma.'

He walked back to the squad car where Garda Bernadette Galvin was waiting behind the steering wheel.

'How did it go?'

'They're all cracked if you ask me.' Breen took off his hat and stashed it on the dashboard. 'But the boy interests me, he reminds me of a duck on water.'

'A duck, Sergeant?'

'Calm on the surface; paddling furiously below.' He scowled. 'You're from around here Bernie. Do you know that young one, Emma?'

'Only by reputation Sergeant, and, from what I gather, she keeps pretty much to herself. I…' Bernadette hesitated.

'What is it?'

'They say she's got a gift.'

'What sort of gift?'

'Animals Sergeant, she can read them…or something to that effect.'

'She *reads* them?'

Bernie shrugged. 'I don't know. I'm only saying what I hear. She works with horses now mostly. Doesn't deal with people hardly at all.'

'Tell me this Bernie, how does a girl who barely communicates with people manage to get herself pregnant?'

'She must have found some way of expressing her wants and needs, Sergeant.'

'Do we know who the father is?'

Bernie shrugged.

'Out with it.'

'There's some talk that it's Dody Molloy.'

'How do I know that name?'

'He owns Sliabh Rua Stud. Emma's father put him in the hospital a while ago, but he didn't press charges.'

'Hmm,' Breen said, thinking again of Anthony's calm, buttoned-down exterior. 'Let's go have a chat with him.'

Pete was emptying sacks of feed pellets into large plastic drums when Ruby started to bark. He looked out the door and sighed when he saw the squad car pull into the yard. He folded the plastic bag, stacked it on top all the other bags and went out to meet the occupants.

'Morning.'

'Does he bite?' a big uniformed guard asked from the passenger seat, eyeing Ruby up with naked fear. Pete recognised him from the Community Centre, the day they organised the search party. What was he called? Sheen, Breen?

'She, and no she doesn't. Ruby, give over.' Ruby stopped barking instantly.

'I can't say I like dogs,' the guard said, 'especially big loud ones.'

'That's funny, mate. It's usually the small quiet ones you need to watch out for.'

The guard hauled himself out of the car using the roof as leverage. He put on his hat and extended his hand. 'Detective Sergeant Jim Breen.'

'Pete Cartwright.'

'I saw you at the search party.'

'That's right.'

'I was wondering if we could have a chat.'

'No problem. Do you want a cup of coffee?'

'No, I'm fine thank you.'

He seemed reluctant to travel too far from the car.

'I was over at the Byrne's home yesterday. I hear you're a good friend of theirs. Especially their daughter.'

Pete's facial expression did not change, but Breen noticed the flint in his eyes.

'Oh we're *friends*, friends and work colleagues.'

'I understand Emma used to work here.'

'That's right.'

'I spoke to her…friend, Dody, yesterday too. You know Jack Byrne put him in the hospital a while back?'

Pete lit a cigarette. 'Look. Is there something you wanted to talk to me about Sergeant? Because half the morning is gone and I've near enough a dozen horses that want seeing to.'

Breen raised his eyebrows and looked a bit taken aback. 'Have I said something wrong?'

'I'm saying Emma's business is Emma's business and no one else's. Not mine, not Dody Molloy's and it's certainly no business of yours.'

'Fair enough. What can you tell me about Arthur Donovan? I heard you had a number of run-ins with him over the years.'

'Heard that, did yer?'

'You knocked him down at a horse market in front of a lot of people.'

'What of it?'

'He deserved it then?'

'He did.'

'You know everyone I've talked to seems to have much the same feelings for that family.'

'Well, they're a type aren't they?'

'A type?'

Pete blew two jets of smoke through his nostrils. 'People like Arthur Donovan would rob the sight out of your eye, sell you the guide dog, then mock you for being blind. I don't like Arthur and, for that matter, I wasn't overly fond of young Gully either, but that's neither here nor there. Nobody would wish on Arthur what he's going through now. You saw how many people turned out to help.'

'I did indeed,' Breen glanced at Ruby again. 'But someone wished Gully more than just harm, Mr Cartwright, and someone carried out that wish.'

'Is it true how he died? Someone garrotted him?'

Breen shrugged. 'It was a cold-blooded act, with *plenty* of malice aforethought.'

'By God, I can tell you now I don't know anyone like that, and I sure as hell don't want to.'

'Or maybe you do and you don't realise it.'

Pete shook his head. 'You'd know. You'd *have* to know. How would someone be able to keep something like that to themselves for long?'

'How indeed,' Breen said. 'You know, maybe I will take you up on the offer of the coffee.'

Anthony walked to Lakelands for his evening shift. Although it was only three o'clock, there was hardly any daylight left, and the temperature was dropping steadily. He replayed Breen's interview over and over in his mind. Breen wasn't stupid, that much was obvious. He also knew from the questions Breen had asked him that more than one person had been talking about his and Gully's shared animosity.

He kicked a stone and watched it skip across the road and vanish into the weeds. Was it possible they'd found something on Gully's body? Some trace of him? Did Breen know more than he was letting on? Why had he been asking people about Emma?

Absorbed in his thoughts, he failed to register a jeep as it drove past, but he could not fail to notice when it whipped into the ditch a few yards ahead of him and Martin Harte jumped out and confronted him.

'You think you've got away with it, don't you?' Martin got right into Anthony's face, jabbing him in the chest with his finger. 'But you won't get away with this, I *know* you did it.'

Anthony slapped Martin's hand away and yanked open the door of the jeep. The Labrador he'd seen with Martin on the day of the search jumped out.

'You know Martin,' Anthony said, 'I always knew you were a gutless fucking piece of shite, but I never realised just how low you can get.'

He clicked his fingers at the dog and the animal approached, wagging its tail furiously between its legs.

'What are you talking about?' Martin asked.

'I mean Gully was a bollox and a bully, but at least Gully would come at you head on. Not like you.' Anthony grabbed the dog by the scruff of the neck so hard it yelped.

'Get your hands off my dog.'

Anthony ignored him and undid the dog's collar. He stood up and waved it in Martin's face. 'Green with a rusted lock. That's exactly what Emma said she remembered. This is the dog that licked her face the day she was raped.'

Martin stared at him. Anthony noticed he had lost some of his cocksureness.

'Nothing to say?' Anthony shrugged. 'Funny that.'

'I don't know what you're talking about.'

'I wonder how long it will take people to put two and two together once Emma's baby is born? I wonder what kind of hair it will have? I wonder will it have black hair? I wonder will it have dimples?' He took a step closer. 'I wonder will it look like a Byrne... or a Harte?

'You shut your face.' Martin looked scared and angry. 'You don't know what you're talking about.'

'Oh I know all right, you raped an unconscious girl and shot her horse. You're scum, Harte, and soon everyone is going to know it.'

Martin snatched the dog collar out of his hand and tried to walk back to the jeep, but Anthony grabbed him and spun him around.

'You're a thief and a fucking low-life.' Anthony spat in his face and wiped his mouth with the back of his hand. 'But you're going to suffer for what you did. When I'm finished with you, even your own family wouldn't piss on you if you were on fire.'

CHAPTER 62

Emma carefully unwrapped Garryowen's legs and checked his tendons, running her thumb and forefinger down each side his fetlock, checking for any sign of heat or swelling. He wasn't lame exactly, but she'd noticed he was favouring his right side earlier that afternoon, as she was working him over poles in the arena. It was always better to be safe than sorry.

She put his foot down, straightened it and felt a twinge in her right side so sharp, she had to lean against Garryowen and take a number of deep breaths until it passed. She waited for a moment or two, but the pain did not return.

She rubbed the top of Garryowen's ears with her fingertips. He grunted with pleasure.

'Your new owner will be here tomorrow,' she told him. 'You can show her everything you've learned. She will be very happy with you. It is possible she will feed you those mint sweets you like.'

Garryowen lifted his head and nibbled at her face. Emma patted the arch of his neck. She was not overly sentimental about her charges, but she liked this gelding a lot. He was gentle and kind and honest, the sort of horse she would like to own herself someday.

She returned him to his stable and rugged him up. She checked the horses had enough water, switched off the lights and made her way across the yard to the house.

She ate a dinner of spaghetti and cheese with Jack and Evelyn and afterwards she read Margaret a story from *Ireland's*

Own. Margaret's eyesight was failing, and she slept a lot more, like Shep had done just before he died, Emma thought. These nights, her grandmother always waited for Emma to pick a story. She hoped Margaret wouldn't die. She had grown used to the old lady's presence, and she quite liked reading to her before she sat down to work on her own book. She found the time that the two of them spent alone together soothing.

She had categorised the notes for her book on horses at last, and she now spent most evenings transcribing them into a foolscap jotter. Evelyn, who could type and who owned an ancient typewriter, had offered to type them out for her, but Emma declined. Instead, she bought a second hand Amstrad word processor and taught herself to type. She found it easy.

That evening, Emma worked on her book for a while. The chapter she was writing was important: she was trying to convey how horses, being herd animals, are conditioned to seek out company, and that humans could use this to their advantage.

She had rewritten that particular section numerous times, but each time she read it back, the language came across as stilted, the factual content inaccurate. It was, she complained to Evelyn, almost impossible to translate her thoughts into something other people might enjoy reading.

A few minutes before ten o'clock, she stopped writing and made herself a cup of hot chocolate in the kitchen. She sat drinking it, watching Evelyn and Jack playing Pontoon for a while. She liked to watch them play cards. She liked their "poker faces" – a strange saying, as they were not playing poker, and one that made no sense to her at all. Card games in general made no sense to her. Jack had tried to teach her countless times but she always forgot the rules or mixed up the different games.

At ten-fifteen she picked up a torch and put on her coat. Jack offered to check the horses for her, but she said no, she wanted to do it herself.

She went to bed not long after that and was asleep within minutes.

When next she woke, the large, luminous dial on her alarm clock read 1.25 am. Evelyn had told her that waking up frequently during the night was not an unusual thing, as the baby was probably pressing on her bladder.

She got up and went to the bathroom. On the way back to her room she heard one of the horses in the barn whinny and she recognised it as a worried sound. The moon was out, and Emma could see from the landing window that the barn door was open. She had shut it before she went to bed.

Making the minimum of noise, so as not to wake anyone in the house, she dressed and put on a pair of boots. She made her way downstairs, grabbed her coat and stepped out onto the cobbles. She made her way across the yard, entered the barn and flicked the light switch inside the door.

Lily was awake and pacing around her stall. Garryowen too.

Emma frowned. Something was not right.

There was blood on the ground by her feet, a dark red splash, then another, and then another. She followed the blood trail to the rear of the barn. She realised her heart was beating very fast. Moving quietly, she checked on each horse as she made her way to the rear. All were present and accounted for.

She heard movement from the tack room. Taking a deep breath she edged closer to the door and peered inside. Anthony was sitting on the floor with his back against the blanket box. His legs were sticking out straight and he had his hands in his lap. He was breathing in a ragged way and there was dark blood on his hands and on his mouth.

'Anthony?'

He moved his head slowly. His skin was extremely pale and he looked slack-jawed and disorientated. Emma went over to him and kneeled beside him.

'What has happened? You are hurt.'

'I made a tactical error.'

His voice did not sound as it usually did. It was weak and scratchy and it made her feel afraid.

'An error?'

'Cockiness I suppose, or stupidity. Maybe both.

'I do not understand.'

'Cornered rats are dangerous.' He coughed and blood stained his lips and chin.

'I will go get Dad. He can help you.'

'No. Listen to me. Stop being afraid of me. I would never hurt you. Please…don't leave me.'

She manoeuvred herself into a more comfortable position and sat beside him on the floor. 'Your blood is very dark. That is bad. Like the time the Flannery's dog got hit by the milk truck.'

'It's okay. I don't mind.'

'Who did this to you?'

'Martin Harte. He was waiting for me after my shift ended.'

'Is he dead?'

'No. I don't think so.'

'Anthony–'

'No, shut up, Emma. I need you to listen to me. You've got to tell them he attacked you.' He closed his eyes for a moment. 'You're not safe.'

'I am safe here.'

'You're *not*. He won't risk you telling people. Emma please, listen to me. He will hurt you. He might even hurt Mam and Dad.'

Emma pulled her legs under her as much as her bump would allow and crossed her arms over her knees. 'I am sorry you are hurt.'

'Me too.'

She shook her head. 'I wish it was not so.'

'If wishes were horses.'

'I do not understand that expression.'

'Actually… me neither.'

She looked at him; his voice was growing fainter and there was more blood coming from his mouth. 'Anthony. I will get help.'

'No.'

'But you are bleeding.'

'Please… stay with me, I don't want to be alone.'

Emma cracked her knuckles one after another. All her life she had done everything her bother had told her to do. But she knew this was different: this was bad. She knew she had to go get help. She knew she had to do something.

She took off her coat and put it over him. 'I suspect you have shock. You are white and you tremble. Shock is very dangerous.'

Anthony barked a laugh. His eyes were half closed; his heavy lashes glistening with tears. 'I've been thinking a lot recently, about us.'

'Us?'

'I think people have got it all wrong. When we were kids I used to hate you because you weren't like everyone else, because you didn't know stuff like me. Now I think I had it backwards all along.'

'I do not understand.'

'That's okay. You don't have to. It's okay… because I get it now.'

'You are not making sense.'

'It's okay. I get…it.'

He closed his eyes. Emma shook his shoulder but he wouldn't wake up.

Emma sprang to her feet and ran for the house as hard as she could. She burst in through the front door and ran up the stairs to her parents' bedroom.

'Wake up!'

Jack snapped on the light and sat up in bed.

'What is it? What's wrong? Is it the baby?'

'Anthony has dark blood in his mouth and I know that is bad because I saw that with the Flannery's dog when he was hit by the milk truck.'

'Oh Jesus.' Jack got up and grabbed his trousers and a fleece. 'Where is he?'

'In the tack room.'

Evelyn was awake now too. 'What's going on?'

'I don't know. Emma says something's happened to Anthony. He's been hurt.'

Anthony had slid down the walls and now lay on his side in a pool of his own blood. Jack ripped open his coat so hard buttons pinged across the floor. He was horrified to see a massive bloom of dark red blood on his son's white work shirt. He rested his head against his chest and then turned him on his back.

'Oh God.' Evelyn stood in the doorway of the tack room, watching him, her eyes huge, her fist mashed against her teeth. 'Oh my God Jack, what's happened to him?'

'Ring an ambulance, quick!'

She turned and ran back towards the house. Jack checked Anthony's airways, pinched his nose shut and blew great mouthfuls of air into his mouth. He did this several times and then checked Anthony's chest again.

He continued to breathe into his son's lungs. He pressed the heels of his hands against his chest and counted out the beats. 'Come on, come on, come on, please, please, son, please,' he pleaded.

After a while he stopped and hung his head. Evelyn screamed at him to keep going.

Emma left, walked across the yard and went upstairs. Without undressing, she lay down on her bed and pulled the duvet over her head. She did not return downstairs, even when she heard her mother weeping loudly.

CHAPTER 63

Jack stood in the doorway of the barn and watched as two sombre men loaded his son into the back of an ambulance and drove him away.

Jack's face was drawn, his eyes empty. They were taking Anthony to Dublin to perform an autopsy. They had been kind enough not to patronise him.

Detective Sergeant Jim Breen, who had arrived an hour earlier with Garda Bernadette Galvin in tow, walked across the yard and offered Jack his hand.

'I am very sorry for your loss.'

Jack stared at his hand for a moment before he shook it.

His loss.

'I will need to speak to your daughter. She's a witness, Mr Byrne. She was the last person to see Anthony alive. I need to know what she knows and time is—'

Jack lowered his head. 'God damn you.'

'I'm sorry.'

They crossed the yard together. Inside in the kitchen, Evelyn sat at the table, a cup of cold tea in front of her. His mother was in the chair by the stove, her eyes were so swollen from crying she could barely see through them. Pat Kinsella was there too, with his wife, Stella. Evelyn must have called them, Jack thought, though he wasn't sure why. What could they do? What could anyone do now?

Stella stood up when they entered. 'I'll make some fresh tea. Sergeant, would you like a cup?'

'No thank you.'

'He needs to talk to Emma,' Jack said, to no one in particular.

'So let them talk,' Evelyn said and lowered her face into her hands.

Predictably, Emma refused to open her door to Breen, who came back downstairs after a few minutes with no more information than he had when he left the kitchen.

'Let me try,' Jack said. He went upstairs and knocked softly on Emma's door.

'Emma, it's me.'

No answer. He rested his forehead against the door and sighed, suddenly overwhelmed with exhaustion. He wanted to weep, he wanted to lie on the floor and die. Instead he waited. 'Emma?'

He heard footsteps and the sound of a key being turned.

'I saw them take him away.' She walked back to her bed and sat on it with her hands in her lap. 'I saw them take Anthony.'

'Get dressed and we'll go take care of the horses.'

She did as he asked and together they fed and watered the animals. Jack was patient and bided his time. He was filling the hay net when Emma began to talk.

'I am thinking that I made a tactical error too.'

'What do you mean?'

'Anthony was alive when I found him. I would call a vet immediately if I found one of the horses bleeding.'

'He was…' Jack swallowed, 'alive?'

'Yes, but he would not let me leave. He said he did not want to be alone.'

'It's not your fault.'

'It is my fault. I should not have told him about the dog. Then he would not have killed that man.'

Jack stared at her. 'What man? What are you talking about?'

'Anthony killed Gully Donovan because he thought he made me pregnant. But it was not Gully. It was the other one. The one with the dog.'

Jack could barely bring himself to say the words.

'Anthony killed Gully Donovan?'

'Yes. He was wrong, Gully did not attack me.'

'Who did?'

'Martin Harte. Anthony said I had to tell you. He made me promise. He was afraid Martin would hurt me. He said he wanted to protect us. He wanted to be sure I told you so that you and Mam were safe too.'

Jack dropped the hay nets and leaned against the wall. He felt light headed, nauseous. 'My God, why didn't he come to me?'

'You told him to fight his own battles.'

'Fight his…'

'When he told you he was being bullied by Gully Donovan. That is what you said to him. To both of us.'

'But that…he was a child then…that's not…'

Jack sagged against the wall, wracked with grief and began to sob. Emma stared at him for a moment, then walked to the other end of the barn and waited there until he stopped.

Detective Sergeant Breen and Garda Bernadette Galvin drove across the village to Ivan Harte's home in silence. Breen parked the squad car beside a stone fountain, and glanced towards the magnificent house.

'I hate this,' Bernadette said.

'You know them?'

'Everyone knows everyone round here, Sergeant. I thought you'd have worked that out by now.'

He considered reprimanding her for her tone, but decided against it. 'Let's get this over with.'

'Why do you need to speak to Martin?' Ivan Harte said, washing his hands at the kitchen sink. His wife, Claire, had called him in when Breen had asked to speak with her son.

'We need to talk to him in connection with a stabbing incident.'

'A stabbing? Would you go on out of that. Talk sense man.'

'Who was stabbed?' Claire asked.

'Anthony Byrne.'

'Jack's lad?' Ivan said, shocked. 'That's terrible. Is he all right?'

'No, he's dead.'

'Oh my God,' Claire said, lowering herself onto a kitchen chair. 'What is going on in this village?'

'An allegation has been made, regarding Martin.'

'What sort of an allegation? Made by who?'

'Emma Byrne.'

Grace Harte, who until that moment had been staring at Breen with rapt attention, suddenly began to laugh. 'That weirdo?'

Breen looked at the teenager. She was a singularly unattractive girl, overweight, with frizzy hair. 'Yes, his sister.'

'But everyone knows she's nuts. God knows what she's talking about.'

'Nevertheless, I want to speak to Martin.'

'He's not here,' Ivan said.

'Where can I find him?'

'He's gone into Arklow to collect some sheet metal.'

'Well, if you could ask him to–'

'What's he driving?' Garda Bernadette Galvin asked.

Claire and Ivan stared at her.

'I'm only asking because his jeep is parked out there by the shed.' She nodded at the window, beyond which Martin's jeep was clearly visible, 'I don't think I've ever seen him drive anything else.'

'Bernie–'

'Garda Galvin if you don't mind, Mrs Harte.'

'Where is he?' Breen said, and this time there would be no brush-off.

They found Martin around the back of the house, shovelling mulch onto raised beds. He looked up when he saw them and, for a moment, it looked like he would bolt, but then his shoulders slumped and he stood his ground, waiting for them to approach.

'Hello Martin,' Breen said. 'I take it you know why we're here.'

'How would I? I haven't a clue what you want.'

Breen thought the kid had a very punchable face. 'Anthony Byrne was stabbed last night.'

'Oh?'

'He's dead.'

'Sorry to hear it.'

'Are you?'

Martin shrugged. 'We weren't friends or anything, but yeah, of course I am.'

'Nice looking gloves, are they leather?'

'Yeah.'

'I've been looking for good pair of gardening gloves. Do they affect your dexterity much?'

Martin glanced at his father. 'Dad, what's this about?'

'They think you've got something to do with Anthony's death. Tell them where you were, so that they can get on and bother other decent, hard-working people.'

'Why would I kill Anthony Byrne?'

'Because he knew you shot at his sister perhaps?' Bernadette Galvin said.

Ivan whirled around to face her.' Now you hold on a fucking minute here–'

'Show me your hands, lad,' Breen said.

Martin glared at him.

'For what?'

'How about for my own peace of mind?'

Martin's jaw muscles clenched.

'I don't have to do that, do I Dad?'

Ivan looked between his son and Breen. 'This is ridiculous.'

'He was a light lad, not much to him, but I'd say he put up more of a struggle than you were expecting. Am I right?'

'I don't know what you're talking about.'

'Did he fight back?'

'Fuck you.' Martin threw down his shovel. He peeled off the gloves one by one and held out his hands, palms down.

'See?' Ivan said, 'there's not a mark on them.'

'Turn them over.'

Slowly, Martin did as he was asked.

'Oh Martin,' Ivan said, 'oh son.'

The palms of his hands were criss-crossed with cuts.

'I think Martin,' Breen said, 'you should come along with me.'

It didn't take long for Martin to start talking, although he tried to put his spin on things. He pinned Emma's rape on Gully, insisting that it was he who had instigated it. He said he was always afraid of Gully growing up, that he was a thief and a blackmailer and extremely dangerous. Through unchecked tears, he said he hadn't wanted to hurt the girl, but she'd been semi-conscious and they'd just been kidding around but it had gone too far. He said he didn't think any more about it, but then she turned out to be pregnant, and Gully was worried that someone would find out they'd had sex with her.

It had got out of hand, he said, over and over again. When Gully was found murdered, he said he'd figured out that Anthony knew about the rape, but he wasn't sure what Anthony was planning to do about it. Anthony had threatened him. It was self-defence, he bawled.

Detective Sergeant Jim Breen let him talk: with every excuse and snot-dribbled plea for understanding, his opinion of Martin

Harte sank lower and lower. 'A consummate actor' is how he described him to Bernadette Galvin after they had left the interview room. She agreed with him fully.

CHAPTER 64

The day after New Year's Day, Jack and Evelyn buried Anthony in a small graveyard, beside the Jack's father, Malachy.

Margaret laid a sprig of holly on his coffin before it was lowered into the ground, and wept as though her heart would never be whole again.

Emma stood to the side, remote and lost in her thoughts. She had not cried since the day Anthony died and she did not cry now. When people went to shake her hand and offer their condolences, she turned away and looked out over the valley until they were gone.

Flicky Gillespie delivered Anthony's belongings to the Byrne's home a few days later. Amongst his things, Evelyn found a diary and a visa for Australia. For two days, the diary remained unopened under her pillow. On the third day, she carried it to the sitting room and settled herself into Margaret's rocking chair. Her hands shook as she opened it.

She began reading.

As she read, she wept for the child who had suffered so brutally in silence. She wept for her son, for his pain, for his loneliness.

When she was finished reading, she closed the diary and leaned her head back against the chair. She thought long and hard about whether to share what she had learned with Jack. In the end, she decided she would not.

She burned Anthony's diary and his visa for Australia, letting the fire take his secrets, as she had taken them to her heart.

It was May 21st; Emma gave her horses one final check, went upstairs to bed and awoke five hours later in labour. With Evelyn's help, she delivered a nine-pound baby boy in the backseat of Jack's car on the way to the hospital, thirty miles away. Gazing mesmerised at the baby, she asked Jack to turn the car around and take her home. Jack insisted they continue on with the journey and Emma was admitted to the hospital shortly afterwards. On the morning of the second day she told Evelyn that someone had better bring her home immediately or she would walk there herself. No one doubted her and she was released that afternoon.

Emma named her son Anthony Klaus Byrne and scandalised Margaret by refusing even to entertain the notion of baptising him.

'Klaus?' Jack said, watching Evelyn rock their grandchild softly in her arms. 'Where the hell did she come up with that one?'

'I have no idea,' Evelyn replied. 'Who knows what goes on in that girl's head? Who knows what goes on in anybody's head really?'

'I've never heard the like. Klaus?'

'It's not important, Jack. It's really not important at all.'

Evelyn lowered her head trying to hide her tears, even as one rolled down her cheek and plinked onto the baby's cheek. Baby Anthony's hand jerked in surprise, but he did not cry. He hardly ever cried.

Jack put his arm around his wife shoulders 'It's all right love, everything will be all right.'

But it wasn't. It got better though and, as Emma always said, any improvement is a good thing.

THE END

ALSO BY ARLENE HUNT